The Messenger

By Andrew E. Shipley

The Messenger by Andrew E. Shipley

ISBN 978-1-4303-2512-3

Author's Note: This is a work of fiction. The characters and incidents depicted herein are entirely fictional and a product of the author's imagination. Any resemblance between the characters or incidents described in this book and any actual person or event is entirely coincidental.

To my father, who showed me what courage looks like,
To my mother, who taught me what poetry means,
To my sister, who made me believe in dreams,
And to my wife, without whom none of this matters

Acknowledgements

To the extent this story has merit, it is largely due to the knowledge and wisdom I have learned from the wonderful friends fortune has bestowed upon me, including Joe Armao, John Dougherty, Doug McElwain, Don Rodgers, Cathy Thompson, and most of all, my wife, Patti. Any shortcomings are due entirely to my failure to learn their lessons well.

**We will walk on our own feet;
we will work with our own hands;
we will speak our own minds…**

Ralph Waldo Emerson

Venice, 1605 AD

His eyes, large and unnaturally black, fixed on the solitary figure moving like a shadow through the foggy courtyard. Rainwater spilled over the side of a clogged gutter and dripped on his head, but he did not move. "From shadow to ghost," he whispered.

A soft chirping sound drew his gaze; a bat had perched incongruously on the lip of the courtyard's ornamental fountain. It distracted him for only a moment as a muffled cry broke from the man he had been watching. A second shadow had joined him. A glint of steel flashed through the mist just before the two grappled and fell. Only the second man rose. The Messenger had been silenced.

The man retreated down the alley from which he had watched the assassin earn his pay and headed toward the Grand Canal. From there, a boat would take him to the mainland and a waiting carriage. If he pushed hard enough, he would reach Florence by dawn. He would follow the river to the sea, make the crossing to Corsica and deliver the news to the Master. Afterward, he hoped, he would return to his life in London.

He saw no reason for the Master to prohibit his return. If the lessons of history held true, there would not be another Messenger for decades, perhaps longer, so it would fall to another to ensure the Order of Mani's preservation.

The Order had existed for over a thousand years, exerting influence from the shadows of power. Not even he, who had been chosen for this singularly important mission, whose intensely black eyes attested to the depths of his initiation, knew the full extent of the Order's reach, or even the Master's true identity.

The Messengers threatened to end it all. He wasn't sure why or how, but the Master had said it was so, and that was enough for him. According to the Master, the Order had kept watch over the centuries, and in every instance, had successfully interceded before the

Messengers could do their work, before their venom could poison the world. He took great pride in having been chosen for this mission, and even greater pride in having accomplished it. The Master would be quite pleased.

Miracles on the Senate Floor?

(The Washington Gazette, October 15)

Do you believe in miracles? Not the U.S. Hockey team, garden-variety, once-in-a-century sports upset, but the hair-raising, water-into-wine, this can't be happening kind?

If you don't, you soon may.

Freshman Senator John Peters, a soft-spoken man from the hills of North Carolina, walked into a nearly empty Senate chamber yesterday morning to give his first speech. The topic, income tax reform, was hardly heavenly. But the way he delivered it? – God only knows.

According to his office, Senator Peters delivered his speech in English. According to his office, English is the only language Senator Peters speaks.

But according to hundreds of amazed people from around the world, he gave his speech in every language in the world, all at the same time.

Many would consider the ability to clearly explain tax reform to even one non-tax person a pretty miraculous accomplishment. But when people who speak Kurdish, Swedish, French, Chinese and Russian all claim to have understood Senator Peters, it's Cecil B. DeMille time.

Some claim it's all just a hoax. A great practical joke made possible by clever software programs and the Internet.

Some claim it's clever politics designed to make Senator Peters a national figure.

Some believe he is the Second Coming. As for me, my parents named me Thomas.

Senator in Critical Condition
(The Washington Gazette, April 20)

Senator John Peters lies in a coma this morning following an assassination attempt. He was shot once in the head. No suspects have been arrested.

Senator Peters' startling rise from an unknown interim Senator has been one of the most widely reported and closely followed stories in modern times, cutting across political, cultural and religious lines.

While the Senator has consistently claimed to be a non-religious figure, tales of miracles have followed him since the day his supporters claimed he spoke in tongues from the Senate floor.

Although there are no official reports on the Senator's prognosis, an anonymous source at the hospital stated that Senator Peters "will need a miracle to recover."

Chapter 1

Janice took more time than usual getting dressed. Although the Senator's speech would be covered by only a small cable network specializing in politics, it was still television, and as the Senator's chief aide, she was likely to be interviewed and she wanted to look her best. She could hardly believe that her boss' first speech from the Senate floor would be her handiwork. He hadn't changed a word – she had tailored it perfectly to fit his soft, southern lilt and understated delivery.

After checking in at the office to ensure no last minute glitches, she made the long walk to the Senate Chamber – junior Senators were assigned the most remote offices – and climbed to the gallery for a bird's eye view. Senator John Peters, smiling as always, walked to the podium, took a sip of water, and looked up at the rows of empty seats facing him. The Chamber was virtually empty, as both he and Janice knew it would be so early in the morning. He looked up at Janice, nodded and smiled.

Then it happened.

He started speaking, but what Janice heard wasn't the speech she had written. Not exactly. She had written the speech in English, but somehow, she heard the Senator speaking simultaneously in English and Spanish.

Janice was confused. What she heard didn't sound like a translation. Besides, if the Senator had wanted his speech translated, he would have told her, and it wouldn't have been done this way. He would have said a few phrases in English, and an *interpreter,* not an invisible, disembodied voice that sounded eerily like his, would have translated what he said into Spanish. She looked about, searching for a second microphone or a tape player, certain they were the victims of a hazing ritual – an impersonator playing a joke on the new Senator.

Senator Peters kept speaking, unperturbed, while she grew increasingly agitated. She and the Senator had worked too hard for this moment to have it made the butt of a sophomoric prank. Another Senator's aide, someone she had seen a few times in the hallways, plopped into the seat beside her. She didn't know his name, but he knew hers.

"Nifty trick, Janice," he said. "How did you pull it off?"

"I didn't," she answered through tight lips. "And I suppose you don't have any idea who did?"

"Don't look at me," he said, throwing both hands up in the air. "I thought this was your way of trying to make the evening news."

"Hardly."

After the speech ended, Janice went down to the Senate floor to a smiling Senator Peters.

"That was interesting," Janice said in an edgy voice.

He looked at her with a puzzled expression. "Was there a problem?"

"Except for the whole Tower of Babel, simultaneous Spanish translation bit, no, no problem at all."

"What are you talking about?"

Janice raised her voice, her irritation evident. "Didn't you hear it?"

"I have no idea what you mean."

Janice started to explain when the unnamed aide that had been sitting next to her approached. "Nice bit, there, Senator Peters. I'll have to tell my boss there's someone in the Club who speaks French better than he does." Turning to Janice, he said, "Catch you later," and walked off.

The Senator and Janice watched him leave through a side door.

"I thought you said it was in Spanish," the Senator said.

"I did."

"I'm confused."

"So am I," she replied. The Senator shrugged it off. Clearly, a practical joke had been played, but he wasn't about to let himself get ruffled by it.

"Don't sweat it," he said.

The media storm hit the next day. A political junkie, who like Janice had been bilingual since early childhood, watched Peters' speech on a cable news show and realized that he heard every word spoken simultaneously in both of the languages he knew. He taped the speech, uploaded it to the Internet, and within hours, dozens of Web bloggers had quickly spread the word. A young wire service reporter who regularly monitored political chat rooms on the Internet noticed the increasingly excited chatter, and his hastily written dispatch turned into the lead story for nearly every drive-time DJ and radio talk show host in the country.

Chapter 2

The rat's nose twitched in nervous anticipation. It could smell food just ahead, and it scampered down the damp, narrow ledge that ran the length of the tunnel. The smell of food always accompanied the appearance of light at the tunnel's end – when it was dark, as it usually was, there was no food to find, not even the slightest crumb.

The rat poked his head into the large circular chamber at the end of the tunnel and sniffed. Dark wood paneling covered the limestone from which the cavern and the tunnel had been excavated; sconces jutted out every few feet, each bearing a large candle that illuminated strange patterns and images carved into the wood behind it: spirals, triangles, squares and circles superimposed on each other in sometimes chaotic, sometimes precise arrangements; figures of angels and demons battling over worlds beneath their feet; earth and sky torn asunder; human bodies split in half -- their left sides scored with fine lines, their right sides smooth.

A large table dominated the center of the room. Seated at its head was an old man with a prominent hook nose, a bold jaw, and large, deeply black eyes. He was dressed in a fashion not so much out of style as indifferent to it, and he wore the confident look of a man who never worried about getting his way because he always did. A much younger man sat across from him. They were deep in conversation when the rat jumped to the floor, its tail twitching. The movement caused a slight stir in the air, and the candle closest to the tunnel's mouth flickered.

"Ah, my old friend, you are back," said the old man in his native Corsican, a language the younger man did not understand. "You are here to greet me, as always. Come." He sprinkled morsels of bread and cheese on the floor. The rat scurried over, quickly devoured the crumbs and looked up for more. The man tossed a few more crumbs to it before turning his attention back to the young man.

"So tell me," he said in French. "What is the news?"

The young man cleared his throat. He had pale blond hair, and his blue eyes had just started to take on the black tint that marked membership in the Order of Mani. He had never before been to this secret room, located deep below a stately villa built at the foot of one of Corsica's many mountains, and he hoped his nervousness wouldn't show in his voice. "We have called Clark."

"Yes, of course you have. That is not news."

The young man stammered. "Clark was not involved in selecting Peters to fill the vacant Senate seat."

"An unfortunate mistake."

"Clark's man, Governor Smith, appointed Peters without consulting Clark."

"That would suggest he isn't entirely Clark's man, wouldn't it?"

The young man shrugged his shoulders in a movement so slight as to be almost imperceptible, a movement designed to say, yes, Clark may have faltered, but he was not certain it was his place to say so. He had never heard the Master speak of Clark with displeasure, and he felt the need to be circumspect.

"Master, Clark understands that he isn't as familiar with Peters as he needs to be. He wants Governor Smith to talk to him to see if there is anything more to this matter than sloppy news reporting or practical jokes."

"Very well. But we shall not depend only on Smith, or on Clark, to learn about Peters. I have another set of eyes that will help me learn what I need to know."

The young man did not know to whom the Master referred and waited for an explanation. When none came, he spoke again.

"Master?"

"Yes."

"Clark asked if there is something he should look for, some way to confirm whether Senator Peters is indeed a Messenger."

"If he is, we will know soon enough. And we will act."

In a building on Pennsylvania Avenue a couple of blocks from the White House, a dozen of the most powerful men and women in Senator Peters' political party, only three of whom held elected office, sat around a conference room table cluttered with coffee cups, sandwiches and newspaper clippings.

Clark reached for his cup of coffee. Never in his long career had he held office, but to those who sought access to the Party's resources – from money to endorsements – he was considered the man to see. It hadn't always been that way. There was a time when Clark was seen as nothing more than another overly ambitious political staffer in a city jam packed with them. But somehow, almost imperceptibly, things changed. He transformed from a middle-aged, mid-level staffer into a man with connections, a man everyone wanted to impress, a man who could make things happen. Even those who thought they knew him best weren't sure how it all occurred or how far his influence reached, and Clark preferred it that way.

The shades were drawn and all the lights except those at the far ends of the room had been turned off. Even with sunglasses, Clark's enlarged pupils couldn't stand the glare of the afternoon sun or the overhead fluorescent bulbs.

Clark stifled a yawn. He didn't care much for these "brainstorming" discussions. He preferred to do something other than sit and listen to a bunch of untalented hacks opine on the state of things. In his view, only a couple of people in the group had risen through their own merits, and they were the only ones who had any sense of history, any flair for the dramatic, or any feel for government. They were the only ones who thought for themselves. They were therefore the ones he was most careful of. Fortunately, neither of them had been able to make it this morning.

The rest of the men and women seated about the table had achieved their prominence through family connections or family money. As if to prove the axiom that all things revert to the mean, they possessed remarkably uninspiring minds – poor reflections of their gifted forebears. They were too stupid even to realize that he needed them more than they needed him. Leaders can't lead if they don't have people willing to follow them. These were his followers. They were the tools of his influence. So while they bored him terribly, he suffered through their chatter. When they were done, he would speak, and what he said, they would do.

Today's discussion focused on Peters' speech. The Peters incident, as they were starting to call it, troubled them. U.S. Senators weren't supposed to be tabloid material. And there were many in the Party that would not tolerate a miracle worker in their midst. That sort of thing belonged in the opposition's camp. Clark did not let on that the matter troubled him far more deeply than it did them. They were concerned only with polling numbers and the Party's image.

He had far weightier things to consider, but he needed time. Time to think. Time to learn more about Peters. Time to see whether Peters would simply be a temporary issue, a novelty that would be forgotten the moment the media found something else to fascinate it, or whether he signified something far more significant, something he had heard about but only as a legend, a tale from long ago, not something he ever thought could be true. The discussion continued around the table, long on worry and short on plans of action. After several speakers repeated themselves, Clark finally spoke.

He began by clearing his throat, and the other voices instantly fell silent. "Who is Senator Peters?" Clark asked rhetorically. "Was he our choice to replace Smith in the Senate when we arranged for Smith to become governor?" – a few heads shook their heads in a communion of disavowal – "*We* don't know much about him. *Smith* does." The same heads nodded in agreement. A few smiled, believing that Clark had just identified their scapegoat should things turn truly troublesome. "But surely," Clark continued, "surely, Smith would not have appointed Peters unless he believed Peters shared our common interests, our goals." Clark leaned back in his chair and turned both palms up as if in supplication. "I think we should send this issue to Smith for handling."

A murmur of approval rolled around the table. Clark placed his hands down firmly on the table and continued, "It's settled then. We'll have Smith meet with our young Senator. We shall learn what he is up to, and what exactly, is on the tip of his tongue."

A few hours later, after Clark had telephoned Governor Smith of North Carolina and directed him to meet with Senator Peters, he placed another call, to someone that only he among the Party leadership knew, a man with blue eyes just starting to turn black, and told him to assure the Master that things were under control.

Chapter 3

Archbishop O'Connell's office hadn't changed much since the days Janice and her father had been regular Saturday morning visitors. As a young girl, Janice would sit in the waiting room, curled into a lush leather armchair with her latest book while the Archbishop and her father conferred in the private inner office. The air was still warm and heavy and tinged with the scent of pine oil. She breathed in and let her memories wash through her.

The thick mahogany door to the inner office swung open and Archbishop O'Connell stepped through. His large round face gave him a boyish look despite the disappearance of the fiery red that had once colored his thick and now white hair. He smiled slightly upon seeing Janice; his curiosity at her visit was evident, but he remained quiet, letting the space between them hang thick with his unasked question.

Janice extended her hand, which the Archbishop held onto for a moment longer than he would have if greeting a mere acquaintance.

"Thank you for seeing me on such short notice," she said.

"I was a bit surprised to hear from you. How is your father doing? I haven't spoken with him in a while, either." He accented the last word, testing to see if she harbored any guilt over her long absence from the church.

"Neither have I, your Excellency." She felt her face flush slightly. "Please forgive me, but I didn't come to speak about him."

The Archbishop studied Janice for a long moment, then took her by the elbow and guided her into his private office. The jumbled room that opened before her, with papers scattered across the desk and stacked in various piles on the windowsills, looked more like the private study of an absent-minded professor than the official center from which the Archdiocese's business was conducted. But the office's personal touches, showing through the clutter, gave it a cozy, Old World feel. Miniatures of classical Greek and Italian Renaissance statues haphazardly dotted the room, and finely crafted, leather-bound books lined the dark mahogany bookshelves. A beautiful chess table adorned with intricately carved pieces of ebony and boxwood sat in a corner.

Archbishop O'Connell was a modest man. As he put it, whatever intellectual talents he possessed reflected a combination of God's gifts and his parents' genes, with his only contribution to the mix being his work ethic, and even that his grade school nuns had helped beat into him. Modesty notwithstanding, his intelligence was considerable and his judgment sound. Thus, people often came to him for advice, and he rarely turned them away.

He motioned Janice to a chair and leaned against his desk. "What brings you here?"

"Haven't you seen the news?"

He smiled and waved a hand across the seeming chaos of correspondence and memoranda piled before them. "Not recently."

"Then you'll have to take my word for it that I am not delusional."

The Archbishop's eyebrows rose slightly and he slid into a chair beside her. "Why would I think you were?"

Janice didn't answer. Her face was drawn tight and she kept fidgeting with the purse strap in her hand – it was obvious to the Archbishop that she was very nervous and even a bit frightened.

"Janice, how can I help you?"

"What can you tell me about speaking in tongues?"

Archbishop O'Connell arched his eyebrows in surprise and slowly clasped his hands together, as if in prayer. "Speaking in tongues?" he asked, "Why on God's earth do you want to know about that?"

"I think my boss, Senator Peters, spoke in tongues on the floor of the United States Senate."

The Archbishop listened carefully, but when he shook his head and suggested in a calm, measured tone that she had been confused, she stopped him short. “I know what I heard,” she insisted. “He spoke in two languages at once. To be more precise, I understood him in two languages simultaneously. I’m not sure how it happened. That’s why I came to you.”

The Archbishop reached for the Bible on his desk and opened it to the Acts of the Apostles in the New Testament. He began to read aloud:

> Now there were dwelling in Jerusalem Jews, devout men from every nation under heaven. And at this sound the multitude came together, and they were bewildered, because each one heard them speaking in his own language. And they were amazed and wondered, saying, "Are not all these who are speaking Galileans? And how is it that we hear, each of us in his own native language? ..."

“That’s exactly how I felt,” Janice said after the Archbishop had finished reading, “bewildered.”

“Janice, whatever you heard, it wasn’t your boss speaking in tongues. Aside from the Bible account I just read to you, there have only been a few instances of people speaking in languages unknown to them. They all occurred hundreds of years ago and they all involved saints.”

Janice gazed past the Archbishop and nodded her head in a silent beat that paced her thoughts. She replied softly, “Maybe it happened to people who weren’t Catholics, too. Maybe the Church only knows about the saints.”

The Archbishop smiled and pulled a pen from his pocket. “I’m confident that whatever you thought you heard has some mundane explanation. But if you’re still the same girl I once knew, you’re not likely to take my word for it, so let me jot down some terms for you, and you can go research this for yourself. You’ll see that I’m right.”

Chapter 4

As Janice searched for answers, and Governor Smith tried to arrange a meeting with Senator Peters, two men, living in opposite parts of the world and ascribing to different political philosophies and religious creeds, reached an identical conclusion: Senator Peters must die.

Abdul Imrahain knelt with his head pointed toward Mecca. He emptied his mind of worldly thought and filled it with the Koran. He was a devout man, awed by the power of Allah, and convinced that with faith came assurance that one's actions were divinely guided.

He had been much troubled by the news of Senator Peters' speech, for it had been heard in Arabic yet he read that Peters claimed to have delivered it in English. Clearly, the United States was once again trying to deceive the Muslim world, pretending that one of its leaders spoke with the voice of God -- the Christian God, of course.

Imrahain had not mapped out all the consequences that would follow widespread belief that Peters had been divinely inspired. He had no need to. Fear, distrust and hatred already ran strong between his world and Western governments. Until now, the American government had relied on the tactics it had used in the past: armed might, economic sanctions, and then handouts to those they had crushed in a pitiful attempt to win their hearts. Peters' speech marked an entirely new strategy. Now America was taking aim at their faith. America, the Great Satan, was using the powers of Satan to corrupt the faithful. Imrahain knew in his heart that if this latest attempt weren't stopped, the people he loved would be pitched into a struggle, not for their lives or for their oil, but for their souls.

He wouldn't let that happen.

Mark Hartson wasn't a happy man. He hadn't been a happy child, and he didn't expect to discover happiness as he aged. But he wasn't sad, either. What he was, what he had always been, what he always would be, was angry. At times he directed his anger toward a particular person or event; more often, though, he couldn't tie his anger to any specific cause. It was just part of his makeup, like the color of his eyes and the bow-legged gait with which he walked.

He was, however, smart enough to control his emotions. He needed to work, and no one would hire a man whose face showed the anger he carried inside. So he had learned to smile, crack a joke, and play the nice guy. But deep inside, his anger simmered.

Recently, he had fallen in with a group of men who seemed to understand who he was better than anyone he had ever met. They too were angry, but they had figured out why and they were going to do something about it. They thought of themselves as dark, dangerous and mysterious men, and although their meetings were informal and infrequent, they hatched great plans and thrilled in the conspiratorial air of their secret meetings.

They blamed the government for many of the ills they believed had befallen America. It had grown too large, too nosy, and too controlling. It had forgotten its purpose; it had neglected the charter laid down by the Founding Fathers. The fiery massacre of David Koresh and his followers at Waco, people trying to live their lives as they saw fit, was just one example of the government's many capital crimes.

The first blow for justice had been struck in Oklahoma with the bombing of the Federal Building. More would follow. They believed that the government's attention had been diverted by the fear of Muslim radicals, and that they could prepare without fear of detection.

Hartson, however, was impatient with the slow progress of their machinations. Senator Peters offered an ideal opportunity. What better example could there be of a government overstepping its bounds than to have a U.S. Senator setting himself up as a prophet? It was bad enough that Koresh was killed for his beliefs; now the government was laying the groundwork for a nationally imposed religion. Worse yet, the government sought to set itself up as the voice of God!

The more he thought about it, the angrier he grew. It would be a challenge to stay in control, to coolly plan out what he had to do, and not betray his thoughts. But he had spent a lifetime holding in his anger – he could hold out for a few more weeks.

Chapter 5

Janice sorted the books she had retrieved from the Library of Congress into the two categories the Archbishop had described. The custodian hadn't been too happy about ferreting out the rather arcane volumes she had requested – the longer books sat undisturbed on the shelf, the more likely they were to collect dust and paper fleas, and retrieving these had kicked up quite a bit of both. But her long, shapely legs, which showed quite nicely beneath her mid-thigh length leather skirt, and her smile, which the custodian decided to treat as sincere, convinced him to gather all the books she wanted.

Janice skimmed the titles piled in front of her and hoped that somewhere in this collection of knowledge, myth and rumor, she might find an explanation. The first stack, by far the bigger one, dealt with glossolalia, which the Archbishop referred to as the "language of the angels" even though it sounded like gibberish to everyone but the person speaking it. The other stack, which contained only a few volumes but seemed far more promising, explored all the reported cases of xenoglossia -- the ability of a person to speak in a language he or she had never learned.

There was one book – a 17th century volume – which the custodian failed to find despite there being no record of it having been borrowed or removed from the stacks for restoration. Its title sounded ominous – *Being a True and Full Account of the Order of Mani and the Slaying of the Man Who Spake in Tongues.* The custodian was convinced that it had been stolen by a black market book dealer. "We had a lot of trouble with book thieves until we started requiring photo IDs. People would give fake names and steal rare books right from under our eyes." Janice nodded in empathy, thanked him for bringing her the books he could find, and turned her attention back to them.

Janice took careful notes of what she read – having learned from experience that initial reactions were often misguided, and that it paid to have detailed summaries for future reference. She wrote copiously about every example of xenoglossia she found, even though she thought the evidence for most of them to be more than a little suspect. The most often cited modern example she came across involved a Jewish woman who supposedly spoke Swedish while under hypnosis, and the incident was repeatedly cited as proof of reincarnation. But the more careful researchers acknowledged that they had relied upon unverifiable tape recordings and could not exclude the possibility that she had learned Swedish as a child.

Janice also found references to the saints the Archbishop had talked about. Three were mentioned most frequently: Saint Hildegarde von Bingen, the Sibyl of the Rhine, born 1098, died 1179; St. Vincent Ferrer, the Angel of Judgment, born in 1350 in Valencia, Spain, died 1419; and St. Francis Xavier, from the Basque region of Spain, born 1506, died 1552. The stories of St. Hildegarde and St. Francis read like medieval versions of urban myths, but the accounts of St. Vincent, who believed that his mission was to warn the world that Judgment Day was at hand, were significantly more intriguing as they included eyewitness reports from a doctor from the University of Paris and a Catholic bishop. St. Vincent preached to crowds of as many as ten thousand people, yet supposedly even those farthest away could hear him clearly in whatever language they spoke.

Every saint she read about had been a member of a religious order. St. Hildegarde headed a convent, St. Francis was a Jesuit and St. Vincent was a Dominican missionary. They not only fervently believed in God, they had dedicated their lives to Him. Her boss was at best agnostic, hardly the miracle worker type; yet he had spoken in tongues – of that she had no doubt.

She kept replaying the events in her mind, as if reliving them would make them turn out differently. Years before, she used to tease her older brother, Jimmy, for opening the refrigerator door every five minutes and staring inside, wishing that cherry pie would magically appear. 'Now I'm the one looking for that cherry pie,' she thought. 'What would he have made of all this?' she wondered. She missed Jimmy, but now wasn't the time to get melancholy.

She had to focus. She had to think about what she would tell Senator Peters or John as she called him in private. Before this incident, he had not been well known on the national stage. He had labored quietly in his community, gradually building up favors by doing everything asked of him by more prominent party members. Then, just two months before, all those favors were suddenly repaid in full. The Governor of North Carolina had unexpectedly announced his immediate resignation, purportedly for health reasons, but the word inside the party was that someone had threatened to disclose rather unsavory information about the governor's sexual predilections if he stayed in office for even one more week. Ned Smith, the senior United States Senator from North Carolina, who believed that with a term as governor on his resume he could obtain the White House, won a hastily arranged special gubernatorial election. Among his first duties as the new governor was the appointment of an interim Senator to fill the seat he had just vacated.

John found himself thrust into an office that he had always held in awe -- his father had raised him on stories about the legendary Sam Ervin, the Bible quoting, Shakespeare quipping North Carolina Senator who book-ended his twenty year career by helping to break first Joe McCarthy and then Richard Nixon. John was proud to be in the office that Ervin held, wanted to do his job as honestly and competently as he could, and hoped that his best was good enough for the short time he expected to be a Senator.

Janice had greater hopes. In her experience, most successful politicians had mastered the art of using physical mannerisms – a hearty arm clasp, a strong wag of the finger, a somber nod of the head. Their every movement was studied, rehearsed and designed to draw a desired emotional response from the public. John was different. He was truly natural. He had a quality the power of which he didn't yet fully appreciate: an ability to make people feel comfortable in their own skin, to believe that good things are possible, and to want to be near him. In others, this would be called charisma, but that was too flashy a word for the quality that made John special. Janice referred to it as the "Jimmy Stewart thing," (she loved old black and white movies) and she was absolutely confident that, before long, the rest of North Carolina would see him as she did and that following his interim term, the voters would return him to office as an elected Senator for a full six years.

Janice closed the last of the books and capped her pen. The Library of Congress offered volumes of information but not a single answer. For that, she decided to trust her own judgment.

Chapter 6

John let his body sag into an overstuffed leather chair. The bourbon he had been sipping for the past twenty minutes had finally started to loosen the knot in his stomach. He set the glass down onto the sheaf of handwritten notes Janice had given him, mating it to the ring of condensation that marked its previous spot. "Docking," he called it, a private reminder of his boyhood dream to be an astronaut, held until fourth grade, when he learned that astronauts were supposed to have 20/20 vision. He watched idly as a thin ribbon of blue ink trickled from underneath his glass. 'She should have made photocopies,' he thought.

Outside, rain fell in steady sheets; its sound blended with the soft strains of Brahms playing on the radio and drowned out the tumble of Janice's voice in his head – the words "saints" and "apostles" faded into faint whispers. Janice had been a huge help to him the past few years; tough, smart and someone he had grown to trust without reservation or hesitation. What was he supposed to think now? He wasn't sure what to do – Janice wasn't taking this in the direction he wanted – and he needed time to think. He had turned off his cell phone and pulled the phone line out of the jack. The thin crack of light outlining the study's door widened as Sara stepped in.

"John, are you okay?"

John shook his head in reply, took another sip of bourbon, and laid his cheek against the cool glass. Light from his desk lamp reflected off the ice cubes and glistened on what appeared to be tears on his face. Sara hadn't known him to cry in the 20 years they had been married. She started to tell him that it was too early in the day to be drinking, but stopped when she realized that if the newspaper article lying on the desk next to Janice's notes had been about her, she would probably be drinking herself.

Instead, she asked, "What are we going to do?"

John slowly rocked the glass in his hand from side to side, watching the clear amber liquid slide over and around the ice. "First thing, I've got to talk sense into Janice. If I can't get her to see reason, there's no way we'll get the press to calm down."

"Is that what the two of you were arguing about?"

He nodded. "She talked to an Archbishop she knows."

"And?"

"She thinks it might have been a miracle." He leaned his head back into the chair's headrest with an exhausted sigh. "I'm not sure of much," he said, "but I'm no miracle worker, that I do know. How about you? Any ideas?"

"I haven't a clue." Sara picked up the newspaper and glanced at the column for a moment before returning it to the desk. "I read the article, but it felt like I was reading about someone else, not you. I don't know. Maybe it was just a very clever practical joke someone pulled off."

She took the glass of bourbon from John, put it on the far side of the table from him, and held his hands in hers. "Whatever the explanation, I think you're going to need a clear head today. I also think you're in the best position to understand what happened. What does your gut tell you?"

"I don't have any idea," he sighed. "I keep waiting for a voice inside my head to tell me what it means, what I'm supposed to do. Yesterday, I would have thought that was crazy. Now, I think it's the only thing that will keep me sane."

That night, after he had spent hours in a frustratingly unsuccessful effort to surf the Internet for information beyond that contained in Janice's notes, John stumbled into bed next to an already sleeping Sara. She had stayed up with him as late as she could, but their son would wake early, and she needed to get some sleep before facing what the next day was likely to bring. She urged

John to go to bed, but sleep was simply not possible for him. His head ached from the questions banging around like pin balls inside it, and neither the bourbon, nor the aspirin he took afterward, nor the thirty-minutes he had spent lying on the back lawn staring at the night sky had been enough to calm the feverish state of his mind. When he finally crept into his bedroom, the darkened lamp on the nightstand – Sara's silent admonishment that he should have come to bed with her – reminded him that she too was impacted by this ... whatever *this* was ... and that just added to his worries.

As he reached over to give her a goodnight kiss on the cheek, he thought he saw a moon shadow flicker against the back wall, but he was too tired to care and instead turned his back to the wall and went to sleep. Long before he was ready to wake, Sara shook him out of his slumber.

"John, get up. There's something in the house."

He murmured in a groggy voice that she was dreaming and that she should go back to sleep.

"John, get up! I heard something moving downstairs."

With great effort, he propped himself up on two elbows, turned to face her, and asked in a voice still thick with sleep, "What? What did you hear?"

"I don't know. I just know I heard something."

"Okay, okay."

John struggled to his feet and pulled on a pair of pants. He first checked Connor's room, then pulled his door shut, flicked on the stairwell light and went downstairs. As he turned the corner toward the kitchen, he saw a shadow flit through the room and knew instantly that it was a bat. The back door was ajar. John swore silently at himself for forgetting to close it and quickly did so. Then he turned on lights in every room downstairs and searched each one, but succeeded only in smashing his toe against the corner of the living room sofa. When he returned to his bedroom, he found Sara scrunched up against the headboard staring at their ceiling.

Hanging upside down halfway up the cathedral ceiling, with its wings wrapped about it, was an extraordinarily large bat. But its size wasn't its most arresting feature. Black eyes glared back at him, eyes that to his exhausted brain seemed full of malice and unnatural intelligence. Shivers

traveled down his back and arms but he willed himself to act and think calmly even as his heart raced. He limped to the bedroom door, certain he had broken his toe, and shut it to keep the bat trapped in the room. He fished an old tennis racket out of the closet, climbed onto the bed, and eyeballed the distance to the bat. The bat's eyes followed John's every movement. Even with outstretched arms, he couldn't reach it from the bed, so he jumped and swung, hoping to knock it to the floor. He didn't come close.

The bat slowly unfurled its wings and swooped across the room. John chased it, hopping on one leg, swinging as hard as he could, but the bat swerved effortlessly around, over and even beneath the racket. Then John had an inspired idea: if he swung the racket up and down quickly enough, the bat's sonar would ping it in multiple places and it might just be fooled into thinking it faced a solid wall.

The plan seemed to work. John slowly forced the bat back toward and finally into the bathroom. He lunged in after it, swinging the door shut behind him. Only when the latch clicked shut did it occur to him that he had trapped himself in a very small room with a very large bat. He switched on the light and saw it, a mere arm's length away, sitting on the floor, watching him watch it. He had the strange sense that it was studying him. He took a deep breath, and forcing his instincts to yield to his reason, dismissed his reaction as the product of too much bourbon and not enough sleep.

He slowly unfolded a towel from the rack behind him, tossed it over the bat and seized it. The bat clicked loudly and rapidly as John carried it to the front door. Taking care not to let any part of his body come into contact with any part of the bat – the mere thought of touching it roiled his stomach – John stepped outside and shook the bat free. He watched it fly off toward the full moon that hung low in the night sky.

John tiptoed quietly outside Connor's room. His six-year-old had managed to sleep through the entire incident. Sara waited in the hall.

"It's a good thing he didn't wake up," she said. "He was already having nightmares earlier tonight. If he knew about the bat, he'd never get any sleep."

"I'm probably going to have a nightmare or two myself tonight. Maybe for a few nights, at least until all this blows over."

Sara slipped her hand through John's arm. His forehead seemed slightly more lined than it had been just the day before. She had often heard it said that lives are changed forever by events that last only seconds – seeing that final lottery number hit, not seeing the red light or the other car entering the intersection. Would John's speech on the Senate floor change their lives forever? She didn't know. And if it did, she didn't know in what ways. Was it a winning lottery ticket or a terrible wreck?

"What if it doesn't blow over?" she asked. "Then what?"

"I'm sure that in a few days, some other story will come along and this will be largely forgotten."

"Do you honestly think so?"

"Yes, I do. People can't deal with what they don't understand, so they tuck it into a neat compartment off in a corner of their minds and forget about it. That's what I'm trying to do. Give it enough time, and everyone else will, too. This will be a faded memory."

Sara's eyes narrowed slightly, as if she were trying to focus on a distant object. "What does Janice think?" she asked after a few moments' pause.

"You know the old saying, 'The only bad publicity is no publicity.' That pretty much sums up her view. She thinks that if we handle this correctly, it could be a good thing."

"Is that what you want?"

"I don't want to be known as the religious freak from North Carolina," John replied. "It's not who I am or what I'm about. I don't even know if I believe in God."

"I understand."

"Then you agree? We should just wait for this thing to die down?"

"I guess I'm not as confident as you that people will forget about it. I worry that if you do nothing, you will forever be remembered as that weirdo from North Carolina because that's the only story about you that anyone will have ever heard."

"What do you suggest I do?"

"I think you should tell the story of who you really are. I think you should introduce the world to the man I fell in love with."

John tilted his head to one side, a habit he had developed as a young school boy when thinking through especially difficult test questions, and as he considered her words, he realized that they dovetailed perfectly with Janice's argument as to why he should make the rounds of the late night television programs and network morning talk shows. If the two women he trusted most came up with the same advice, even if guided by different motives, he knew he had to consider it carefully.

"Janice wants to book me on some network shows out of New York. She even had an itinerary planned out. Six a.m. shuttle to

LaGuardia to shoot the morning shows live, then hang around till the afternoon to tape the late night programs."

"How soon could she get you on?"

"This week if I want. They've already been calling her, requesting interviews."

"You'd be great, you know."

John shook his head. "I don't know about that. I'm not even sure what I'd say. It's not like they'll want to hear more about my views on tax reform. They're only going to be interested in one thing. What am I supposed to say when I'm asked what it all means?"

"You'll think of something. You always do."

John chuckled. "I guess I'm going to have to take back the 'No way in hell' comment I made to Janice when she first asked me to do it."

Chapter 7

Mark Hartson walked along the black granite wall of the Vietnam Memorial, dragging the outstretched fingers of his right hand across its polished surface in the casual way that a young boy drags a stick across a fence. He watched his reflection pass over the names etched into the wall, stopping when it came to 'Sgt. Robert Hartson.'

He had never before visited Washington, DC, so this was his first opportunity to see in-person the source of the name rubbing that a family friend had mailed to his mother several years back. His father, a career soldier, had been killed on the first day of his third tour of duty. Mark had been conceived between the second and third tours, so he had never seen his father except in old photographs from which the color had long faded. It had been hard for his mother to raise him alone, and while she had tried to fill his head and heart with stories of what a wonderful and brave man his father had been, to Mark he was nothing more than a shadowy fiction, less real and less heroic than the comic book characters he cherished.

As a boy, he had collected comic books; through odd jobs, smart trades, and successful forays into flea markets and second-hand shops, he had managed to acquire some valuable ones, including first issues of *The Justice League of America* and *The Green Hornet.* His favorite superheroes were ones that had potentially fatal flaws. The Green Hornet, for example, was helpless in the face of anything yellow – if someone shone a yellow flashlight on him, he'd crumple to the ground. Flaws made the story more suspenseful; there was always a chance the bad guys would win.

One day he came home from school to find that all his comic books had been thrown away. His mother had tossed them out during one of her annual spring-cleaning days as if they had been nothing more than old newspaper bundles. She approached spring-cleaning week as if it were a religious holiday, scheduling the days months ahead of time. She planned many events that way, marking her calendar an entire year in advance with things she had to do. Mark never understood that was how his mother coped with her husband's death – it gave her something to look forward to, tasks on which she could focus.

In retaliation for the loss of his comic books, Hartson threw away his father's baseball card collection. His mother had been keeping them for him, so she said, but he didn't care about sports and he knew that stripping away another memory of his father was the best way to get back at her for what she had done.

He walked away from the wall and headed to the steps of the Lincoln Memorial, where he sat down and took from his backpack the list of cheap hotels he had ripped from the pages of a tour book. He wasn't sure how long it would take to accomplish his mission, so he needed a place he could afford for an extended stay.

A commotion immediately to his left startled him. Two teen-aged boys with skateboards under their arms started screaming at each other. One shoved the other into Mark, toppling him backward. Mark pushed the boy away, and was surprised to see the two run off together. Then he noticed that his backpack was gone. Another teen-ager, running in the opposite direction, had it slung over his shoulder.

Cursing, Mark jumped to his feet and started after him. He ran ten miles each morning, so he wasn't too concerned about the boy's head start or quick pace. As long as he could keep the thief in sight, he was confident he could run him down. That backpack contained a thick collection of newspaper clippings about Senator Peters, a detailed itinerary of Senate hearings for the next two weeks, and his gun. He couldn't afford to let it get away. He certainly couldn't afford to have anyone discover his plans.

The boy was fast. He repeatedly crossed against the traffic light, darting in and out of moving cars with the nonchalance of someone used to city streets. Mark maintained his steady pace, tracking the ripple in the crowd whenever he lost direct sight of his target. After several blocks, the boy's legs gave out. Mark grabbed him and dragged him into a narrow alleyway. Mark was too strong for the boy to entertain any thoughts of fighting, so he tossed the backpack to Mark and tried to talk his way back to the street.

"Shit, man. I'm sorry, all right. No harm no foul. We're cool now, okay. "

Mark said nothing, but squared his body to prevent the boy from sliding past.

"Man, what you got in this bag, anyway?"

Mark slapped the boy's face so hard his head snapped back. A thin line of blood trickled from the corner of his mouth. Mark hated thieves. No good, lazy bums who'd rather get money the easy way than buckle down and earn a dollar. Mark never had any money growing up, but he never stole. Not even when stealing would have been the easiest thing in the world to do. When he needed money, he found an honest way to get it, like the time he had to buy a Christmas present for a classmate. Every year, the class picked names from a hat, and everyone would hold their breath when it was Mark's turn to pick because he never had enough money to buy a decent gift. But one year, Mark scrimped and saved for months just for this event, and when he presented Bob Tobias with a Daniel Boone flintlock cap gun, the look of awe and joy on the boy's face erased the shame he had felt for so long. For a moment. Then someone piped up, "Wow, can you believe Mark actually bought a decent gift?" He had known that was what everyone had been thinking, but to hear it said, out loud, in front of everyone, that was a hurt that never went away. But still, he never stole.

Mark slapped the thief again. The boy threw his hands up over his face to ward off the blows, and pleaded for Mark to stop, but

Mark didn't hear him. Mark had no use for jerks like this, and he was too absorbed in the act to pay attention to anything the boy said. He enjoyed the stinging sensation in his hand; it gave him a sense of release, so he kept slapping. The boy crumpled to the ground under the blows, and by the time Mark finally stopped, the boy was curled into a ball, whimpering for help.

Chapter 8

Abdul Imrahain's view from his window seat on the shuttle flight from Boston to Washington DC was obstructed by the portside wing and its single engine. A better seat would have done little to improve the view given the heavy cloud layer below, but the lack of a stationary marker against which the plane's course could be measured made it seem as if the aircraft floated calmly in air. He knew that the air outside was anything but calm, that it swirled and churned in dizzying eddies and if caught, was pulled with tremendous force into the engine's voracious turbine.

As Abdul looked out, it occurred to him that the seeming calm outside his window was a metaphor for the presence of Allah in the world. He was everywhere; His will surrounded everyone, moving about them in powerful currents. Yet nonbelievers blithely, and at their peril, ignored the force of His presence. They confused the primacy of Allah with the manufacture of their own imaginations. They could see the engine and the wing, but not the wind that held them up and made them move.

Abdul was in a contemplative mood. He had stood in a long security line with fellow travelers in Boston's Logan Airport, and he found their nervous reactions to him sadly amusing. The copy of the Koran in his hand and his bearded face made him look like a figure from the FBI's most wanted posters. He understood that they couldn't help but stereotype him -- men who looked like him had hijacked an airplane from this very airport -- and felt guilty for doing so. These poor Bostonians, champions of liberal values and self-professed haters of prejudice, despised themselves for being human.

They feared him because they didn't understand him. He wasn't a suicide bomber. He wasn't a terrorist. He was on a holy mission, and in this, he continued a tradition that dated back centuries to the cult of the Assassins. Western histories, misinformed by the writings of Marco Polo, described the Assassins as drugged out zealots who killed for the promise of Paradise, and even described the word 'assassin' as a derivative of the word 'hashish.' The word actually meant 'follower of Hassan,' an 11th Century warrior who seized a castle in the mountains near the Caspian Sea and became known, perhaps incorrectly, as the scourge of the Crusaders. No, Abdul didn't see himself a terrorist who randomly and wantonly murdered innocent people to further political aims. He was a defender of the true faith.

Most Americans badly misunderstood the nature of Islam. Devout Muslims were not 'medieval barbarians,' an ironic phrase he had heard on an American news program, ironic because the only barbarians during what the West called the Middle Ages were Christians. Most Americans didn't understand that it was the Christians who invaded Muslim lands, and that the great Muslim leader, Saladin, had shown charity and mercy to the invading armies he defeated, only to have Christian leaders brutally massacre Muslim women and children in return.

The West failed to appreciate how the memory of these early Christian atrocities lived on in the Muslim world, communicated from parent to child, generation after generation, serving as continual reminders of the need to be on guard against the avarice of Western power. Americans in particular paid little attention to history, preferring to focus on the future and treating the past as little more than 'yesterday's news.'

Life was very different for those who moved more slowly through the currents of time. Imrahain believed himself to be shaped as much by the distant past as by his personal history; his destiny inextricably linked to his heritage.

He didn't hate Americans; he actually found most of the Americans he had met to be quite friendly, although largely superficial and not worthy of respect. It was the American government he feared and despised; that was the great Satan that sought to force its will upon his people. One could not ask for a higher honor than to confront Satan to save one's people and he gave thanks for the opportunity to prove his worth.

Trusting that he would be forgiven a minor detour, in light of the sacrifice he was about to make, he had decided to fly first to Boston where he had spent three wonderful years at Harvard Law School. 'The Law School,' as it was known, housed one of the world's largest international law libraries. Even more important than the books, however, were the minds that surrounded him. For three years he studied with and debated the brightest, most inquisitive law students in the world. Not all of them were Muslim, but he didn't have to share their beliefs to respect their intelligence and enjoy their company.

Harvard Square, the busy intersection just outside the campus, was as frenetic a place as he had remembered, in which people of all sorts milled about, from businessmen in impeccably tailored suits to teen-age boys with spiked purple hair. Chess tables dotted the central square, ringed by bistros, coffee shops, and the college bookstore.

Abdul loved chess. His father had taught him the moves when he was only four years old, and he had displayed a natural aptitude for the game. By the time he was seven, he regularly beat his father's friends and started playing in local tournaments. Occasionally, someone claiming that chess was Haraam, 'useless play,' and therefore forbidden, would accost him. But as his father noted, chess had a long and proud history in the Islamic world: it was a Muslim caliph who first paid professional chess players, and it was the Moors who introduced chess to Europe when they arrived in Spain in 712 AD.

He sat down to play the local chess master, who charged two dollars a game, refunded only to that rare person skilled enough to draw or win. Abdul drew the white pieces and the first move. He started cautiously. He had never liked the wild, attacking style of chess typically played by the trash talking teenagers who frequented the tables in Harvard Square, boys who would insult their opponents' every move and punctuate their own by slamming their pieces on the board.

Abdul preferred a defensive game in which he lay in wait like a coiled python, biding his time, positioning his pieces so that they could fend off any attack but strike quickly at the first sign of weakness. It was a cold, calculated style that required great patience, as it did not actively provoke weaknesses in the opponent's position. The chess master mistook Abdul's preparatory maneuvers for timid play and attacked prematurely, thinking that Abdul would wilt under the pressure. Instead, Imrahain coolly exploited the growing weaknesses in the black position. A crowd gathered around the table, watching with surprise and increasing respect as Imrahain logically and methodically choked the life out of Black's pieces. Finally, the master tipped his King over and resigned. The crowd applauded, Abdul shyly nodded his thanks, and waved off the two-dollar refund.

He crossed Massachusetts Avenue and entered the university campus. He climbed the marble stairs of Widener Library, a temple-like edifice built by distraught parents in memory of their freshman son who drowned on the Titanic, and looked out over Harvard Yard, the grassy expanse in the middle of the campus. His graduation ceremonies had been held in the Yard. Then he crossed the campus to the Law School and walked through the corridors of Langdell Hall, the Law School's main building, where priceless 18th Century portraits of renowned English jurists had once hung unprotected and undisturbed on the walls. They had all been replaced with contemporary prints and posters – paintings of dead white men no longer seemed to be in vogue. He sat in the back row of a class in session and smiled as one of the students worked the word 'turkey' into his answer, provoking laughter from his classmates.

He had played turkey bingo during his days at the Law School, continuing a tradition that pre-dated the tenures of even the most senior professors. Each bingo card contained the names of students who repeatedly volunteered to answer questions in class. Whenever one of these 'turkeys' answered, their bingo-playing classmates would search their cards for his name. When someone got bingo, he had to answer the professor's next question and work in the word 'turkey.' Abdul had to give such an answer in his Criminal Law class.

Imrahain would miss Harvard. He would miss his wives and two sons. He would miss his life. But some things were more important than even life itself, and he knew in his soul that the quest on which he had embarked was such a thing.

Chapter 9

John was in the limousine on his way to the studio when his cell phone started ringing. A very annoyed Governor Smith was on the other end.

"What the hell are you doing, John? I thought you agreed we'd meet and map out a strategy before making any public statements."

"I'm just trying to calm down some of the hysteria I've been dealing with ever since that speech. I've got people grabbing my coat as I walk by, hoping it'll cure their cancer. I've got to put a stop to it. I'm not going on TV to talk about politics, Governor, I promise."

"I've known you a long time, and one thing I always thought was that I could count on you. I don't know what this 'tongues' thing is all about – I'm not buying this miracle bit, so I'm assuming you have a logical explanation and I hope to God it isn't some practical joke or publicity stunt that somebody on your staff pulled off, but you can't go on national television yet, not until we've talked. Christ, John, when you're a Senator, everything's politics, and you should know that by now. You have to cancel the interviews. You can't go on national TV without meeting with me first. I'm afraid you don't quite understand the consequences of your actions."

"I can't cancel. Don't worry. I won't say anything stupid. And I still plan on meeting with you."

"John, there are some very powerful people who are really pissed off. Cancel the interviews."

"Who are you talking about, Ned? What powerful people?"

"Not over the phone, John. I need to speak with you in person, in private. I'm asking you to do us both a favor. Cancel the interviews."

"Too late. I'm already here."

The limousine pulled up to the studio and the producer who greeted him as he stepped out of the car led him to a small waiting room. She tried to make casual conversation, but John was too distracted by his call with the governor to pay her much mind, so she left him alone with his thoughts. 'Powerful people,' the governor had said. 'Who was he talking about? Why would they be pissed off?'

He didn't have much time to dwell on the questions as a few minutes later he found himself ushered into a chair across from the nation's highest paid television personality, Melanie Kraft. She barely acknowledged his presence; she was far too busy berating her hairdresser for not pointing out the run in her pantyhose until it was too close to airtime to change. The stream of invective that poured from Kraft's mouth would have made a grizzled longshoreman blush, but the hairdresser seemed unfazed and continued adjusting loose strands of Kraft's hair. John stared in amazement.

Then the producer called out, "Going live in ten, nine, eight ..." and Kraft transformed. Instantly, everything about her was perfect: her hair, her smile, her legs (she adroitly crossed them in such a way as to completely hide the tear in her hose). She became much prettier, much more pleasant, and much less real. She looked directly at him and wished him a good morning. John felt as if he were looking at a plastic doll.

As the seconds to airtime counted down, Kraft kept her eyes and her smile fixed on him, and that made him feel even more nervous and unsettled than he already had been. He was sure that his legs were trembling, but when he looked, they seemed quite still. He couldn't imagine how he could appear so calm when it felt like every muscle fiber in his body was twitching. The green light went on and Kraft turned to talk to the camera.

"Today we have with us Senator Peters, whose speech the other day turned heads, grabbed headlines, and even brought some people to their knees. Good morning, Senator."

"Good morning, Melanie." With those first words out of his mouth, his nerves melted away and he focused entirely on the moment.

"So, are you a messenger from God?"

"No. Hardly. I'm not even a very religious person. I mean, I believe in God, but I'm not a preacher or anything like that. I don't wear my religion on my sleeve. I don't hear voices. I don't see angels."

"So what happened?"

"Hell if I know," he laughed.

Melanie smiled. "Surely, you have thought about the significance of your speech. What do you want to tell America, tell the world?"

John had been prepared for this question – it was entirely predictable given Melanie's interviewing technique, which was to smile and ask the guest to emote.

"At first I was in shock. Denial, really. Then I started asking myself the same question you just asked – what did it all mean? Was I supposed to change my life, become a minister, join the Peace Corps? I kept thinking that if God were really trying to talk to me, I'd know it, feel it in my bones. Remember Charlton Heston in *The Ten Commandments*, how his hair turned white after he had seen the burning bush, and how after he came down from the mountain, his face glowed? Well, that didn't happen to me. I was the same guy after the speech as I was before. I didn't even know what had happened until my staff told me. I started looking for signs as to what it meant. I looked everywhere. I even poured some of my son's alphabet soup into a bowl to see if it would spell out a message. Nothing happened." John smiled, "I ate it, though. I had forgotten how good alphabet soup tastes."

John took a deep breath and nodded his head solemnly. "Then I started to think that maybe the message was the speech itself.

Everyone knows that politicians use words to shade the truth. We don't outright lie, at least most of us don't, but we all play the 'it depends on what 'is' is' game. And we rationalize what we say by claiming that everything is political and that everyone does it all the time – 'Yes honey, that's a pretty dress,' and 'No honey, you haven't gained weight.' We've white lied ourselves into a habit of deception. I've done it, too. I admit it.

"So there I was, preparing to give my very first speech on the floor of the United States Senate. It was about tax reform, an issue I believe in, one that everybody advocates, but no one wants to really tackle. I wanted to get something done so that middle class America doesn't have to keep carrying the unfair burden it's been saddled with for years. I crafted my speech into a piece of advocacy, and to do that, I manipulated facts. I didn't lie; I chose the facts that helped my argument. There were other facts I left out. That's what you do. You use the statistics that work and ignore the ones that don't. It happens all the time. Just listen to the rhetoric after each monthly job report. Did the administration's economic policies create jobs or lose jobs? The truth is, both. It depends on how you slice and dice the numbers.

"So I started thinking, maybe the message behind the 'miracle speech,' as I've heard some people call it, is simply that it's time for all of us in government to stop shading the truth. We should speak our own minds; we should say what we actually believe, not what is politically expedient. If we have disagreements with our colleagues, whether in our own party or in the other party, let them be honest disagreements over policy. Let's end the practice of spinning. Truth is a straight arrow. You can't spin and be honest at the same time."

Chapter 10

Reverend Creighton B. Jones, known to his followers simply as the Reverend, jammed his thumb into the power button on the remote control and flipped it onto the empty seat beside him on the sofa. He continued to look at the darkened television screen as a wry smile played across his lips. Not a strand of his perfectly coiffured and heavily sprayed salt-and-pepper hair moved as he shook his head in disbelief.

"Damn it all to hell," he chuckled, "that's all we need – a frigging U.S. Senator playing on our turf. Have to hand it to him, though, this stunt makes our revival tent meetings look like Amateur Night at the corner café."

"What if it's not a stunt?"

The Reverend turned to see who had asked such a naïve question. Darnell Edom. He should have known. Darnell, tall, lanky, somewhat unkempt, a bit taciturn, but obviously bright, was the newest member of the entourage, young enough to be idealistic but greedy enough to share in the take. 'Suffer the children,' the Reverend thought.

His own faith had faded many years before, but he didn't consider himself either jaded or cynical. The Reverend was a pragmatist, and he had made a deal with the world. He ministered to those who yearned for something more than the daily creep of their routine lives by giving them something too sublime to understand and too powerful to ignore. He gave them God, from 8 pm to 9 pm, Fridays and Saturdays, and from 10 am to Noon on Sundays, the last hour of which was broadcast on local access cable TV. In exchange, they gave him money. It was a fair trade, he thought. In fact, one could argue they got the better of the bargain. By forging a daily community of souls who would otherwise spend their money on lottery tickets, cigarettes or booze, he saved his flock from themselves.

They left his prayer meetings feeling better about their lives and their souls, and that alone was worth whatever they contributed to his church. He didn't need to believe in a personal God to believe in the value of preaching about Him.

"Say again?" the Reverend asked Darnell.

"What if it's not a stunt?" Darnell noted that everyone else in the room had adopted the same smile the Reverend wore. His chin dropped to his chest, his ears now flaming red – they always glowed when he felt embarrassed. "I mean...what if he really spoke in tongues. It's happened before, hasn't it?"

"The Bible makes several references to the act of speaking in tongues," the Reverend intoned in the smooth bass voice he used to drive home a sermon's moral point. "Acts, Chapters 2, 10 and 19. First Corinthians, Chapter 12, and if I recall correctly, Chapter 14 in its entirety." Then his voice lightened and a chuckle rippled through it. "But I think you'll find, my boy, that there has never been any mention of it in the Congressional Record."

Everyone but Darnell laughed. Darnell persisted; apparently, he had not yet mastered the Reverend's Second Commandment, "Go Silent," which the initiated understood to mean that when the Reverend disagreed with you, the proper response was to say nothing. "Just because no Senator did it before..." Darnell stopped when the Reverend stood up.

"Your faith threatens to overwhelm your judgment."

"I'm sorry, Reverend."

The Reverend held his arms open wide, and with a stately swivel of his head, captured everyone in the room with his gaze before turning back to Darnell. "You are surely not the only one confused and uncertain about the meaning of all this."

The Reverend once more surveyed the entire room. "What is the community of the faithful supposed to do with this Senator

Peters? How are they supposed to interpret this so-called miracle? He raised both hands to his chest. "Who better to help our fine young Senator understand the miraculous than one who has himself heard the Voice of our Lord?"

Nervous laughter rippled around the room as his staff, save for one person, fidgeted uncomfortably. The Reverend played wonderfully well along the dusty country roads they traveled and in the market squares of the small towns in which they often stayed. Their traveling show provided a nice, comfortable living and promised to do so for quite some time. To leave what they had behind and dive into the glaring spotlight of national politics was to court disaster. They knew the Reverend for what he was. If he somehow managed to get anyone's attention in DC, it wouldn't take long for the Washington press corps to figure him out. Once exposed, he'd be a laughing stock not only in DC but also to the very crowds that now came to see him, crowds they'd worked hard over the past five years to cultivate. The best that could be hoped for was that no one in DC, neither Senator Peters nor the press, would give a damn about the Reverend or what he had to say, and that he would come limping back to where he belonged, perhaps a bit humbled, but with no harm done to his ability to earn their daily bread.

The one person who thrilled at the Reverend's words saw things quite differently. Darnell didn't care about making money. If Senator Peters had worked a miracle, if he was an instrument of God, then Darnell wanted very much to meet him, and the Reverend provided the best chance for making that happen.

The Reverend knew how most of his staff felt. He realized full well that they saw him as a caricature, the stereotypical Bible-thumping preacher portrayed in poorly written TV shows and low-budget movies. They thought he was a smug, self-important showman with more pizzazz than brains. But they were wrong.

In his private locker in the back of the RV that served as both his home and the means by which his show traveled, he kept dog-eared copies of books on philosophy, history and literature that he pored over late at night after everyone else had gone to sleep. He read them not with the light heart of a student who loves learning for its own sake but with the unflagging determination of a farmer clearing poor soil of stones and weeds. Creighton Jones played the Reverend because he could do it better than anyone, but if he had a chance to move beyond the caricature, well, the world would see the depths he had in him.

Chapter 11

Janice burst into the office the morning after John's interview with Melanie Kraft waving a couple of faxes.

"Great news, Senator! Your interview with Melanie was a huge ratings success."

"Really?" John replied. He hadn't been certain what to expect.

"Senator, the numbers were unbelievable. Right up there with the Super Bowl."

John grabbed the faxes from her hand and started looking at rows of what were to him completely unintelligible numbers. "What are these? I can't make heads or tails of it."

"I'll tell you what to make of it once we get the favorable /unfavorable numbers in, but I just know they'll be good – you were amazing in all your TV appearances – and if they come in anywhere close to where I think they might, Smith is going to forget all about your going on television without meeting him first. He'll want to be your new best friend. I bet you even start getting calls to help other politicians out on the campaign trail. Who knows, maybe you'll find yourself on a few of the more desirable Senate committees."

John smiled. Janice's enthusiasm always gave him a lift. "Let's not get ahead of ourselves, Janice. I'm still the *junior* Senator from North Carolina."

John's private line rang. Sara was on the line, but she had a difficult time speaking.

"Sara, what's wrong? Is Connor okay?"

"Connor's fine. But your interview with Melanie ..."

"What about it?"

"It happened again, John. People are claiming you spoke in tongues. Word is spreading across the Internet. It's been picked up on the cable news shows. You'll probably be getting calls any minute now from the press."

"That's ridiculous." John hit the speaker button and brought Janice into the conversation.

"Janice, you listened to my interview with Melanie, right?"

"Of course I did."

"You didn't hear me speak in tongues, did you?"

"No. Of course not. I would have said something if I had."

Sara's voice crackled through the speaker. "This time, apparently, it wasn't every word you spoke, John, just some of them. And the story floating around is that not everyone can hear it."

"People are imagining things," John said.

"Maybe, but it's causing a stir ... John, turn on Channel 7. They're doing a piece on it right now."

Janice flicked on the television. A reporter stood next to a group of a dozen people of mixed ages, races and gender sitting in two rows of six. The reporter was speaking, "We have gathered an informal cross-section of the community and we're about to play the controversial clip from Senator Peters' interview yesterday with Melanie Kraft that has generated so much controversy."

Janice interrupted with a sniff. "Controversy. That's a reporter's favorite word. When they can't think of the right adjective, they call it controversial. Idiots."

"Shhh," John admonished.

The reporter continued, "Afterward, we'll ask each of our panelists whether they heard anything unusual."

The clip played. John and Janice looked at each other. Neither of them had heard anything strange.

"Sara, did you notice anything odd?" John asked.

She knew from the mere fact that John had posed the question that neither he nor Janice had heard anything unusual.

"No," she lied.

One of the panelists on the television program, an elderly black man, had clearly been taken aback by what he had heard. The rest had quizzical looks on their faces, as if they were wondering what the fuss was about. The reporter directed his question to the entire group, "How many of your heard anything other than English?"

The one man who had reacted to the clips raised his hand, pulled it back, and then raised it again. The reporter put the microphone in front of his face. "You seem a bit unsure. What did you hear?"

"Well, I only speak English, so I heard the whole thing in English. But there were three words that sounded different, almost musical. I can't explain it better than that, but those three words jumped out at me like they were saying, 'Pay attention, Gus. Pay attention.'"

"What words jumped out at you?"

"Hear. See. Believe."

Chapter 12

The blue in his eyes was nearly gone; only the outer rim of his irises showed their original color, the rest had disappeared into enveloping black pupils. He had recently started wearing tinted contact lenses when venturing outside, both to protect his eyes from the sunlight and to conceal them from curious onlookers.

He had never been to America before. Its sights, smells and sounds were strange, a bit off-kilter, starting with the police sirens he heard shortly after he got into the taxi at the airport. Their wails were deeper and longer than the short, pulsing sirens of France. The people were deeper and longer, too, he thought – fatter and taller, to be more accurate. He found the thought amusing; he enjoyed the feeling of superiority it gave him. As the taxi worked its way slowly through downtown Washington, DC traffic toward Clark's office, he observed tourists bustling from one monument to the next. Many wore jeans and t-shirts with windbreakers against the slight chill, dressed not very differently from his French countrymen. He, in contrast, wore a sharply tailored black suit, a white shirt that did not appear to have lost any of its starched crispness on the transatlantic flight, and a black tie. He was always impeccably dressed.

When he arrived at Clark's building, he was shown into a conference room adjoining Clark's office and asked to wait. He could hear two voices through the door. Clark's he recognized; the other he did not.

Clark threw a newspaper to the man seated across the desk from him. "Read this," Clark spat. "This is your guy causing all this commotion."

Governor Smith picked up the paper and looked at the story dominating the front page. It was the same front- page story in newspapers around the world:

Last call for prayers has been pushed back a few hours lately. Churches, synagogues and mosques have been staying open late, tending to overflow crowds. Many come to worship because they believe they have heard the voice of God speaking through Senator Peters during his interview with TV personality Melanie Kraft.

One such woman, Julia Schwartz, who has prayed at the Mount Zion Hebrew Temple for three straight days, claims she never heard anything so beautiful. "It was like a song in my heart. I've been on the street, you know, for the last five years, but I'm done with all that. God is calling me to something better."

Others come because they did not hear God's voice and want to know why. Father Thomas, a Roman Catholic priest at St. John's Church in Old Town Alexandria, has been answering such questions from his parishioners for several days. But he himself heard nothing unusual in Senator Peters' interview, and he is a bit mystified by all the excitement.

"I know many, many God-fearing people who watched the interview and heard only Senator Peters' voice," he said.

"I understand that God works in mysterious ways, but this just doesn't make any sense. I have a hard time believing that the world is witnessing a miracle. I think it's probably more a case of people who desperately want to believe convincing themselves that they've heard a miracle. People think they see ghosts, too. That doesn't mean they're there."

At least one noted psychologist, Dr. Bernard Willis from Stanford, has proclaimed the worldwide reaction to Senator Peters' interview as the greatest

> example of mass hysteria the world has ever known.
>
> "Things like this have happened before," said Willis. "A few centuries ago, entire towns fell prey to the belief that women cavorted with demons in the middle of the night. In their hysteria, leading citizens swore they saw it with their own eyes, and as a result, innocent people burned at the stake. Today, we have the ability to transmit such hysteria across the globe at the speed-of-light. But just because hysteria spreads farther and faster than ever doesn't make it true."
>
> But as Julia Schwartz put it, those who claim they heard God speak believe that they "know what He sounds like, and no amount of psychological mumbo-jumbo will change that fact."

Governor Smith finished reading the article. "I thought John would be a good soldier," he said, "someone who would do what he was told, and mostly keep his head down."

"Yeah, well, the ability to keep his head down and his mouth shut don't seem to be in his repertoire. I want to find out what the hell is going on, and I want to find out from the source. Have you set up a meeting with him yet?"

"All my calls are being routed through his assistant, Janice Baxter. She keeps telling me she'll get it on his calendar, but so far no date has been set. I'm going to call his wife, Sara. I've known her a long time. She'll set it up for me."

"Make sure Sara understands that if her husband doesn't play ball, there will be a heavy political price to pay."

Smith stared long and hard at Clark, but Clark pretended not to notice and started shuffling papers from one pile to another. "Clark." Smith's voice had a hard edge to it. Clark looked up and smiled, but it was a smile that chilled rather than warmed. Smith felt his stomach twist and almost took a step back but managed to stand in place.

"Something bothering you, Ned?" Clark asked.

"I understand that we need to talk to John, but I don't appreciate your trying to give me orders, Clark. Remember, I'm the governor, not you."

Clark's smile widened. "That's right, Ned. *You're* the one in office, not me. An office I obtained for you." Then his smiled disappeared and his voice became hard and clipped. "You're nothing without me, Ned. You remember that."

After Smith left, the door leading to Clark's private conference room opened and the young man stepped through the doorway, taking the seat that Smith had just vacated.

"Hello, Emile. That was our governor who just left," Clark said.

"I heard." His voice was low and gravelly. "It doesn't appear that you have him completely under control."

"He's not a problem. He just needs to mouth off now and then to feel important. To feel like a governor."

"All talk, eh?"

"They usually are."

The man leaned forward in his chair. "Peters is a Messenger, isn't he?" he asked.

"Perhaps. I'm not sure."

"This latest incident hasn't convinced you?"

"Peters himself doesn't hear it. How can he be a Messenger if he doesn't even know what the message is or hear himself giving it?"

"What other explanation can there be?"

"If we act prematurely, and it turns out Peters isn't a Messenger, we could trigger consequences we may not be able to control."

The man pulled his jacket away from his hip, revealing a small pistol tucked into his pants. "The Master is growing impatient for answers."

"Where did you get that gun?" Clark asked.

The man simply smiled and shrugged in reply.

"The Master sent you here to assist me. I don't need a gun to do my job."

"He sent me here to do what needed to be done."

Clark gritted his teeth at the young man's disrespectful attitude – he would not have acted so rudely unless the Master had indicated some dissatisfaction with Clark's handling of this problem.

"You will not do anything foolish. Can you imagine the scrutiny that would follow any ... precipitous action? The police? The press? That's hardly the type of attention we want to bring on ourselves."

"Perhaps you should go to Corsica and make your explanations in person."

"If asked, I will. In the meantime, we wait. Sometimes things have a way of working out, if only you have the patience to let them."

The young man eyed Clark suspiciously. Clark shook his head and sighed. "People in this town get chewed up and spit out every single day. You don't need a bullet to destroy a man. You only need a good sound bite."

Chapter 13

John pulled a large cardboard box from his closet and leafed through the mementoes he had collected over the past twenty years, a flyer from his first campaign, ticket stubs from the Royal Shakespeare Company's production of *Hamlet* that he and Sara had attended in Stratford, England on their honeymoon, a program from one of Connor's school pageants, and he wondered where the time had gone. He reread each of the letters that Sara had written to him during the year of their engagement and found tucked among them the draft of a poem he had written to her the year before. He smiled as he recalled the look on her face when she saw it folded inside her birthday card.

I love you most in the rush of morning
Shaking sleep from our drowsy son
Shepherding him through pre-school rituals
Of clothes, cereal and carpool lines

I love you most in the noisy afternoon
Thoughts of you sneak through the clutter,
Clatter of emails, faxes and conference calls.
And for a moment stop the world

I love you most in the quiet of the night
Cares of the day have set with the sun
Sleep has not yet lidded our eyes
We embrace in a communion of souls

I love you most

He still loved her most. He was a lucky man and he knew it. Sara had been there for him and with him through every challenge, every setback and every victory. Although they were both different people than they had been as students at the University of North Carolina, they loved each other as much as ever. He knew that Sara still had a hard time believing that she was the wife of a United States Senator – it was a long road she had traveled from the ramshackle farmhouse in the hills of Appalachia where she grew up. She was the first person in her family, let alone the first woman, to finish high school, and fortunately, she had a sponsor in the name of John Desmond Smith, the richest man in her part of the state. Smith's oldest son, Neville or Ned as everyone called him, had graduated from the University of North Carolina before going to law school, and Smith had made some healthy contributions to the college's coffers. When he heard about Sara's board scores, he made inquiries. After learning that she was not only an excellent student, but a good athlete and most importantly, a good person – she spent long hours tutoring other students without charge – he put in a call to some friends of his on the university's board of trustees, and an offer of a full academic scholarship soon followed.

Sara met John at a new students' mixer sponsored by the Honors Department. He had been standing off in a corner by himself, wearing a bemused smile. She wandered in his direction and waited to see if he would strike up a conversation. When he didn't, she did, and they took an instant liking to each other. Sara and John started spending so much time together that by the time they were sophomores, their friends hardly ever mentioned one of their names without throwing in the other, as if their two names were as intimately linked as any other person's first and last name.

They married soon after graduation. She became a teacher while he worked on various political campaigns and on various politicians' staffs. By the time Connor was born, John had run for and won office in a local election. Sara's connection to the Smith family helped get him involved in Ned Smith's first Senatorial campaign and ultimately led to John's being appointed to the U.S. Senate when Ned became governor.

He depended on her more than she probably knew. As John sat paging through memories of their time together, he realized how much of what he had said to her over the years he had said in letters or poems. His thoughts always came more freely and clearly when he wrote them down. He picked up a pen and wondered whether, if he let his hand float across the page, the words that flowed would bring order to his thoughts.

Sara,

Remember when I used to lay my head in your lap. You would gently stroke the hair behind my ear and I would gently drift into pleasant dreams. Such sweet, little things are the colors of young love. Thinking back on them is like looking at old photographs – the images are there but the colors have faded to sepia. Sepia isn't bad; it's a heartwarming tone. Soft. Comforting. But it makes me feel old.

It's hard to believe we've been married twenty years. I remember so clearly that wonderful morning when you promised to take me, in sickness or in health, for richer, for poorer, for better, for worse. You have kept your promise. But am I still the man to whom your promise was made? Am I still the man to whom you offered your heart?

Sara, my head hurts. Worry and fear keep pounding at me. I try not to let it show to you and never to Connor, but it takes its toll. Sometimes it seems that it's all chaos; my thoughts are unmoored and lack compass. I cannot think clearly.

How can it be that what I speak and what people hear are not the same?

In every day conversation, we say one thing, but people, hearing what they want to hear, interpret our words in a way entirely different than what we intended.

But what's happening to me is something altogether different. There are no crossed signals or debates over the meanings of words. This is something I can't explain. I've tried. I've looked up everything I could find on any subject that comes close. You know how I can be about that. That time you had to go in for surgery, I read so much medical literature I started arguing with the doctor about the procedures he planned on using. Remember how flustered he got with me. I suppose I was being a pain, but I wanted to be absolutely sure you were getting the best possible treatment. I can't find anything that explains what has happened to me.

It would be easy to say it was God, if only I were a religious man. But I'm not, Sara, and never have been. Too much random pain and suffering in the world for me to believe wholeheartedly in an omniscient, all-loving God.

There's a piece of advice that gets passed around to freshmen Senators – I don't recall if I mentioned it to you before: "Be careful you don't speak more clearly than you think." Is that what has happened to me? Are my words getting ahead of my thoughts? Have I tapped into some ability that perhaps we all have but haven't understood how to use? If so, will I ever learn how to control it?

I have always relied on the power of words to make my way in the world. In high school, I was the star of the debate team and the editor of the school newspaper. You've witnessed my history since then. You know full well that words have always been my allies, my tools. Now I'm learning something entirely new about them. Words can betray you.

I think that later tonight I will lay my head in your lap and pretend for a few minutes that things are as they used to be.

Love always,

John

John took the letter and placed it in the box with his memories. Someday, he would share these thoughts with Sara, either by telling them to her or giving her the letter. Someday. But not yet. She was already worried enough – he didn't need to add to her burden.

Chapter 14

Janice and Archbishop O'Connell walked slowly along the footpath hugging the Potomac River. The air was cool and crisp, a perfect October day. The brilliant foliage of red, orange and yellow leaves burst forth from both the trees and from their reflections in the sun-dappled water.

"I take this walk almost every morning," said the Archbishop, "but I enjoy it most this time of the year."

"I love the fall, too. Reminds me of the times I would jump into the piles of leaves my father had raked. He didn't do much yard work, but every year, he raked the leaves."

"Maybe he enjoyed watching you play in them."

"Maybe."

"What happened between you?"

"I disappointed him. He doesn't forgive that very easily."

"That is true," the Archbishop said. "He neither forgives nor forgets easily. He was so angry when he learned that some of the money he had donated over the years was used to …" The Archbishop exhaled loudly and turned his palms up in a supplicating manner, "I'm afraid I disappointed him as well." The Archbishop paused, shaking his head. "I've tried to explain the difference between God's perfect Church and the imperfect men who run it, but he didn't want to hear it."

"He's smart enough to see the difference, "Janice replied. "He just doesn't want to. He prefers absolutes. With him, you're either right or you're wrong."

"Perhaps. Or perhaps he just lives by a higher standard than most of us are capable of meeting. But you still haven't answered my question. How did you disappoint him?"

"It's not something I'm ready to talk about, yet. Maybe later. And that's not why you called me. Why did you want to meet this morning?"

"I have some information I want to share with you, but you must promise that you won't tell anyone other than the Senator and his wife what I'm about to tell you. And you can only tell them if you trust them as much as I trust you to keep it secret."

"Maybe you shouldn't tell me."

"You were the one who brought all of this to my attention in the first place." The Archbishop stopped walking and took Janice's hands into his. "I've known you since you were a little girl, and this is something you should know. Something that might help you and the Senator with any doubts you may have."

"Okay. I promise."

"The Vatican did some tests on the Senator's interview."

"Tests? What do you mean?"

"Whenever there is a credible claim that a miracle has occurred, the Vatican checks it out. The Vatican Academy of Sciences has a team of highly ..."

"The Vatican Academy of Sciences?"

"Yes. The Vatican is quite heavily involved in the sciences, has been for a long time. Most people don't realize that we have one of the oldest observatories in the world, dating back to the 16th Century. In fact, the Vatican Observatory currently funds and operates a working observatory in the Arizona desert. But we have other types of scientists, too. And we have a strong Intelligence group, about which I know little and can say even less. What I can tell you is that the United States trusts us, in part because of the Vatican's role in bringing down Communism, and is sometimes willing to share intelligence and other assets with us. I've even heard stories about how angry the French got during the Balkan War. The U.S. showed the Vatican some aerial shots it wouldn't show France, and when the French ambassador heard about it and asked why, he was told, 'Because we trust the Pope.'"

Janice stared at the Archbishop. He was obviously a much more significant and powerful figure within the Catholic Church than she had ever imagined. "I had no idea you were so well connected within the Vatican."

The Archbishop chuckled, "You don't have to be *at* the Vatican to be *in* the Vatican. Anyway, the point is the Church borrowed some software from the CIA that analyzes voice samples at the phoneme level, the smallest unit of speech. This software authenticates a speaker's identity and can trace pronunciations back to a speaker's place of origin."

"Sounds like that character from *My Fair Lady* who could tell where people came from based on the way they talked."

"Precisely."

"And you ran the Senator's speech through the program?"

"Actually, we tested his interview with Melanie Kraft. We weren't as confident of the integrity of the recordings we had of the income tax speech."

'And?"

"According to the computer ... remember, we're talking about each phoneme as it's pronounced ... the only sounds were those made by Senator Peters. No anomalies, no deviations, pure North Carolinian speech."

"Okay, so what you're telling me is that we're dealing with a huge case of mass hysteria, just like some of the talking heads on cable news want us to believe."

"No, I'm not saying that at all."

"Then I really don't understand."

"Even though the computer program could not detect anything other than Senator Peters' voice, two of the scientists running the analysis claimed that they heard the same three words, 'Hear ... Speak ... Believe' in their native languages. One was Italian. One was Spanish."

"So what does it mean? The computer was wrong? The scientists were hearing things?"

"Neither. The computer wasn't wrong. It analyzed the only sounds that were actually on the tape. But the scientists weren't imagining things, either."

"Both statements can't be true."

"Yes they can. We did one further experiment. We chopped up the tape of Senator Peters' interview into short clips and ran them out of order to an Italian deaf man who doesn't read or write English. He was born deaf and has communicated in sign language his entire life. We wired electrodes to him to monitor his brain activity as he watched the clips. For a while, he didn't understand a thing and was complaining about the point of the experiment. Then, suddenly, he started signing frantically to the interpreter that he understood the word "Believe."

"Did he hear it, or see it in sign?"

"No. Somehow, the word was communicated directly to that portion of his brain that handles language. The electrodes registered a high level of brain activity consistent with speech recognition."

"So this deaf man heard the word 'Believe' without actually hearing it."

"I would put it a bit differently. I don't think we're dealing with language at all, but with thought that transcends language, or perhaps precedes language. Somehow, what Senator Peters says is communicated directly to the mind, but since we humans are not sophisticated enough creatures to understand thoughts unless they're reduced to language, that's what we've done. That's why non-English speakers think they hear him in their native language, and that's why English speakers notice a musical vibrancy to his words. They're not actually hearing him."

"You're going to have to walk me through this slowly."

"The computer can't analyze what isn't physically present on the tape. When John "speaks" in tongues, he's not actually making any sounds beyond that which he hears himself making."

"What is it, then? Telepathy?"

"Not the way we normally think about it. It's not mind reading. And you've told me that Senator Peters neither realizes it's happening, nor notices anything unusual about his speech when he hears himself on tape. So he isn't generating it. Someone else is using John to communicate directly with our minds."

"Who could do such a thing?"

"That, Janice, is the question."

"Is it God?"

"I don't know. I'm not ready to go there yet."

"Why could only some people hear it this time? Why couldn't I hear it?"

"I don't know."

"Did you?"

"Hear it?"

"Yes."

"Yes, I did."

Janice stopped walking and leaned against one of the many large boulders scattered along the river bank. Her hands slipped into her jacket pockets, her chin dropped to her chest, and she looked absently at the ground, kicking away a leaf that had fallen on her shoe.

The Archbishop put a comforting hand on her shoulder. "I wouldn't worry about not hearing it, Janice."

She looked up at him. "I'm worried about a lot of things...I don't know ... At first, I thought only about what this would mean for the Senator's career, my career. But with this last one ... I don't know. It's easy for you to say not to worry – you heard it. You were asked by ... whoever is doing this ... to believe. I wasn't."

"You're a good woman, a woman of faith," the Archbishop said. "You have nothing to worry about."

"How do I know that my faith is strong enough?" Janice started walking back toward the parking lot without waiting for a reply.

Chapter 15

The Reverend snapped his cell phone shut with a flourish. Water spots dotted his sleeve from the rain that sprayed through the open window of his Georgetown hotel penthouse suite. He detested hotel air-conditioning, and didn't mind getting a little wet in exchange for breathing fresh air. Darnell sat on a sofa well back from the window. He was the only staff member the Reverend had brought with him to Washington. He liked Darnell – there was something about him that the Reverend found both intriguing and beguiling. Normally, the Reverend trusted his ability to read people, and he had earlier thought that he had pegged Darnell fairly cleanly. On the surface, he presented as both bright and gullible – a combination of traits that marked a con man's favorite target, someone too smart to believe that he could be tricked. But the more time the Reverend spent with Darnell, the clearer it became that there was something different about him, something the Reverend couldn't pin down. Something that his instincts told him might come in useful some day.

"We're in," he said to Darnell. "That was Senator Peters' assistant. It took some doing – she doesn't exactly trust us 'religious types,' as she put it – but she's willing to hear me out."

"What do you plan on telling her?" Darnell asked.

"Peters is in over his head, Darnell. There are Christians calling him the Second Coming. There are Jews calling him Elijah. He isn't either of those, and there is no one that a crowd hates more than a hero who doesn't live up to his hype. The Senator needs someone who can help him manage expectations, someone who knows how to navigate the tricky waters he has found himself in. I want to be that person. I plan on being that person."

"So you still don't believe he's for real?"

"I stopped believing in miracles a long time ago."

Darnell shook his head as a smile crossed his face. "There are more things in heaven and earth than are dreamt of in your philosophy."

The Reverend fixed Darnell with a curious stare. "I wouldn't have guessed you to be a fan of Shakespeare."

"You mean I'm smarter than I look?"

"No. Not that. I mean, yes. Oh, you know what I mean."

Darnell shrugged. "How do you explain his interview with Melanie Kraft?"

"Listen," the Reverend replied, "I don't know what happened during Peters' interview with Kraft– I didn't hear anything unusual. But just because I can't explain it doesn't mean that the answer must be God."

"Apparently, Senator Peters agrees with you."

"That's why he'll listen to what I have to say. I won't be one of the people fawning all over him, hoping that blessings will rain down on my head if I can only touch his sleeve."

"Why did you want me along on this trip?"

"You're my pulse on the people, Darnell. You're just like those folks out there," said the Reverend, pointing out the window onto the crowded street below. "You believe the Senator performed a miracle because you want there to have been a miracle."

"My personal wants don't change the fact that something happened that no one can explain. A miracle seems as likely an explanation as any other."

The Reverend crossed the room to the mini-bar and fixed himself a whiskey on the rocks. "This," he said, swirling the amber color liquor around the ice, "is the kind of miracle I believe in. Aqua vitae – the water of life. I ought to baptize people in this. Talk about getting filled with the Spirit. Would you like one?"

"No thanks. I don't drink."

The Reverend smiled. "You should try it sometime. Relaxes the mind. Unburdens the soul. The first glass warms the heart, the second the belly, the third..."

"A place a bit lower down."

"It's a generous spirit that flames the passions."

"'O thou invisible spirit of wine, if thou hast no name to be known by, let us call thee devil.'"

"Shakespeare again?" the Reverend asked.

"I like to read." Darnell pulled a soda from the small refrigerator. "I'll stick with this, if you don't mind. Alcohol doesn't mix well with my prescription."

The Reverend hadn't been aware that Darnell was on any medication. "Suit yourself."

"Are we still going to meet with Mr. Clark?"

"Apparently, he is the man to see in this town, so it would hardly seem appropriate not to pay our respects."

Chapter 16

It was going to get harder and harder to line up a clean shot at Peters. Reporters and television cameras shadowed his every move, and crowds gathered around him whenever he appeared in public. Mark Hartson realized that he'd have to be ready to strike quickly.

Originally, he had thought he could shoot the Senator and melt away undetected. He now understood that such an outcome was unlikely, but he remained determined to see this through to the end. He wasn't the sort to give up just because the road to success proved tougher than initially imagined.

A few blocks away, Imrahain sat on his hotel room bed sharpening a knife he had purchased at a pawnshop near the courthouse. To him, pawnshops perfectly symbolized the weakness of the American spirit. Their windows and counters were littered with the detritus of overindulgent people who spent more than they could afford simply to impress their neighbors or convince themselves that they were better and more important than they truly were. What need did anyone have for a $25,000 wristwatch? What was the point of a $5,000 fountain pen? Men of faith had no need for such baubles, but all men were subject to temptation. He did not want the decadence of this culture to infect his home, and as long as Senator Peters remained alive and able to 'speak' to his people, that risk remained high. With every pass of the sharpening stone across the blade, the end of that risk drew nearer.

Chapter 17

Sara brushed back a lock of hair that had fallen over John's eyes. He looked peaceful as he slept, a look he now rarely had when awake. She loved this man so much, and she was so terribly afraid for him. No one understood what was happening, or why, and no one could predict where it would lead. She, Janice and John could plan and plan, almost fooling themselves into believing that they had anticipated every conceivable contingency, but reality had a way of circling back to them, reminding them that they were helpless in the face of events.

She, alone among the three of them, had heard those three words from the Kraft interview spoken with a resonant tone not her husband's, and it made her angry and afraid. Afraid because she couldn't begin to fathom the power capable of such an act, angry because someone was using her husband without his consent, and no one, not even God – if it was God – had the right to do that. Wasn't God supposed to be about free will? Where was the free will in this bit of showmanship? John was being treated like a puppet. The story Janice told about the Vatican testing only deepened her disquiet. John had shrugged it off, as usual, though she couldn't help but think that it bothered him more than he let on.

Sara reflected on the sometimes meandering, sometimes dramatically conflicting paths her thoughts had taken over the past few days as she tried to make sense of events that defied reason. She knew her doubts bordered on and perhaps crossed into the blasphemous, but they came nonetheless, and she wasn't in a mood to pray for forgiveness. She cared more about John than she did about the fate of her soul.

She brushed another lock of his hair, and John's eyes opened slightly. He slipped his hand around Sara's waist. "Good morning, honey."

“Good morning,” she answered. She forced a smile to her face. He was under enough stress and didn’t need her worries filling in the only moments of peace he was likely to have this day.

“Is Connor awake?”

“Yes, he came in twenty minutes ago for a good morning hug.”

“Too bad,” he said with an impish grin.

“Why?”

“I was hoping he was still asleep. I wouldn’t mind some private time with you.”

“He’s watching a cartoon downstairs. Not much is going to distract him.”

“I may have to revisit my opinion of cartoons.”

Later, after the cartoons had ended and John and Sara had dressed, they brewed a pot of coffee, made waffles, and talked. They talked about taking a summer vacation at the Outer Banks, what gift to buy for a birthday party Connor would be attending later that week, and whether Connor was getting too little or too much homework. They talked long after their third cups of coffee had grown cold, each treasuring the feel of a routine morning.

When the phone rang, Sara suggested that they let the answering machine take the call, but John pushed away from the breakfast table and picked up the receiver. It was Janice.

“Good morning, John.”

“It’s Saturday. You’re supposed to be off.”

“I’m never off, and neither are you.”

John chuckled. “Fine, fine. What is it, Janice?”

“Clark called.”

“Who?”

“John, don’t be dense. I’m talking about Clark. *‘The man to see’* Clark. ”

"Oh. That Clark," he replied in a voice as cheerful as the smile on his face. "What did he want?"

"To talk to you."

"Why?"

"I'm not sure, John, but this can only be good news."

"Should I mention this to Ned?"

"I don't see why it's any of his business."

"Go ahead and set it up. Now can I get back to my coffee?"

"I'll call you later."

Sara was clearing the table and about to put John's cup into the dishwasher. "Do you want me to brew a fresh pot?"

"No thanks."

"What did Janice want?"

"What else? More politics."

"She's not still floating that crazy idea about having you run for President is she?"

John faked a hurt look. "What's so crazy about it?"

Sara smiled and continued to load the dishwasher. "Nothing. Nothing at all. If you want to be President, John, you've got my vote." She crossed over to John and poked a playful finger in his chest. "And you'll have Janice's vote. As for the rest of the country ..." She scrunched her face and shrugged her shoulders, "...let's just say they may not be ready for someone as remarkable, as young, and as handsome as you."

"You know, Janice was only half-joking when she suggested it."

"And only half sober, too. We'd all had a few glasses of wine that night."

"Seriously, she thinks if we floated a trial balloon, we might be pleasantly surprised at the results. Apparently, a lot of people liked what they saw during my TV appearances."

"John," Sara said, "One thing at a time. Remember why you got into politics in the first place: to serve. You always said that wasn't just an empty phrase to you. You're brand new in the Senate. Do this job first, and do it well, before you think about anything else."

Sara put her hand on John's shoulder. "Look at this from a practical viewpoint: you'd ruin the goodwill and the connections that you spent years building if you cross Ned. He wants the nomination and he is probably going to get it. All you'll get from running against him is grief. Besides, he has always been a friend to us – he appointed you to the Senate – let's not be ungrateful."

"I know, I know. But to tell you the truth, Ned has been getting on my nerves lately. He keeps asking me to explain this tongues thing, and I don't know how many different ways to tell him I haven't got a clue. He just doesn't seem to believe me. Besides, he's been after me to do all sorts of favors for him and others in the party, but hasn't done a thing to help get me on any of the more important Senate Committees. He could talk to his buddies in the Senate if he wanted, but he told me those positions traditionally go to senior members."

"He's right, isn't he?"

"Seniority shouldn't be the only test for appointment to those committees. Merit ought to have something to do with it."

"Have another talk with Ned. He's a friend. He'll help you as best he can."

John nodded, but did not share with Sara his suspicion that Ned would find ways to avoid helping him, in part because he feared being overshadowed, and in part because he was uncertain how long John's popularity would last. Helping John's star to shine might cause his own to dim; conversely, if he lobbied hard on John's behalf to secure an important committee membership, only to watch John's popularity fade, he wouldn't get much of a return on the political capital he had spent. The bottom line, John thought, was that Ned would act pursuant to a political calculus, not as a friend.

Chapter 18

"Tell me, John ... do you mind if I call you John?" Clark didn't wait for a reply before continuing, "tell me why you got into politics in the first place."

Clark's voice sounded smooth and friendly enough, but John could feel hardness lurking in the words he spoke, as if they were elastic bands that could be pulled taut in an instant.

They sat in a cafe next to the National Theater, where John and Sara had recently taken Connor to see a Disney musical. The three of them had been at the same table following the matinee, with Connor chattering excitedly about the show between sips of hot chocolate. That had been a much more pleasant experience than it appeared this was going to be.

"Why does anyone get into politics?" John answered.

Clark smiled. He had a haunted face, but the warm light of the setting sun softened his wrinkles, making him look for the moment as gentle as a kindly grandfather. John could sense the keen intelligence at work in his eyes, even though they gazed at him from behind smoky gray lenses.

Clark wagged a crooked finger at John. "I'm not asking just anyone, John. I'm asking you."

"It will sound trite."

"Try me."

"To help people."

"That's it?

"That's it."

"No little boy who dreamed of being president?"

"My dream was to be an astronaut."

Clark picked up the oversized white porcelain mug from which he drank his coffee – he refused to drink out of cardboard cups – and took a slow sip.

"So how is it that you spent your life laboring away in a local district instead of blasting off to space?"

"Lousy eyesight. If you can't see, you can't fly. Without my contact lenses, I'm blind as a bat."

Clark flashed a smile, rose from his seat, and took his cup over to the counter to have it refilled. A noisy crowd of teenagers pushed into the café. Two squeezed into the already crowded table next to John and knocked John's jacket off the back of his chair. One of them, a teen-aged girl about 16 years old, wearing a tight T-Shirt with the logo of a rock band he had never heard of, apologized and put it back on the chair.

"Oh my God! You're Senator Peters," she exclaimed in a voice that sounded straight out of a movie parody about empty headed, cash rich girls. "It's really you! Can you say something for me? Anything? I'm bilingual." Her friends crowded around him, waiting eagerly for him to speak.

"I'm sorry," said John, in as soft and understanding a voice as he could muster. "It's not a magic act. I can't do it on cue, and I honestly don't think it's going to happen again."

They looked disappointed, but only for a moment. The girl quickly regained her smile and asked for an autograph. The others echoed her request, and after he had signed each of their T-shirts, he turned back to Clark, who had returned with a steaming mug.

Clark picked up their conversation where it had left off.

"So you're blind as a bat. That explains why you're not an astronaut. Now how about filling me in on how you wound up in politics."

"I started thinking about it when I was a kid, actually. After I had figured out I wasn't going to the moon. I was fifteen years old, and I'd gotten a weekend job at a movie theater near my house, doing stuff you'd expect a teenager to do – selling popcorn at the snack counter, taking out the trash, cleaning the theater between showings. Most of the employees were teenage boys like me, but one was a grown man who was kind of slow," John pointed to his head, "upstairs, if you know what I mean.

"We all called the guy 'Superman' as a joke. I never even learned his real name. I'm not sure who gave him the nickname, but it wasn't hard to figure out the joke. The comic book Superman could do anything, but this guy ... well ... he couldn't do anything right, and actually didn't do much at all except stand around the lobby all day holding a dustpan and broom."

Clark squinted. Even with his tinted glasses, it seemed bright in the room. "How did he keep his job?"

"The manager of the place, a guy named Dottie, kept him on."

"So let me guess. Something happened with this guy that changed your life; made you dedicate yourself to public service?"

"Pretty much."

"What was it?"

"Dottie was always playing jokes on Superman, telling him that some of the women who worked at the theater liked him, stupid stuff like that, just to get a laugh. Then one unbelievably cold night, Dottie told Superman that we were running out of steam. He said the whole place was powered by steam and that he'd have to shut down if they didn't get some fast. So he asked Superman if he would do a huge favor and walk to the firehouse a few blocks down the street to get some.

"Superman bundled up and walked down to the firehouse with an empty bucket, planning to bring it back full." John paused and took a deep breath. This was not a memory he enjoyed reliving, and on each of the few occasions that he told the story, he had to gather himself for a few moments before he could finish. "He didn't come back for a while, long enough for even Dottie to start to get worried.

Finally, he walked in the door, his glasses frosted, his face beet red from the cold, and with tears frozen on his cheeks. He told Dottie that when he arrived at the firehouse, they didn't have any steam. They just laughed at him. But since he knew how important it was to get steam, he kept looking. He walked in the freezing cold to gas stations, restaurants, shops, anyplace he could find open. He didn't want to let Dottie down."

"What did Dottie do?"

"He just laughed and said, 'Oh, that's okay, Superman. After you left, I remembered that we don't use steam. We use electricity.'

"Everybody laughed, even Superman, everybody except me. I lost it. I started screaming at Dottie, telling him what an awful person he was to take advantage of someone like that."

"And?"

"Dottie looked at me like I hit him in the face with a wet fish. After he got over the shock of my yelling at him, he fired me. First, though, he lectured me on how if it wasn't for him, Superman wouldn't have had a job; that no one else would hire him; that he kept Superman on out of the goodness of his heart; and who the hell was I to tell him off. I grabbed my coat and headed out, but before I went through the door, I turned to wave good-bye to Superman. He was by the snack bar, standing next to Dottie, wearing a bigger-than-life grin as Dottie patted him on the back and whispered something funny in his ear."

Clark took his glasses off for a moment to wipe away the condensation caused by the steam from his coffee. Although he kept his head bowed while he cleaned his lenses, John saw his eyes for a brief moment. His pupils were arrestingly large, making his eyes appear almost entirely black, set off by the red tinge of the most bloodshot corneas John had ever seen.

"You're lucky," Clark said. "You learned an invaluable lesson far earlier in life than most people do. I'm not even sure most people ever learn it."

"What lesson is that?"

"That there's often more to people than you can see from the surface and that it's not so easy to figure out what's beneath. What you think you know about a person often proves to be wrong."

John shook his head and chuckled. "Is that your profound insight for the day?"

"It's deeper than you might think. I've been in this business a whole lot longer than you, and I'm reckoned a pretty good judge of people, but I've stopped believing that I can figure people out. Every time I thought I had, they went and did something that completely surprised me."

"Are you trying to figure me out?"

Clark laughed. "I wonder if that would be a hopeless quest."

"So why did you want to meet with me?"

"I'll get to that. But I want to finish off the Superman story, first. How did it lead you to politics?"

"I couldn't stand the thought that someone like Superman, someone who could be taught to do so much more than he was doing, was so dependent on the charity of a man like Dottie. I wanted to do what I could to see that others like Superman could go to school, get decent jobs, live with dignity."

"We're not that different, then. Helping people is what I'm all about. John, we live in a harsh world. Dog eat dog. It's up to people like you and me to make it a kinder, gentler place."

"How?"

"For my part, I help the right people get elected."

John studied at Clark for a long time. "Let me ask my question again. Why did you want to meet with me?"

Clark took another sip of coffee.

"Did Ned Smith ask you to do this?" John continued.

Clark leaned forward to speak, and his face came closer to John than it had been the entire evening. John reflexively backed away, and Clark quickly and gracefully eased back into his chair. A thin-lipped smile stretched across his face.

"Ned? Come on, John. Don't be so naïve. Ned does what I tell him to do. I wanted to talk to you myself. You've turned into one of the most recognizable people in the country" – he nodded to the teenage girl whose T-shirt John had autographed – "and you're a Senator in my party, but I don't know who you are other than what I've seen on TV, and they just keep showing the same clips again and again. Perhaps it's a hopeless quest, but I would like to know who you are. I'd also like to know why you speak in tongues."

"Christ, not that again!"

"It's a fair question, John. It is the thing that sets you apart."

"I'll tell you the same thing I've told everyone else. I have no idea. I don't even hear it."

"I believe you, I think."

John scoffed. "Thanks. I can't tell you how much that means to me."

"Don't thank me yet. I'm not done. Let me see if I have this right. First, you claim that this tongues thing is not a hoax. Second, you claim not to understand how or why it happens. Third, you make a point of saying in every interview I've seen that you are not a religious figure and you'd rather everyone just forget about the whole thing and take you seriously as a politician. Have I got that right?"

"Yes," John said as emphatically as he could.

"Interesting, isn't it, though, how you seem to have thoroughly exploited your 15 minutes of fame, getting yourself on news shows, talk shows, who knows what else. I understand you're even trying to leverage your notoriety into a seat on some important Senate committees."

"It's not quite like that."

"It isn't? Then the rumors I hear about you considering a run for the White House can't be true, either."

John stared at Clark but said nothing in reply. After a few moments of silence, Clark continued. "I believe that somewhere inside you is the young man who got into politics to help his slow-witted friend from the movie theater. But I'm having a hard time finding him. On the surface, you seem to be in this for you and only you."

John forced himself to remain calm. He did not want to argue with Clark. "Just what is it you're asking of me?"

Clark lowered his glasses and fixed his black eyes on John. "I don't want you to get ahead of yourself. I want you to stop pushing for positions you don't deserve and bide your time. Let this tongues thing, whatever it is, die down. I want to be your friend, John, so believe me when I tell you that for your own good, you need to lay low."

As John climbed into one of the taxis lining the curb outside the café, Clark started to walk back to his office, wondering how best to ease the pressure the Master, through his French errand boy, was starting to apply. A sudden movement at the periphery of his vision distracted him; turning toward it, he saw a muscularly built man with a surprised, angry look on his face hurriedly jamming something that appeared to be metallic inside his pants. The man spun around and walked off with a noticeably bow-legged gait.

Clark watched him for a few moments, vaguely curious, before continuing on, his thoughts returning to the French visitor who threatened to turn his life upside down. Clark did not want to have

Senator Peters killed – it carried too much risk – but he wasn't sure he could prevent it. His best chance was either to convince the Master that Peters wasn't a Messenger, or to so thoroughly discredit Peters that it would make no difference if he was. In the meantime, he hoped that Peters would take his advice and lay low for a while.

His office light was on. A thin ribbon of smoke drifted below the ceiling and suffused the room with the pungent odor of unfiltered tobacco. "Good evening, Monsieur Clark."

"Good evening, Emile."

The young man flicked ashes into a paper cup and smiled. "So, how did your evening go?"

"Fine. It went fine."

"Did you learn anything?"

"Nothing that convinces me that he is a Messenger."

"Ah. And what would it take to convince you?"

"I'm not sure, but I think I'd know it if I saw it."

"Perhaps you don't want to believe it is possible?"

"I want to be convinced."

"I have been reading this book of yours," Emile said. He pushed an old, leather bound volume across the table. The faded gilt lettering read, *Being a True and Full Account of the Order of Mani and the Slaying of the Man Who Spake in Tongues.*

"How did you find it?"

"You've been gone for a while. I went exploring."

"You must have explored some interesting places. That book wasn't out in plain view."

Emile shrugged his shoulders. "I was bored. What can I say? I apologize. The book is a very interesting read, if not quite accurate."

"It explains the Order's official doctrine fairly well. More importantly, it reveals the Order's existence. That's reason enough to keep it out of sight."

"Hah," Emile laughed, "as if the Master cares about official doctrine."

Clark frowned and raised a warning hand. "Take care, Emile."

"My eyes are also black now, Clark. I'm not just any member. I know the truth."

"There are many truths, Emile, and each truth has many layers. What you know of the truth would cover no more than a grain of sand on an infinitely wide beach.

Emile scowled and slouched into a chair. "I have a question for you, Clark."

Clark returned the book to his desk drawer. "Well," he said, "what is it?"

"If the Order killed that man ...," Emile pointed to the desk drawer holding Clark's book, "for speaking in tongues ... and we know that much of the book is correct ... why isn't that enough for us to act?"

"That man wasn't a United States Senator. And I'm not going to make a decision based on a 400 year old story."

Emile stretched his arms lazily behind his head and looked at Clark with a broad grin across his face. "You forget yourself, Clark. It will be the Master who decides."

Chapter 19

"What did Clark want?" Sara sat at the vanity with her back to John, brushing her hair in the mirror.

John walked up behind her and took the brush from her hand. He pulled it through her hair in long, slow strokes, then set it down and started combing her hair with his fingers, letting the silky strands slip softly across his hands, occasionally rubbing her scalp. Sara's head tilted slightly back and forth under his gentle pull.

"That feels nice," she said.

He slid his hands down to her shoulders and began massaging them. He could feel the knots start to loosen under his fingertips.

"You're pretty tense," he said.

"It's been a long day. Connor was in a real mood when I picked him up after school."

"Really? Why?"

"He won't say, but I'm guessing he had a run-in with some kids at school. You know how kids are. "

"Run-in? About what?"

"I don't know."

"Was it me?"

"Maybe. You've been in the news a bit, lately. Kids hear their parents talk. Who knows what they've said about you."

"Should I talk to him?"

"He's sleeping. Don't wake him up."

"I meant tomorrow."

"No, I don't think so. If it happens again, but for now, let it be. Let's get back to the subject. What did Clark want?"

John crossed the room to their bed, sat down, and started to loosen his tie.

"For me to be patient."

"Meaning what, exactly?"

"Somehow he got wind of Janice's trial balloon idea ..."

"How?"

"Good question. I need to talk to Janice to see who else she has shared it with. I assume you haven't talked to anybody about it?"

"No, of course not."

"Well, anyway. He knows. And he's blown it all out of proportion. He thinks we were serious about it."

"Didn't you set him straight?"

"At that point, I was pissed off, so I let him think what he wanted to think."

"That may not have been the smartest thing to do."

"It is what it is."

"Well, I agree with Clark – on the need to be patient."

"Are you sure you didn't accidentally let Janice's idea slip out?"

Sara stared at John for a long moment, shook her head and walked out of the room. John chased after her.

"I'm sorry, Sara. It's been a long day for me, too."

"John, my only concern is for my family. The more I hear you talk, the less sure I am that the whole Presidency idea is just a joke."

"I'm not serious about it."

"Well, just in case you are, think about this: if you run for President, we'll be put under even more intense media scrutiny than we're under now, and I can barely handle it as it is. Think what it would do to Connor. Not to mention what it would do to your career if you lost."

"If Smith wins, it will be a long, long time before I'll be able to throw my hat in the ring."

"A few weeks ago your biggest concern was how many people would show up at your spaghetti dinner fund raiser. Now you're talking about throwing your hat in the ring for the Presidency of the

United States? What happened to the guy who couldn't believe how lucky he was to be made an interim Senator, the guy who just wanted to do his job the best way he knew how?"

"I spent a career watching people with less talent rise higher."

"That's Janice talking."

"Maybe. But I wouldn't be repeating it if I didn't think there was some truth to it."

"John, you're a United States Senator. It doesn't get much better than that, so if you need your ego stroked, walk through the halls of Congress and watch everyone suck up to you. Go out in the street and listen to those folks who think you're a prophet from God. But if you want to do the right thing, then think long and hard about what Clark said. Think long and hard about Connor and me."

After Sara went to sleep, John returned to his study and placed a blank sheet of paper at his desk. He stared at it for a long time, wondering why he hadn't been able to share with Sara everything that had been on his mind.

Dear Sara,

You're sleeping now, exhausted from a long day of worrying about Connor and me, about our family, about what will become of us. We're a long way from North Carolina and I know that in your heart, you want nothing more than to go back home and return to the life we had. There are times when I want nothing more than that, either. But we can't turn back the hands of time, and even if we could, I'm not sure I would. I can do so much more good here and I don't want to turn my back on the opportunity that now lies before me. It won't be easy. It will test our patience, yours more than mine, but it's worth the effort.

I got some sense of the challenge ahead during my meeting with Clark. It was a good introduction into the way politics is played in Washington. This city is a different place than I had imagined. It's not just that it's bigger and faster paced. There's a different feeling in the air. You know the saying, 'Tension so thick you could cut it with a knife'? That's how if felt when I met with Clark tonight. I'm not the superstitious type, but frankly, he gives me the creeps. It's hard to sit with him for very long.

I would have thought that to be as influential as he is supposed to be, as he claims to be, you'd have to be able to get along with people, but I can't see how anyone could get along with him. He's not that likeable. Maybe he's nice to people within his circle, and just doesn't bother being nice to people who aren't. He doesn't put it that way, of course. He claims he's looking out for the good of the Party, but I think it's a lot more personal than that, and it's pretty clear he doesn't see me as part of his coterie.

He said that I don't have the Party's best interest at heart. He even accused me of being selfish, of being in this for myself. Unbelievable! As if he knows anything about me. Sara, you know all too well how many opportunities in the private sector I've passed up, opportunities that would have paid a lot more than I make even as a U.S. Senator. I'm a Senator because I believe in the call of service to one's country. I don't think Clark understands that. I don't think he believes that's possible.

Maybe Clark isn't friendly with anyone. Maybe he simply tries to intimidate the hell out of everyone to get them to do what he wants. He certainly tried that approach with me. I wonder how influential he really is. He could make life difficult for me if he does have a lot of sway with other Senators, especially the more senior ones. It would be hard to get any legislation passed or get on any important committees if I don't have allies in my own Party.

Clark even claims that Ned Smith is at his beck and call. I didn't mention that to you because I know how you feel about his family and everything they've done for you. I don't want to believe that it's true, but I can't imagine Clark saying it so matter-of-factly without there being something to it. He has to know that we both go back a long way with Ned and that it would be natural for us to mention to him what Clark said. Maybe that's what he wants us to do. If it is true, then perhaps Ned's refusal to help me in the Senate had less to do with his own feelings in the matter and more to do with Clark's influence. I'm not sure.

One thing is clear. Clark has got to be worried about me. He wouldn't have insisted on meeting with me otherwise. It also makes me wonder if there isn't more to Janice's plan than I originally thought. If it had no hope of succeeding, Clark would just let me toss my hat in the ring and flame out.

Tomorrow, I'm supposed to meet with a minister that Janice thinks we should talk to. I hope he's not a Bible thumper. The religion angle is not one I want to deal with any more than I already do, but Janice says this guy represents the sort of people we'll need to win over if we're going to have any chance at pursuing the Presidency. She's probably right, and I suppose it can't hurt to meet with him. I should at least hear what the guy has to say.

There's a lot to think about.

I love you,

John

John pulled his cardboard box of memories from his closet and placed the letter inside.

Chapter 20

Sheets of loose-leaf paper lay in a jumbled pile atop John's desk. Janice reached over and grabbed the top sheet.

"What's this?" she asked.

"Nothing. Just put it back, please."

Janice glanced quickly at the page in her hand and smiled. "I didn't know you wrote poetry."

"I wouldn't dignify it by calling it poetry."

Janice started to read aloud, but John interrupted. "Please, it's bad enough you're invading my privacy, the least you could do is read it to yourself."

"Poetry should be read aloud. This is great stuff. Reminds me of Keats."

"Sarcasm doesn't become you."

Janice read in a soft voice as a partial palliative to John's wishes, but still loud enough for him to hear:

'I do not believe in ghosts,'
He whispered.
I stared as the sounds he made
Coalesced into words
Among the drift of my thoughts.
'Neither do I,' I finally replied.
A soft chuckle
Breathed from his lips,
A spectral finger wagged
'Then how do you explain me?'

Janice cocked her head and gave John a quizzical look. "Okay, what does this mean?" she asked.

"Nothing."

"Oh, it's a bit more than nothing, isn't it? You still don't believe what happened to you, even after all the news reports, even though I told you what Archbishop O'Connell said."

"Let's just say I have questions."

"Don't we all?"

John stared at Janice. "Don't you get it? People are hanging on my every word, waiting to see if there's going to be another miracle. I feel like the main attraction at a carnival freak show."

"At some point, you've got to stop complaining about it and focus on the good it has done you."

"We have no idea what's going on, and you're pretending that's not a problem. It scares the hell out of me."

"I'm not pretending anything, John. I am afraid, too, but I've never been one to let fear stop me. I don't know any other way to deal with this than to keep pressing ahead."

John let her words hang without a response for a few moments. "So, are you going to ask me about my meeting with Clark last night?"

"Eventually."

"Someone tipped him off to your trial balloon idea. He told me I should forget about it."

Janice's eyes widened with surprise. "Who told him?"

"I haven't a clue."

"I didn't breathe a word of it to anyone but you and Sara."

"I believe you."

"Was it Sara?"

"No."

"Are you sure?"

"Leave Sara out of this. It wasn't her."

"Then someone must have been eavesdropping. Damn that Clark. He has spies everywhere."

"Apparently."

"I'm going to grill every person in the office."

"Let it be."

Janice shook her head. Trust was the most important component of any working relationship. She couldn't let something like this slide, but it was clear that ferreting out the informant wasn't the Senator's highest priority, so she would revisit the issue later. When she did, heads would roll like apples from an overturned cart.

"What did you tell him?" she asked.

"That I'd think about his request."

"What's there to think about? I thought we agreed it made sense to test the idea."

"No, we agreed it merited further thought."

"John, you can't keep agonizing over this. We either move ahead with the plan, or we forget about it and get back to being a U.S. Senator."

"It's a tough decision, Janice. It's not just me I have to think about."

"I came to work for you because I believed in what you stood for. I believed in you. And now the best opportunity you've ever had to make a difference, to have a real impact on this country, is waiting for you to seize it, and you can't make up your mind?"

John rubbed his face in his hands, pressing on the spot just above his nose. His headache was excruciating. "I want to start with a whisper, okay, a not-for-attribution hint to one of your reporter friends. Something we can plausibly deny if things don't work out. Something I can explain away to Ned, and Clark, as the premature and careless remark of an overly zealous staffer."

"I can do that," Janice said with palpable relief in her voice. "What do you want me to do with this?" she asked, waving the poem in her hand.

"Give it to me. " John crossed the floor to Janice, removed the poem from her hand, and tossed it and the other poems scattered on his desk into the trashcan.

Janice chuckled. "I'm no literary critic, but I feel safe in saying that if what I read fairly represents your skills as a poet, you're right not to give up your day job."

John shot her a grin and replied, "At least I can't get fired from my day job until the election. You, on the other hand ... "

Janice spun smartly on her toes and stepped through the door into the outer office, pausing only long enough to look back over her shoulder and say, "You'd be lost without me, and you know it. Now straighten your tie. The Reverend will be here any minute."

Chapter 21

John slid a bundle of mail across the table to the Reverend.

"What would you do with these?" he asked.

The Reverend picked a letter at random and started to read out loud:

> Dear Senator Peters:
> I must ask you to stop bothering me. I didn't mind when you started talking to me at the breakfast table. The newspapers are so awfully boring these days – all they ever talk about are murders, scandals and sports – so listening to you was a welcome change. I didn't even mind when you started whispering into my ear after I'd gone to bed. I've seen your picture and you are a handsome man. But now that you have started following me into the bathroom, I have to draw the line. I do need my privacy.
> Yours truly,
> Jenna Smythe

"That's one of the nicer ones in that pile," said Janice. "Some are even crazier, and a few are downright threatening."

The Reverend handed the letter to Darnell, who sat beside him. The Reverend noticed that Darnell had forgotten to fasten a button, but fortunately the loose buttonhole lay under his tie where the Senator and his assistant couldn't see it. He would have to remind Darnell afterward of the need to take pride in how one dressed. Being smart and well-read wouldn't take you very far if you didn't present well to others.

"There are always some loose screws in the crowd," the Reverend said. "I've even had people come up to me crying that aliens were stealing their thoughts and they needed God's help to stop them."

"What did you tell them?" John asked.

"That God helps those who help themselves, so keep praying, but in the meantime, wear tinfoil hats."

"What about the more threatening letters?"

"My experience has been – now I'm not an expert in this area, although I've gotten enough crank calls and letters to have a sense of things – is that the folks you need to look out for don't necessarily advertise themselves by sending letters first. They try to sneak in under your radar screen. But if you get a letter that worries you, then you might want to call the authorities."

"I don't want to sound like Chicken Little."

"I understand, and I'm not here to offer security advice."

"What are you offering?"

"Guidance. We have a lot in common, you and me. We've both dedicated our lives to helping everyday people, listening to their problems, trying to find solutions. But we've done it in different arenas. You're the politician. I'm the man of God. You've wandered into my territory, whether you wanted to or not, and the rules we play by are a little different than what you're used to. The people who come to us are a little different than those you're used to. If you want to make a success of this, if you want to be more than a replacement Senator, you need to understand what you'll be facing. I can help you with that."

"What makes you think I have any aspirations beyond the office I hold?"

"I'm not saying you do. I'm saying that if you do, I can help."

"What would be in it for you?"

The Reverend smiled, "Other than the opportunity to help a fellow human being, you mean?"

"Yes. Other than that."

"I am a man of God, Senator, but I'm also a man of the people. You're a man of the people who is seen as a man of God. I think the two of us would make quite a team. I can help you, and if that helps me get my message out to a wider audience, that would be fine, too."

"I'm not interested in proselytizing."

"I'm not asking you to preach. You do your thing, you stick to politics, and I'll give you good, solid, honest advice on how to deal with the religious side of your celebrity. If you find I don't, we'll part company. But I don't think that will happen. And if in being associated with you, my message reaches a wider audience, well, that would be fine, too. God does work in mysterious ways. This is proof of that."

"What do you make of him, Janice?" asked John. The Reverend and Darnell had just left.

"Reminds me of Matthew Harrison Brady from *Inherit the Wind.*"

"Okay, now answer me in normal English." Janice was continually making literary references that John didn't understand. When they first met, he had thought it a bit affected, but he eventually understood that such allusions came naturally to her and he had grown accustomed to it.

"*Inherit the Wind* is a play about the Scopes Monkey Trial in Tennessee back in the 1920s. Tennessee had outlawed the teaching of evolution in the classroom, and after a young teacher named Scopes had been imprisoned for breaking the law, Clarence Darrow, who some say was the greatest trial lawyer of all time, came down from Chicago to defend him. The prosecution brought in a former presidential candidate and evangelical Christian, William Jennings Bryan, to try its case. In the play, Brady was based on the real-life Bryan, who was known as a silver-tongued orator. He could pound the pulpit with the best of them; raise a crowd into a frenzy of fear about eternal hell-fire; and moments later quiet them down and have them straining to hear the sound of angels' wings."

"Sounds like quite the effective preacher. Does that mean you're impressed with the Reverend?"

"In the play, Brady collapsed in the courtroom and died shortly after Drummond – that was the Darrow character – exposed him as a pretentious blowhard."

"Oh. And in real life?"

"Bryan lasted for a few days after the trial."

John twiddled with the pen in his hand as he thought about Janice's comments.

"I'm not sure I agree with you," he said after a long pause. "I have the sense there is a very smart man lurking under that smooth-talking surface. If we're going to press ahead with your idea, I'd rather have him in my corner than not."

"He strikes me as someone you can't entirely trust."

"Aside from you and Sara, I can't think of anyone I do trust."

Janice smiled, but persisted. "I think he's dangerous."

"Do you know what Lyndon Johnson used to say about dangerous men?"

"No."

"It's better to have them inside your tent pissing out, than outside your tent pissing in."

Chapter 22

Sweat beaded across the Reverend's forehead and soaked through his cotton T-shirt. It was a perfect morning for a run. The cool autumn air seemed to give an extra lift to his legs, and he had already run a mile farther than his usual three-mile distance. He nodded as he encountered fellow runners or early-rising tourists strolling around the Mall, the long grassy expanse in the heart of Washington ringed by the multiple museums of the Smithsonian Institute.

When his legs could go no farther, he lay down on the grass, enjoying the feel of the soft green blades that brushed his palms and the back of his thighs. He clasped his hands behind his neck and thought about where he was. Nowhere else in his travels had he seen the elegance and grandeur of ancient Rome so nearly recaptured. With the gleaming white dome of the Capitol at one end of the Mall, the gigantic obelisk of the Washington Monument dominating the other, and spectacular memorials to Lincoln and Jefferson nearby, one could imagine how it must have felt to walk through the Forum of Rome two thousand years before, awed by its stunning marble temples, elegant colonnaded buildings and gigantic Egyptian obelisks.

The Reverend longed for ancient Rome, believing it was a time when a man like he would have excelled. A time when the gifts of oratory were valued more in a politician than in a preacher. A time when a man with such gifts would be courted by all, when a man like Cicero could befriend Brutus and defend the Republic one day, and survive the rise of Octavian and the Empire the next.

The Reverend wanted very much to be a latter day Cicero, a famed orator who moved easily within the inner circles of power and even held its reins for a while. The ministers who presided over the funerals of presidents weren't any holier than him, but they clearly had better connections. This visit to DC was his effort to build on some tenuous contacts he had made in the past, and to create at least two important new connections. Now it appeared that by coming to the capital, he may have done himself far more harm than good.

The Reverend's daily morning runs helped him clear his head, think about what lay ahead, and plan accordingly. Never had he needed a clear head more than today. His meeting with Clark had not gone well. He had completely misjudged the man, a type of mistake he didn't often make. He couldn't believe he had made the incredibly stupid error of stereotyping someone he didn't know.

The Reverend had prepared for his meetings with both Senator Peters and Clark by ensuring that he had inside information as to the Senator's plans (it always amazed him how careless people were with their trash, and how willing janitors were to let others comb through what they had collected -- for an appropriate fee, of course). He had foolishly thought that the handwritten note taken from Janice Baxter's trashcan would engender both Clark's interest and gratitude as it revealed Peters' desire to be far more than the interim Senator from North Carolina. But instead of showing either surprise or gratitude, Clark simply handed the note to the young Frenchman seated by his side – a man Clark did not even bother to introduce – who glanced at it, smirked and tossed it into the trashcan. Clark ended the meeting by wishing the Reverend and Darnell a good day.

It had been such a damned stupid mistake. Despite the fresh air and the invigorating run, he had a sick feeling in his stomach that his own ambition may have done him in. Senator Peters was his best hope to attain a position of prominence, but Clark could ruin that by telling the Senator what had happened. It would take a true miracle to save him now, the type of miracle that he had often promised the members of his congregation would follow hard on the heels of earnest prayer. How many times had he exhorted them to offer up their desires because God was there among them, proclaiming to them the words of the New Testament, “Whenever two or three are gathered in My name, I am in their midst.”

A grim smile crossed his face as he looked first to the empty expanse of grass to his left, then to a similar view on his right, and said silently to himself, “Creighton, old boy, there is no one in this midst but you.”

Chapter 23

Darnell reread the piece of paper in his tightly clenched hands for the third time, and with each reading, his fingers squeezed the sheet even harder. He grimaced at the arrogance contained in Senator Peters' beautifully penned script. Following the dismal meeting with Clark, the Reverend had instructed him to stop combing through the Senator's trash, but Darnell had his own reasons for peering into the unguarded thoughts of a man who may have been touched by the Divine, so he continued to pay the janitor out of his own pocket for a nightly look at the wastebasket.

The night before, he struck gold: a few pages of handwritten poetry that promised to offer an insight into the man's mind and soul. But what he found shocked him. The very first line of the first poem he read came straight from The Book of Genesis – the answer God gave when Moses asked the burning bush with whom he should say he spoke – only Peters used it to refer to himself:

I am Who I am
Are we not each
Circularly defined?
Searching for self,
I am my own Odysseus
I explore the diameter of my ego
I trace the circumference of my mind
I return to zed
I am alone and I am all.

These were not the words of a humble messenger from God. These were the words of a man who confused himself with his Maker. The Senator was no better than the Reverend. No. He was worse. At least the Reverend hadn't fooled himself into believing he was someone other than who he was. He may have told the world he was a holy man, but when he looked at himself in the mirror, he saw a con artist.

It would have been okay if the Senator had simply been confused about his identity, his purpose – the holiest men were the most humble, the most unwilling to believe that they had been chosen by God.

But no true man of God ever feigned his confusion to the world and privately told himself he was "all." A true man of God felt his insignificance in a most profound way, a true man of God humbled his ego; a true man of God delivered himself unto God's will.

Darnell had been looking a long time for a true man of God. It had been his only hope for salvation. He didn't have it within himself to save his soul – there was someone else sharing it with him, someone too powerful for him to drive away unaided. Someone who had entered during a dark moment many years before, who had grown side-by-side with him into adulthood, and whom Darnell had pushed into a corner of his mind but could not drive out. The prescription he took every day quieted the ugly whispers the intruder tried to breathe into Darnell's mind, but Darnell could still feel his chill presence, the way a closed-eyed sunbather feels a cloud pass overhead.

All of Darnell's hopes slouched like whipped puppies out of his heart. The man he hoped would exorcise his demon proved to be a blasphemer instead. Anger welled inside him. He could not let this fraud continue. Such hubris had to be brought to the world's attention. It had to be punished. Holding the poem in one hand, he picked up the phone with the other. He knew exactly who to call. It was a man he hadn't spoken with in years, a man he thought (no, hoped) he'd never speak with again. The reporter wouldn't recognize Darnell's new name – not many people from his prior life knew it. Darnell braced himself for the painful memories the call would dredge up, dialed information and waited for the operator to come on the line.

“Savannah, Georgia, please. Yes. The Savannah Dispatch. Thank you.”

Within a day or so, Senator Peters would have a lot to explain to an angry public.

Chapter 24

It started as a murmur, a single paragraph on a muckraking reporter's daily blog. But like a distant gurgling brook that flows inevitably into roaring white water, the murmur grew into a deafening noise as rumors of the Senator's state-of-mind spread and copies of his poem appeared in print. Within days, the front pages of the leading tabloid newspapers trumpeted "He Thinks He's God" at checkout counters across the country and cable news shows aired debates about the poem among psychologists, Biblical experts and English professors. There were even a few made-for-TV demonstrations in which the poem was burned.

Sara and Janice quickly overruled John's initial wish to respond with a statement decrying the invasion of his privacy and the unauthorized publication of his poem. They recognized the need to deal with the charges of megalomania head-on, and not through a sideways attack on the people who published them.

First, Janice squelched the rumor she had an intern plant with a gossip columnist that John was considering a run for the Oval Office. They would circle back to that plan later, after controlling and gauging whatever damage had been done by the publication of John's poem. John, in the meantime, sought advice from both Governor Smith and Clark, but as Sara had predicted, neither of them returned his calls. Phones at both his office and his house had been ringing non-stop, but most of the calls were from reporters looking for quotes.

Then a call came in from a greatly agitated Reverend Jones. Janice fielded the call, but after listening quietly for several minutes, waved John over and silently mouthed, "You need to talk to him."

John took the phone and listened as the Reverend explained how Darnell had confessed to bribing the cleaning staff for access to the Senator's office trash, and to sending the poem to the press.

"Obviously, I fired him and sent him home, but I just feel awful about this. I trusted that boy. I want to make up for this. If there is anything I can do, please, just ask."

"Thanks, Reverend. We'll get back to you."

John hung up the phone and plunked down into his chair. "I need a drink," he said, and got back to his feet to pour one.

Hours later, after a long evening in which she had lined up a press conference for the next morning and helped John draft a statement to read at its outset, Janice started to walk home. Normally, she'd take a taxi to the townhouse she rented, but she needed the fresh air, and the exercise would help her decompress. She wasn't going to be able to sleep tonight no matter what, and dawn had almost arrived anyway. The air had a bite to it, signaling the approach of winter, and she zipped her jacket up to her chin.

As she approached the front steps of her home, a hand grabbed her arm from behind.

"Hello, Ms. Baxter," whispered a man's nervous voice into her ear. "Don't make a scene." The voice sounded familiar, but she couldn't quite place it. "We're just going to walk up to your door together, okay."

Her legs quivered uncontrollably and her heart pounded so hard her chest hurt. "Let me go, please."

"I need to talk to you."

There was something about the voice, different than what she remembered, edgier, but not one to be afraid of. Recognition clicked in and she spun around to face him. "Darnell, just what in the hell do you think you're doing?"

Darnell flashed the gun in his hand. "Open the door and I'll explain everything."

Janice felt as if the air had been sucked from her lungs, and a small trickle of urine leaked down her leg. He had a gun. She hated guns. There was no reasoning with a gun. "Please, just let me go and leave. If you do, I won't report this, I promise."

"I'm not going to hurt you. I just need to talk to you. Please open the door."

"Why the gun? Put away the gun and I'll listen to whatever you have to say."

Darnell shook his head no. "I need to make sure that you will listen to me. Now open the door." His voice took on an urgent tone. Janice fumbled through her bag and fished the keys out, but her hand was shaking too hard to insert the key into the keyhole. Darnell grabbed it from her with his free hand and opened the door, then pushed her through the doorway into her living room.

"Turn the light on," he told her, "and sit down, please." He drew the blinds on her front windows and disconnected the phone. "Don't move," he said as he crossed into the adjoining dining room and pulled the shades down.

"What do you want?" Janice asked.

Darnell took a deep breath. He had been treated for years by psychiatrists who specialized in violent youths. They had drugged him, analyzed him, counseled him, and eventually pronounced him fit for release from the mental health facility to which he had been confined. The state expunged his record when he turned 21, and he had changed his name from Leonard Clough to Darnell Edom, so as far as the world was concerned, he was a perfectly normal man with a perfectly normal past. But Darnell knew that he wasn't normal, that he wasn't cured, and that he could only be fixed if that thing lurking in the corner of his mind, the Bad One, was destroyed. That was his original reason for hooking up with the Reverend; it was why he had placed such hopes in Senator Peters. Someone who had been touched by God might be able to deliver him from his evil.

Of course, the Bad One had a different view of things. It was the Bad One who had first whispered to Darnell that the Reverend was not such a holy man after all. He was right. That was the scary thing about the Bad One, the danger he posed. The Bad One was quicker to pick up on things than Darnell, and even though his whispers were full of malice, full of lies, they had enough truth in them to make Darnell listen even while telling himself he shouldn't.

Darnell took a seat across from Janice. His knees were shaking. "Comfortable chair. I wish I had one like it." Normal conversation calmed him down. Forcing his way into the house had keyed him up, and he needed to back his heart rate down, to slow the adrenaline rush. The Bad One thrived on adrenaline.

Darnell knew that he had taken a risk when he stopped taking his medication, but he hated being so dependent on drugs. He started counting silently backward from 100 to moderate his breathing.

He just needed to explain himself to Janice, to explain that it wasn't entirely his fault, and to apologize for leaking the poem to the press. Confession was good for the soul.

Janice didn't say anything for a while. Her thoughts raced as she desperately tried to figure out what to do. Nothing came to her. She couldn't believe this was happening. Darnell sat oddly silent, and when she couldn't take the quiet any longer, she asked, "Please, why are you doing this?"

Darnell had only reached 67, so he counted out a few more numbers before answering, just to be safe. "I didn't come here to hurt you. I came to explain things."

"You could have found a gentler way to deliver your message."

Darnell frowned. The gun had been the Bad One's idea, but he wasn't ready to talk about him yet. "Like I said, this way you're sure to listen."

She felt the warmth of the urine on her leg and only then realized what had happened. "I need to use the bathroom."

"Where is it?"

She pointed to a door near the kitchen. "Right there."

"Okay, but don't lock the door."

Janice closed the door behind her and took a deep breath. If Darnell didn't mean her harm, then why the gun, why the drawn shades? She didn't know whether to keep him talking and try to persuade him to leave, or whether to take more aggressive action. She wasn't even sure what action she could take. She wasn't expert in the martial arts, she didn't have any concealed weapons lying around the house, and she didn't have a dog she could loose on him. Suddenly, she remembered her cell phone, and feeling like an idiot for not recalling it sooner, she dialed 911 while keeping the phone stuffed deep in her bag to muffle the sound.

The emergency operator came on the line, but since Janice couldn't speak directly to her, she instead started talking to Darnell. "Darnell, I don't understand why you followed me home. I don't understand why you have a gun. Please, just leave. I've never done anything to you."

Janice prayed that her enhanced 911service, a service that enabled the police to track a transmitting wireless phone to within yards of its location, worked as promised.

"I think you need to come out of there now," he said. He juggled the doorknob. "I told you not to lock the door," he yelled, and banged his shoulder into it. The door crashed open and Darnell saw Janice sitting on the toilet, her slacks and panties around her ankles. He grabbed the open purse on her lap and saw the cell phone transmitting a signal. Quickly, he shut it off and threw it to the floor. His mind roiled, his vision went black, then red, as the Bad One muscled his way to the front, elbowing Darnell to the sidelines.

Darnell watched the Bad One seize Janice's arm and throw her sprawling onto the floor. He watched the Bad One roll her over and force his knees between her legs. He watched the Bad One lower his pants, push himself into her and grimace when the release came. He saw Janice's eyes stream with tears and he felt so terribly bad for her.

He dimly heard the sounds of the police banging on the front door. He saw the Bad One stand up and level the gun at the officer standing in the doorway, and he distantly felt his ribs shatter as the policeman's bullet crashed through and pierced his heart.

In his last moments, as darkness descended upon him, Darnell felt the relief of knowing that he had finally been cured.

Chapter 25

The glare from the television camera lights was brighter than John had anticipated, and he couldn't even count the number of microphones arrayed at the podium. From the wing of the studio where stood, he could see the packed audience of reporters jostling for position, anxious to put their questions to him. He didn't think they cared about the man behind their stories, or the anguish they had caused his wife and son, or the damage they had done to his career. They cared only about sound bites and bylines.

John knew all the clichés about the freedom of the press and the public's right to know and about how a free press safeguards the citizenry against governmental misconduct, but these reporters weren't acting out of such high-minded civic duty. No, they were playing a game, a game of interest only to themselves, a game in which winners and losers were determined by who got the exclusive interview or the great quote.

How many times had he seen commercials touting a news show's scoops? 'You saw if first right here,' or 'Exclusively on this station,' or some other trite phrase that meant the same thing: we beat the other guys and got the story to you first. But how many people outside the press cared? The public didn't keep score with a stopwatch. Most people he knew wanted their news delivered accurately, and if journalists truly cared about serving the public, they would focus more on getting the story right and less on getting it first.

He would have to face them soon. John breathed deeply. He knew he was being overly harsh, that it wasn't fair to castigate the entire journalistic profession. The stress of the last 24 hours was getting to him, and he worried about Janice. She should have been there, she hadn't called, and she wasn't answering her home or cell phone. She couldn't have overslept; knowing Janice, she hadn't even gone to bed and wouldn't think about sleep until the press conference had ended.

He couldn't put it off any longer, and he stepped onto the platform in full view of the reporters. They started firing questions at him immediately, not even giving him a chance to reach the microphone stand. He strode across the platform silently rehearsing the words he and Janice had carefully crafted, but as he reached into his coat pocket for the most recently edited version of the statement, it dawned on him that the reporters' questions buzzing around his head had nothing to do with his alleged delusions of godhood.

They asked about Janice and a Darnell Edom, a name he didn't recognize, and when they saw his confusion, pinged him with what they had heard while the cameramen captured the look on his face for the noon broadcast.

John felt suddenly nauseous, as if a rank odor had been waved under his nose. Clenching his teeth, John slipped the statement back into his pocket and gripped the podium, leaning his body into it to steady his legs. He paused for a moment to calm his stomach, sort through the noise and survey the hungry eyes before him, hoping to find a friendly face, someone he could pull aside and speak with in private. He was not about to have an on-the-record conversation about Janice. Two men, both in the back of the room but in opposite corners, caught his attention, as they were the only two not raising their hands or shouting out questions. One appeared to be of Middle Eastern origin. He wore a well-tailored, expensive suit and stood with a quiet dignity that separated him from the energetic crowd in front of him. The other man wore blue jeans and a tight-fighting sweater through which well-defined muscles showed. Neither man seemed to be a reporter. Neither man seemed to belong at the press conference.

The wireless email device in his pants pocket started buzzing against his leg. It was configured to his personal email address, not one that many people had, so he assumed Sara was trying to contact him. He had turned his cell phone off prior to the press conference, and had meant to shut the email device off as well. He pulled it out and saw that there was indeed a new email from Sara: 'Janice is at Washington General. Reporters everywhere. Meet me at Room 610. Hospital security will let you through.'

John leaned into the bank of microphones and said, "As some of you are aware, my friend and colleague Ms. Baxter is in the hospital. She is a dear friend as well as a valued associate. Under the circumstances, I think it only appropriate to postpone this press conference. We will reschedule as soon as possible. Thank you." He then strode out of the room, his heart pounding, with reporters hurling questions about Darnell after him.

Chapter 26

The sheer curtains were drawn, filtering the sun's afternoon light and tinting it a melancholy gray that matched Janice's emotional state. The teapot whistled, and as she walked toward the stove to turn the burner off, her feet shuffled along the floor, making the soft, scuffing sound her grandmother used to make in her slippers. She had not felt this exhausted, this emotionally drained since her brother's death. At times, she felt so angry she almost wished Darnell was still alive so she could shoot him herself. At other times, she felt so ashamed that she thought she would never be able to face her friends again. But mostly, she just felt tired and alone.

She made her tea, took it back to her most comfortable chair, and sank in, her thoughts circling back to how lonely she felt. She missed her father. She missed her brother, Jimmy. Janice didn't remember her mother, who had died while Janice was still a young girl. She picked up the phone and started to dial her father's number, but halfway through, she gently placed the phone back in its cradle. She just couldn't bring herself to call him. And she couldn't call Jimmy, who had been dead now for ... how many years was it? How could she forget? Jimmy was supposed to have been the successful one. His good looks, quick wit and easy-going charm had won him friends and marked him for fame and fortune. Jimmy did well at nearly everything, in school and at sports, and seemingly without much effort. And he had always been lucky. He was one of those people to whom good things just happened. She still couldn't believe he was dead. It was so out-of-synch with how things were supposed to have been.

Janice had her own successes, but they were hard earned. She stayed up late studying to ensure that she got A's on her tests and ran extra laps to make the cross-country team. And unlike Jimmy, her greatest joys didn't come from being in the spotlight. She much preferred designing the sets for her school plays than starring in them, and took quiet pride in knowing they were the most professional part of the production. Her father made sure to congratulate her on each accomplishment, but no matter how sincere he seemed, she always worried that she suffered in comparison to her brother, and that nothing she ever did, no matter how hard she had tried or how well she had succeeded, would generate the kind of pride her father felt for the son who would carry on the family name.

When it came to Jimmy, she had often struggled with the line between hero worship and envy, but Jimmy, knowing how she felt, never made her feel bad about harboring sibling rivalries. Instead, he encouraged her to excel, not in competition with him or to please their father, but to prove to herself how good she could be. He was as good at being a big brother as he was at everything else.

Janice blew across the surface of the tea steaming in her mug and took a small sip. She had made tea for Jimmy during the last days of his illness when he couldn't keep much else down. By the time his cancer had been diagnosed, he had only a few months left, and he declined rapidly from a young, vibrant man with occasional night sweats to a frail, nearly skeletal man who looked like a concentration camp inmate.

Jimmy's best friend from his teen-age years, Eddie Taylor, flew in to attend the funeral. Years before, on a Saturday afternoon so hot that no one crossed the street because the asphalt had turned gummy enough to stick to shoe bottoms, Jimmy and Eddie had come running through the house to grab a couple of sodas from the kitchen refrigerator. Janice had been sitting at the table wearing a tight fitting halter top that all the girls her age wore back then, and Eddie came to an abrupt halt in front of her, wearing a look of surprise tinged with embarrassment and suddenly developed shyness. No one had ever looked at her like that before.

When Jimmy emerged from the refrigerator clutching two cold sodas, he took in the scene, smirked, said "Come on, Eddie," and the two ran out as quickly as they had come in. Janice realized at that moment that she had more than intelligence and drive working in her favor when it came to dealing with men. Whether she would deliberately choose to use her looks to her advantage was another issue, but just knowing that she could gave her a sense of confidence she hadn't enjoyed before.

Eddie stayed after the wake to help clean up and to listen to Mr. Baxter tell stories about Jimmy's many exploits. Then he and Janice went out to tell each other stories that wouldn't have been appropriate to share with her father. They both had a few too many drinks, and they both made a mistake. She got pregnant, but neither she nor Eddie was ready for parenthood, so when he offered to pay for an abortion, she quickly accepted. The doctor who performed the abortion, a friend of a friend of Eddie's father's, botched it, causing serious damage that precluded the possibility of Janice ever getting pregnant again.

When her father found out what had happened, he paid for her surgery, paid for the malpractice lawsuit against the doctor that left her financially well off, but stopped being 'Daddy.'

He was a devout Catholic. The fact that she had sex outside of marriage was hard for him to take, that she got pregnant was harder still, and that Eddie was the father and that it happened after Jimmy's funeral was even more upsetting. But he would have been able to forgive all that, in time. The abortion, however, that, he could not forgive. He believed whole-heartedly that life began at the moment of conception and that abortion was murder. Janice knew how he felt and that was why she hadn't sought advice or comfort from him prior to having it done. But his withdrawal from her life, coming so soon after she lost her brother, after she had lost the ability to have children ... even now, years later, she still couldn't tell which wounds from the abortion hurt most, the physical or the emotional.

Her doorbell rang, shaking her from her reverie. Standing on the doorstep, wearing a Georgetown Hoyas sweatshirt with a bouquet of flowers in his hand, was the Archbishop. He smiled weakly as she opened the door.

"I brought these for you," he said. "If you're not up for company, I'll understand."

She took the flowers, gave him a hug, and motioned him inside. "Thank you. Would you like some tea? The water in the pot is still hot."

"Yes, that would be nice."

"It was the strangest thing," Janice said. She nestled into the pillows thrown about her sofa and took another sip of tea.

"Perhaps you shouldn't talk about it yet," said Archbishop O'Connell.

"No. I want to. The police made me talk about it, several times, which didn't make sense to me. It's not like I can press charges. So I want to talk about it with a friend."

"I'm glad you see me that way."

"There are some people you know will always be your friend, even if years go by without a 'hello.'"

The Archbishop smiled to mask his anguish. It broke his heart to learn what had happened to Janice, and even worse, who had done it.

"What was so strange?" he asked.

"When he attacked me ... you know," she looked down at her lap, angry with herself for feeling shame when she had done nothing to be ashamed of, "it was as if he was a different man than the one I had met before. Not just because he turned violent. There was something else, something in his eyes. I almost felt that the Darnell I had met was in there, somewhere, and that he wasn't the one ..." Her voice trailed off.

The Archbishop sat silently. He could not bring himself to confess to Janice what he knew. Years before, he had reassigned a priest accused of sexual predation to a new parish and prayed for his cure. His prayers didn't work. The priest targeted a new victim, an adolescent boy named Lenny Clough. But Lenny did not yield. He grabbed a knife and fought back with the rage of one possessed. He cut off the priest's genitals, stuffed them into his mouth, and slit his throat.

Lenny was found mentally incompetent to stand trial, and the Church, as part of the settlement reached with Lenny's parents, paid for all of Lenny's psychiatric care. Although the medical records were supposed to be private, the Archbishop read them regularly. Immersing himself in Lenny's suffering was his own private penance. He knew Lenny had changed his name after being released, but hadn't kept tabs on his whereabouts. He hadn't known that Lenny had changed his name to Darnell Edom.

Archbishop O'Connell rose slowly to his feet, pushing down on the armrest for leverage. "These knees just don't want to work any more," he chuckled. "Too many marathons. You know, once upon a time, I was known as 'the running priest.' One of my staff even referred to me as 'the miter miler.' I liked that one, you know, the bishop's miter..." His hands formed the shape of a pyramidal hat in the air above his head. "The word 'miter' comes from the Persian myth about Mithras, the god of light and defender of truth. That appealed to my vanity – even we priests suffer from that – until I learned that I was being made fun of. Turns out that a miter is also a type of snail."

Janice smiled. "Thanks for coming over."

Archbishop O'Connell stroked her gently on the head. He had often wondered what it would have been like to have children and what type of father he would have been. Janice would have been the type of daughter he would have wanted. "I was just going to put my cup away. Would you like me to pour you another one?"

"No thank you. Actually, if you don't mind, I'm going to get some rest. I'm feeling very tired."

"Of course. I'll check in on you again tomorrow, if that's okay."

"I'd like that."

He started toward the door, when Janice stopped him.

"Father, can I ask you something?"

"Of course."

"I know it's selfish to wonder, I mean bad things happen to good people all the time, but I can't help it." She paused. "Why me? Why did God let this happen?"

"Janice, I know you understand that what happened isn't your fault. But it isn't God's fault, either. Don't lose your faith. It's times like this when we need our faith most."

Janice pulled her blanket around her shoulders. "I remember my catechism lessons from grade school. I remember being told that when people do bad things, it isn't because God wants them to. My second grade teacher, Sister Mary, used to say that if God forced us to be good, then we wouldn't really be good, we'd just be puppets, and that God didn't want a bunch of Pinnochios, he wanted real boys and girls. That's why He gave us free will. It's up to us to choose wisely. We have to choose to be good. And some people don't."

"You remember your lessons well."

"But I don't know if Darnell had a choice." Janice stirred her spoon slowly in her tea, watching the leaves swirl about. She refused to use ready-packaged tea bags, preferring to brew her tea the old-fashioned way. "When I was a little girl, I used to pretend that I was an old gypsy woman who could see the future in the tea leaves at the bottom of my cup. Sometimes, I even convinced myself that I could tell the future, and I imagined all sorts of wonderful things happening to me. I never saw this coming."

Archbishop O'Connell sat down next to Janice and took the cup from her hands. "People always want to know more than can be known, more than should be known. If it's not tea leaves, it's palm readings. If it's not palms, it's horoscopes. I for one don't want to know the future. I don't want to know if good things are going to happen, because it would ruin the joy of the surprise. I don't want to know if bad things are going to happen, because I'd live in constant dread of their approach, and I'd be tempted to disregard my responsibilities to the present. Living in ignorance, I know that each day might be my last; that death, like our Lord, may come like a thief in the night. Not knowing the hour of my death is my daily reminder to do what is right."

"I think Darnell welcomed death. I could see it in his eyes. I think it was his way to do what was right."

"Perhaps it was. Perhaps in his final moments, he found salvation. Let's hope that he did."

The Archbishop found himself concealing something else from Janice, his suspicion that Darnell's attack was not a coincidence. He had seen much in his life, and what he had seen convinced him that evil was more than an adjective. It was a thing, a separate, independent and malignant force. He believed that he knew better than the psychiatrists what had troubled the boy he knew as Lenny. He had read everything he could on schizophrenia, but he did not believe that diagnosis explained what had happened to Lenny. The Archbishop was convinced to the core of his soul that evil had taken hold of Lenny, exploiting the vulnerabilities created by the priest for whom he bore responsibility, and that it had never released him from its grip. He thought Lenny had known this to be true, and that was why he always sought to be in the company of men of faith. He wanted to be freed.

Could it be mere happenstance that the woman he attacked worked for a man that may have been touched by God? The Archbishop didn't think so. As he looked at Janice, he remembered the little girl curled up in his office chair, fast asleep with an opened book on her lap. He had failed Lenny. He had failed Janice once, now he would do everything in his power, both as a man of this earth and as a servant of God, to see that she stayed safe.

Chapter 27

Diary of Janice Baxter

It's been a long time since I kept a diary. One of my doctors told me it would be good therapy, so I thought I should try. It will take some getting used to. I haven't kept any sort of diary (save for day calendars) since college when one of my English teachers made us keep a daily journal as part of a section on autobiographical writing. I remember not being completely honest because I didn't like the idea of some lecherous old fart of a professor drooling over anything I wrote. I was 19 and living in a sorority house, so if I were really going to put down everything I did or saw or heard, there would have been plenty for him to drool over. I wouldn't have minded so much if he had simply asked us to keep a journal, but to collect them and grade them, ugh. On the other hand, I suppose I wouldn't have really kept it if it weren't going to be collected. But anyway, I'm still not comfortable with putting down my innermost thoughts on paper. I suppose I'm still worried that someone else will read them.

Enough stalling. Where to start? Archbishop O'Connell has been a dear. He comes to see me every day, it's almost as if I were his daughter. He has a calming influence on me, and he gives me things to think about. Funny how the world works. I hadn't seen him in ages, but when this whole thing with John came up, he was the first person I thought of. That makes sense. I mean he is an Archbishop, so who better to ask for advice from. But this whole experience I'm going through helped me understand why he is an Archbishop. I'm seeing his spiritual side and that's something I never really appreciated as a young girl. Back then, he was a mysterious, scary figure that was a very important part of my father's life.

Dad gave a lot of money to the church and I suppose that bought him a lot of influence. In many ways, being active in the church is very much like being active in politics, and giving money gets you a long way in both. Maybe that's why I stopped going to Mass for so long. Politics became my new religion and I didn't have time for two. I don't suppose the Archbishop would like to hear that. 'Render unto Caesar' and all that.

I'm still stalling. I haven't yet written anything about the thing that I'm supposed to write about. Well, to be fair, the doctor didn't say I had to write about what happened, just to write. Maybe it's supposed to come out in drips.

What to say? That I'm scared. I am. That I have bad dreams. I do. That I feel ashamed even though I know it wasn't my fault. I can't help it. That I feel like a broken teacup and I don't know how to glue all the pieces back together. That's exactly how I feel.

How long before I stop feeling so angry? I don't know.

How long before I feel like myself again? I don't know.

Will I ever get over it? I don't know.

What am I going to do in the meantime? Sometimes I feel like I could just stay in bed all day and let the world turn without me. But I have to fight that. I have to get my life back. That's the point, isn't it? It's my life. I'm not going to let it slide by me.

Chapter 28

John and the Reverend sat side-by-side at the dais. They had met the night before and agreed that a joint appearance made sense: John would address any lingering issues about his alleged megalomania and reply to queries about Janice's condition in a way that didn't invade her privacy, while the Reverend would handle inquiries about Darnell. He would also, at an opportune moment, add that he had come to know the Senator and had found him to be as humble and God-fearing a man as he had ever met.

The first question, from one of the more aggressive reporters in the room, tied all three issues together. "Senator, there are rumors that Darnell Edom, the man who attacked Ms. Baxter, is also the man who leaked your poem to the press. What was your relationship with Mr. Edom, do you know whether he was the man who leaked your poem, and if so, did your poem have anything to do with why he attacked Ms. Baxter?"

"I'm not sure we'll ever know why Mr. Edom attacked Janice ... Ms. Baxter," said John. "If anyone is in a position to offer insight into Mr. Edom's motives, it would be the Reverend, so I'll let him address that question. He can also confirm that Mr. Edom stole the poem from my office, along with some other papers, for reasons that will probably never be understood."

John leaned back from the bank of microphones as the Reverend leaned forward.

"First," the Reverend began, "let me say that Senator Peters and I have both prayed for Darnell's soul. That's how I knew him, as Darnell. And when I asked Senator Peters to join me in prayer, he got down on his knees without hesitation. The Senator ... John, " a brief smile flickered across the Reverend's face as he said John's first name, hinting that he and the Senator had grown close through this difficult time, "... is as humble, decent, and God-fearing a man as I have ever met. The stories that you in the media have spread about him thinking he is God are nothing but pure, unadulterated nonsense.

"As to Darnell, he was a troubled young man. There was something restless about his soul, as if he were plagued by inner demons that in the end must have gotten the best of him. I believe he hoped to find peace through faith, and it was my hope that I could help him do so. Sadly, it seems that I failed. But I pray that God forgives him and that his soul finds peace in the hereafter.

"I don't know for sure why he stole John's poem, but I know that he believed John had been touched by God. I can only imagine what Darnell thought when he read the poem that has caused so much commotion. He was a simple man, not highly educated. He probably had never heard of Odysseus, and he certainly would not have understood the poem's reference to him. To the extent any of you confused the Senator's private explorations of his inner self with delusions of godhood, the same can be said of you."

The press was not particularly interested in hearing a lecture about ancient Greek poetry, and with the Reverend's denial that the Senator thought he was God effectively killing that story, the reporters tried to focus on the more salacious details of Darnell's attack on Janice. Neither John nor the Reverend would provide any details, however, and none of the bilingual reporters planted in the room to detect any further speaking in tongues noticed anything unusual in John's remarks. The buzz that vibrated through the room at the outset faded away, and the press conference ended slightly earlier than planned.

As John and the Reverend stepped off the dais, the Reverend noticed a ripple through the throng of reporters. Suddenly, an olive-skinned, bearded man broke out of the crowd and lunged at them. The Reverend saw metal flashing in his hand and for a panicked instant he froze like a deer caught in the glare of headlights. Then, just as his mind registered 'knife,' he tried to back away from the assailant, but his foot caught on a microphone cable that hadn't been properly fastened to the floorboards. He spun and fell between the attacker and the Senator, his body intercepting the knife as it plunged down. As the blade pierced the Reverend's upper chest, the sound of a gunshot exploded in the room and the would-be assassin crumpled to the ground, blood spilling from a bullet wound in his back.

Screams broke out and people pressed toward the exits. John knelt by the Reverend, who lay moaning with the knife still protruding from his chest. Blood covered John's hands, and he shouted for help. He offered the Reverend words of comfort and assurances that help would be there soon, and thanked him repeatedly for saving his life. It had looked as if the Reverend deliberately jumped between John and his attacker. Part of the security detail circled the fallen Imrahain while others seized Hartson, who had been standing in the back of the room with a gun dangling from his hand and a surprised look in his eyes, and put him in handcuffs.

Chapter 29

Clark and Governor Smith shared a slow limousine ride through rush hour traffic from downtown DC to the Reverend's hotel, where he had been recuperating since his discharge from the hospital. Notwithstanding the stretch limo's cavernous interior, Governor Smith felt a bit claustrophobic, as Clark sat a little too closely beside him. Clark's limousine was, as always, incredibly well stocked with top-shelf liquors, from 25-year-old single malt Scotches to small batch Bourbons, premium French and California red wines, Cognacs, Armagnacs and other liqueurs. Governor Smith leaned over to pour himself a glass of Grand Cru Burgundy.

"You should try the grappa," Clark said.

"No thank you. I had it once. Never again. Do you know that stuff was made for peasants? Tastes like it, too. Personally, I think it's ridiculous that it's priced like a rare brandy. There are simply no standards left."

Clark pulled a bottle of grappa from the liquor rack and turned it slowly in his hands. He removed the cork and smelled deeply then held it out to Smith.

"Take a whiff."

"No thank you."

"Too edgy for you?"

"I just don't care for it."

"Funny, I would have thought you'd appreciate a good grappa. In fact, I think you have a lot in common with grappa."

Smith took a sip of wine before asking, "How so?"

"The first grappa was made in a little village called Friuli in the Alps of northern Italy. The peasants took all the leftovers from grapes that had been pressed for wine, from stalks to seeds to skins – the word 'grappa' comes from the Italian word for grape stalk – and distilled it. Early on, the stuff was pure moonshine. Then someone came along and polished it up. Cleaned out the stalks and the seeds, smoothed it out and started selling it as premium grade liquor. But here's the kicker – all the marketing for the stuff pays homage to its humble origins. 'Keeps it real,' as they say."

Smith finished off his glass and poured himself another. "Thank you for that history lesson," he said in a somewhat flippant tone. "I'm always amazed at how much you know. Would you like anything from the bar?"

"I don't drink alcohol."

"I guess I knew that. I've never seen you drink anything but coffee. So getting back to grappa, why do I remind you of the stuff?"

Clark tilted his head so that his lips were only inches from the Governor's face, "Come on, Governor. Isn't it obvious? You come from the sticks, a genuine North Carolina hillbilly. Oh sure, when I met you, you already had your law degree, and your Daddy made sure you had a bank account full of cash, but you were plenty rough around the edges. We cleaned you up, smoothed you out, and got rid of the hayseed. Then we packaged you and sold you as a premium grade politician who never lost sight of his roots. You're a human version of grappa. So you'll understand why I think it funny that you won't touch the stuff. I think it ought to be your drink of choice."

Smith gritted his teeth and gently swirled the wine in his glass, holding it to his nose to smell the bouquet. "The French take great pride in their wine. They take great credit, too, as they should. But they couldn't make grape juice let alone a Grand Cru without the grapes. I appreciate what you did for me, but don't forget that I had something to do with my success, too."

"Of course you did," Clark replied. "You did everything we asked of you, except pick the right person to take your Senate seat. You made that decision without us, and that was a mistake."

"You didn't complain at the time. You thought he was perfect. Small town guy, easy to control ... he absolutely fit the bill."

"He wouldn't have been our first choice. I hardly knew who he was. And he certainly hasn't turned out as you planned."

"Are you suggesting I should have known he'd be some kind of miracle worker?"

This time it was Clark who gritted his teeth. "That's not the problem. I don't know what the hell that speaking in tongues bullshit was all about. What I do know and what I do care about is the fact that Peters didn't play ball when we asked him to. He wouldn't stay off the news. He wouldn't shut up."

"Then why did you tell me not to return his calls after the poem story broke? He came to me asking for advice. He would have listened to me then."

"I couldn't tell how that poem story was going to play out. If he was going down, I wasn't about to have you dragged down with him. I've worked too hard to set you up for the nomination."

"Then why are we going to see the Reverend? He seems to be identifying himself pretty closely with Peters."

"I've put a call in to my friend at the paper. He's writing a piece that should nip Peters in the bud. But I always like to have a Plan B, and that's where the Reverend comes in. Now that he's got himself in with Peters, he could prove quite useful. He came to see me a little while ago, offering inside information on Peters, but I didn't want his help on his terms, and I knew that a guy who would do something like that has probably done other things that he'd rather not have uncovered. I set out to find those other things. I succeeded."

"What did you find?"

Clark grinned, "Apparently, the Lord isn't the only thing the Reverend brings to his flock. He left his personal mark on at least one young lady. I imagine the Reverend would rather not have news of that girl, or her baby, surface any time soon."

"What are you going to do?"

"I'm going to advise the Reverend that we can help him keep his past quiet in exchange for a few favors. He needs to understand just how we do things in this town."

Chapter 30

John peered through the metal gate separating the guard station from the cellblock in which Abdul Imrahain had been incarcerated following his release from the hospital, but he could not see Imrahain's cell. The jail cells stretched in parallel rows perpendicular to the corridor in front of the guard station gate, each row watched by guards stationed at various points on a catwalk that ran above the corridor, and Imrahain was in the second row of cells from the back.

The warden had been surprised by John's request for a visit; normally, victims didn't ask to see their assailants. He was even more surprised that John wanted to meet with Imrahain in his cell rather than in the prisoners' visiting room, which offered the safety of a bullet proof glass divider. Visitors weren't even supposed to be in the guard station, let alone the cellblock, but not every visitor was a United States Senator. The warden drew the line, however, at letting the Senator into the block itself. He wasn't going to have the wounding or death of a Senator occur on his watch. The Senator could take a look at the jail cells to satisfy whatever morbid curiosity drove him, but he'd have to talk to Imrahain by phone through the glass, just like every other visitor.

The loud clanging of the cellblock gate as it closed behind two of the guards jarred John back to his senses. He had been in a daze, thinking about the man who had tried to kill him. He was disappointed that the warden would not permit him an up-close talk with Imrahain. Attempted murder by stabbing was, in its own grotesque way, an extremely intimate act, and John wanted to get in the face of the man who wanted him dead, to discover his motives, and to put to rest any fears that there would be others like him lurking in the shadows.

Imrahain's court-appointed lawyer had advised strongly against the interview, for reasons Imrahain could have predicted. He remembered enough from his law school days to know that anything he said to Senator Peters could and most probably would be used as evidence against him at his trial, but he didn't care. He didn't expect to find justice in an American court. According to American law, he was guilty of a serious crime, but if American definitions of crime had mattered to him, he wouldn't have undertaken this quest. No, he would seek justice from a higher authority. He would fire his lawyer and present his own defense, abjuring his lawyer's ridiculous insanity defense to instead explain to the world the just cause for complaint that his people and his faith had against the American government.

Imrahain wanted to meet the Senator. He was not afraid to look the instrument of the Devil in the eye. He had been confident that Allah had called him to his task, but if it had been Allah's will that Senator Peters die at his hand, it would have happened. Imrahain did not presume to know the mind of Allah; he hoped only for some limited understanding as to what he had been called to do if it was not to kill the Senator.

The guards walked Imrahain to the visitor's center. Imrahain had to step slowly and carefully to avoid dislodging the dressing to his wound. The bullet had lacerated his liver and caused substantial blood loss, but Imrahain was a strong man, both spiritually and physically, and the wound, although severe, would not kill him. He would wear the scar as a badge of honor.

John watched the prison guards usher Imrahain into the seat opposite him on the other side of the glass. The man walked slowly but proudly, and his face betrayed no sign of anger, insolence or madness. John had imagined his assailant possessing some or all of these traits, and his inability to discern the slightest trace of any of them left him a bit unnerved. If Imrahain's face hadn't belonged to a man who tried to kill him, John would have described it as intelligent and refined. Those were not virtues he wanted to ascribe to his attacker.

Imrahain eased himself into the chair, careful not to brush his wound against the seatback, crossed his arms and waited. John looked at him for a long moment and then picked up the telephone. Imrahain did the same.

"Let's just cut to it," said John. "You know who I am, or at least you think you know enough about who I am to want to kill me. I want to know why. I've seen your bio. You come from an upper middle class family, you're well educated, no history of violence. It doesn't add up."

"What I have done, what I do now, what I shall do, is as Allah wills."

"Is this a recent conversion? I didn't see any sign of radicalism in your past."

"What you call radicalism is simply a servant's surrender to the will of Allah."

"Why do your beliefs lead you to want me dead? I'm not your enemy. I've never done you any harm. I don't understand."

Imrahain's eyes opened wide. He sat absolutely still and the phone slowly slipped from his hand, clattering to the table in front of him.

"What is it?" John demanded, his heart racing with the adrenaline rush that came with the sudden knowledge that it had happened again. This time, however, there was only one man who heard it, only one man who could tell John what had come out of his mouth. "What did you hear?"

Imrahain continued to stare at John as he pushed the chair back from the glass divider. He stood up, and without ever taking his eyes off of John, motioned for the guard. A few minutes later, he was in his cell, on his knees, forehead to the ground, praying to Allah for guidance and understanding, confused as to whether Satan had once again played a fiendish trick, or whether he had indeed heard something of the Divine through the mouth of a non-believer.

It had been one thing to hear the Senator speak in tongues on the television news. It was altogether different to be alone with him and hear a voice say, in Arabic, "Why do … you … not … understand?"

Chapter 31

This was a morning unlike any other Hartson had ever known, and it followed a night unlike any he had ever experienced. The television network had treated him to a marvelous dinner at Le Cirque, the upscale French restaurant near St. Patrick's Cathedral in New York that provided as much a feast for the eyes as the stomach, with its vibrant wall colors, fantastic art deco interior, and exquisite food. Toward the end of the meal, when he thought he couldn't take another bite, a team of waiters carried in a gigantic bird's cage made of spun sugar housing an array of impossible to resist desserts. He had never been so full.

Afterward, his escort, Mary, a twenty something and very pretty staffer for the network's morning program, took him to the luxuriously appointed Campbell Apartment bar tucked away in a hidden corner of Grand Central Station. In days gone by, it had been the private office of a railroad tycoon, used for business by day and pleasure by night. Mary explained that for years it had been in a sad state of disrepair, used as a holding cell for the city's drunks and vagrants. Fortunately, someone with vision restored it to its original glory and turned it into a hot spot for the young and trendy and anyone else willing to pay high prices for the pleasure of soaking in the ambience. Hartson thought the bar was interesting, with its 25-foot-high ceilings, stained glass windows, and eclectic clientele, but not nearly as impressive as Grand Central Station itself, which, with 44 platforms and 67 tracks, still reigned as the largest train station in the world.

At the end of the evening, Hartson checked into the most luxurious hotel room he had ever seen, a far cry from the four walls and a bed he had rented in DC. He had tried to talk Mary into spending the night with him, but she made it clear that her job to show him a night on the town ended at the hotel front desk. He wasn't surprised and only mildly disappointed.

His room overlooked Times Square in the heart of mid-town Manhattan, the very spot where the city counted down to midnight every New Year's Eve. The gigantic television screens, flashing neon signs, and streaming news tickers kept the square pulsing late into the night. For a while, he left his drapes open, taking in the city's electric feel.

Hartson arose well before his scheduled wake up call. He looked at the clock by his bed and grinned. In two short hours, Melanie Kraft would interview him on national television. He would be famous, and all because he did something that he had never done before – miss what he had been aiming at.

It had been a harrowing few weeks leading to this moment. Immediately after the shooting, he had been arrested and charged with illegal possession of a firearm as grounds for keeping him locked up while other charges were investigated. He knew enough to keep his mouth shut until his court-appointed lawyer showed up – he wasn't one of those idiots who have to brag about everything they do. As far as the police were concerned, it looked like he had intended to shoot Imrahain to stop him from killing the Senator. That was the story he told his lawyer, and he explained the gun by stating that he always carried one in self-defense and thought that as long as he wasn't trying to board a plane with it, he wasn't doing anything wrong. It was a thin story, he realized, but the best he could come up with. Fortunately, the press had been spinning him as a good, old-fashioned American hero, a modern day John Wayne who had risen out of nowhere to fight the forces of evil. Heroes sold newspapers, and heroes didn't belong in jail.

Hartson and his lawyer worked out a deal with the prosecutors in which he surrendered his gun and agreed to perform 40 hours of public service – visiting high schools to talk about courage and the need to stand up for what is right – in exchange for no jail time and no fine.

He endured a brief moment of self-recrimination over the ease with which he had abandoned his original mission, but the lure of celebrity and the thrill of being worshipped as a hero quickly dissipated his remorse. Hartson saw his errant shot as a remarkable opportunity to redefine who he was and where he was going in life, and he would do everything he could to ensure that it gave him more than just fifteen minutes of fame. He had already taken the first steps to a new life by renting an apartment in DC and doing commercial TV and radio spots for local businesses in DC and its Northern Virginia and Maryland suburbs.

Time to get ready for his interview. He put on the new blazer he purchased the day before in a Fifth Avenue department store, and the silk tie and fake Rolex watch he picked up from a street vendor on the corner by the store's display window. He had never looked or felt so good.

Melanie Kraft greeted Hartson with a smile and a firm handshake before the cameras went live, and showed him where to sit. She turned to her notepad while he crossed and re-crossed his legs, anxiously awaiting the start of the interview. He heard someone say, "Five, four ... " and watched Melanie's face light up.

"Good morning," she said. "Today we have with us a man who is being hailed as a hero, Mark Hartson, who with a single shot stopped an assassination attempt on Senator Peters. Good morning, Mr. Hartson, it's a pleasure having you with us today."

Hartson felt a nervous tickle in his throat, and he barely squeaked out the words, "Thank you for having me."

"Can you tell us, in your own words, exactly what happened?"

"Well, I was at Senator Peters' press conference when I noticed this guy pushing through the crowd, and he didn't look right to me, you know, so I kept an eye on him. Then the next thing I know, the guy whipped out a knife and jumped at the Senator, so I pulled out my gun and shot him."

"Amazing. I'm sure that both Senator Peters and Reverend Jones were extremely grateful."

"Yeah. I got a call from Senator Peters a few days after, thanking me. "

"The entire country thanks you, Mr. Hartson. Here, in NY, we live daily with the terrible reminder of terrorism, and we celebrate our heroes who stand up and fight back. Mr. Hartson, we'd like to give you a little something to show how much we appreciate what you did."

Melanie turned to face someone standing behind the cameras, and on that cue, the Reverend strode across the set holding a gift-wrapped box. He approached Hartson and handed him the gift.

"Mr. Hartson," he said, "Both Senator Peters, who unfortunately couldn't be here this morning, and I want you to know how extremely grateful we are to you for saving both our lives. With the help of Ms. Kraft and her staff, we did some checking to find out how best to express our gratitude. We spoke with your mother..."

Hartson sat in stunned disbelief. He had no idea what his mother would have said, as he hadn't spoken to her in several years.

"...And she told us," the Reverend continued, "that you absolutely loved comic books, superhero comic books, to be precise. She also told us that, unfortunately, some very rare comic books you had owned as a child had been lost. With her help, we've been able to identify those issues. Mr. Hartson, it gives us great pleasure to give to you, a real-life hero, this collection of superhero comic books."

Hartson opened the box and saw, at the very top of the pile, in protective plastic sleeves, mint condition first issues of the *Green*

Hornet and *Justice League of America,* the two most prized possessions of his childhood. Tears rimmed his eyes. He had never in his life been treated so specially.

Later that morning, after the segment had finished airing, the Reverend and Hartson found themselves alone in a studio waiting room. The Reverend contemplated Hartson the way a self-important art critic might contemplate a sculpture, with his arms folded across his chest and his head cocked slightly to one side.

"What is it?" Hartson asked.

"Somebody important wants to meet with you," the Reverend replied.

"Who?"

"His name is Clark, and he is a very, very important man. Very powerful, too."

"Why does he want to meet me?"

"That, I'm afraid, I don't know. What I do know is that it's never wise to turn him down."

Chapter 32

The initial response to the possibility of a Peters' Presidential candidacy was overwhelmingly positive. Polling data showed, to no one's surprise, that he had enormous name recognition across the country, but what especially reassured John and Janice were the high favorability ratings he had among self-styled conservatives who normally voted for the opposite party, and the minimal negative reaction from the more left wing members of their own party.

The polling results amazed John. Janice chalked them up to a combination of Peters' own natural gifts and charm, religious fervor by those who thought he was heaven-sent, sympathy arising from the attempt on his life, and pure physical attraction. History had shown that both men and women voters were biased in favor of handsome candidates.

Encouraged by this preliminary reaction, Janice formed an exploratory committee to see how much money they could raise. She and John both realized that name recognition and early favorability ratings could take them only so far. They needed staying power; simply put, they had to generate enough enthusiasm and sufficient cash to last through the long and grinding primary season.

The committee started a web page dedicated to a Peters' Presidential campaign and before long they had to switch to a more robust server to handle all the people logging on to the website. Checks started arriving, mostly in small amounts, ranging from $5 to $25, but in a constant stream. Even Sara started to warm to the possibility that, if events played out as hoped, she would be First Lady.

Then, one morning, they woke to the first hard-hitting salvo fired at their plans, and it was an attack aimed not by the other side, but by their own party.

"This has to be Clark's handiwork," said Janice, handing John a folded newspaper with the opinion page facing out. "Everyone knows Richard Braun is his hack."

Braun was a nationally syndicated and very widely read columnist who could always be counted on to spin issues and candidates exactly the way the Party wanted. He could also be counted on to viciously attack positions and candidates with which the Party disagreed. Usually, he saved his personal attacks for politicians from across the aisle. In fact, John couldn't remember ever seeing a piece of Braun vitriol directed at someone within the Party. Even so, he wasn't entirely surprised by the column.

"We expected some pushback when we formed our exploratory committee," John replied. "So I guess we should have known something would be coming our way."

"But this is vicious. Have you read it?"

"No." John made no effort to look at the paper now sitting on his lap, so Janice snatched it back.

"I'll read it to you," she said.

> Word on the street and on the Web is that interim Senator John Peters plans to run for President.
>
> But just who is John Peters? Someone who ought to be President?
>
> No way.
>
> A life-long small timer, John is, in his own description, just a guy from the neighborhood with holes in the soles of his shoes.
>
> He has been a Senator for only a little while, barely long enough to get new shoes, so forgive me for doubting whether he has the stuff, the goods, to be the leader of the free world. I haven't had time to assess his leadership skills, or lack thereof; I haven't had time to gauge his intelligence, or lack thereof. What I have seen in Peters' short time on

the national stage is an unbelievable and frightening amount of ambition.

And, oh yeah, there's the 'tongues' thing.

I'm as respectful of faith as the next guy, but it doesn't belong in politics. Whatever happened to the separation of church and state? Our Presidents are supposed to inspire us with the ideals of our founders, not infuse us with the zeal of our pastors.

I don't know what happens when Peters speaks. I've never heard the angelic voices so many people have made such a fuss about, and frankly, it doesn't bother me a bit that I haven't. I don't need to witness miracles to be a good person, and in my book, it's just as likely that Peters summons demons, not angels, when he opens his mouth, and I put the chances that either event happens at fairly close to nil.

I suspect that some day science will reveal the cause of this mass hysteria, and until that day comes, we'll just have to live with the mystery. But living with the mystery doesn't mean we have to coronate it. Our society has succeeded by championing civilization, embracing science, and emphasizing facts. Religious fanaticism has no place in the modern world; it should have no role in choosing our Presidents.

So let's get back to basics. Let's get back to picking Presidents in whom we can place our trust. Let's get back to moving ahead to brighter tomorrows. Let's not slip back to yesterday's dark superstitions and irrational fears.

Senator Peters, stick to fixing your soles. Leave our souls alone.

John laughed. "He does have a way with words, don't you think?"

"I think he is a miserable, sad, small human being."

"Then you should feel sorry for him."

"Aren't you even the slightest bit angry? This is beyond the pale, even for Braun."

Her voice sounded a few notes higher than normal, bordering on a screech. John struggled to find the proper balance between appropriately expressing concern for her well-being and overstepping his bounds by prying into areas she deemed private.

"Janice, I don't want this to come out the wrong way, but are you okay? I'm worried about you."

"What are you talking about?"

"Look, I know it's none of my business, and I don't want to pry. But you know how I feel about you. You're more than just someone who works for me. You're a friend, and as a friend, I'm concerned that you're not ... you're not ready to get back into this yet."

Janice's cheeks flushed. "I still don't know what you're talking about."

"Janice, come on. You went through a horrible experience, but you hardly took any time off. You just jumped right back into work like nothing had happened. You never talk about it, and I understand that, but maybe you should take some more time off, ease your way back into work."

"I don't need to take any more time. And I don't want to talk about it."

"Okay. I'm sorry. I didn't mean to pry. But I need to know that you're up for this."

"What makes you think I'm not?"

"This Braun piece, for one. It's typical Braun. It's not personal, so don't take it that way."

"How can you say it's not personal? It's nothing but personal."

"Janice, how serious are you about making a run for the Presidency?"

"You know better than to ask that. I'm dead serious."

"Then you need to develop a thicker skin. This is only the beginning. The more viable our candidacy becomes, the nastier the attacks will get. If you can't stomach this, you won't be able to make it through to the end."

Janice slammed the paper into John's chest. "So you're just going to lay this off on my overwrought emotions? You're going to laugh this column off? Treat it like it doesn't matter?

"John, don't you get it? This isn't just an insult someone shouted at you from across a barroom floor. You've been called out in a nationally syndicated column. Braun described you as a backwoods hick, a religious zealot, a political neophyte with no business seeking higher office. You can't sit silently by and let this slide. This is the kind of personal attack that builds up steam. It generates copycat columns in other papers. It gets on the evening news and Sunday morning talk shows. It plants doubts in people's minds. They need to see a strong response. Otherwise, the campaign is as good as dead."

"You don't think you're overreacting just a tiny bit?"

"No, not even the tiniest bit."

"And what is it you want to do about it?"

"Fight back. Schedule interviews with the network news. Send in your own opinion piece. Post something on our web page and mention it on TV – that'll get us even more hits. Let's get your message out there."

"First, maybe we ought to figure out exactly what our message is."

"Excuse me?"

"Right now, the thing most people think of when they hear my name is that I'm some kind of miracle man. I have no faith at all – no pun intended – that will translate into actual votes on Election Day. I need something else that sets me apart, plays to my strengths, and connects with the voters. Up till now, you've focused on name recognition, likeability, all the stuff that you need to focus on in the early stages of a campaign, and you've done a great job. But we need to move past that. If I'm going to respond to Braun's column, I want to be able to do more than simply say I'm not the man he describes me as. I want to say who I am and what I stand for."

Janice tilted her head and looked quizzically at John. A long moment lapsed during which neither said a word, and then Janice broke the silence. "I know you think I'm in denial about what happened to me. Trust me, I'm not. Darnell is dead; maybe that helps, as horrible as that sounds, because it made it easier for me move on, but that doesn't mean I pretend it never happened. You want to pretend that nothing happened to you, that nothing has changed since your speech on the Senate floor. But something did happen, John, something extraordinary, and you can't undo it."

Janice paused again and took John's hands in hers. "But I think I understand why it bothers you so much. It's not what you've been telling me –that you're afraid of being seen as a religious nut – because anyone who listens to you speak knows you're not like that. It's because you feel that you're not in control of what happened to you. It was as if someone used your body for his own purposes without your consent. I understand what that feels like.

"But I also believe that what happened to you was not a violation. I have been thinking about it a lot. So has Archbishop O'Connell. He visited me every day after I got out of the hospital, and we've talked quite a bit. He believes, as do I, that you were specially chosen to deliver a message. I don't know what that message is. I hope that in time I will."

"You've got me confused with Moses," John said. "I'm not a prophet. Check your Bible. All the prophets spoke with God; they had two-way conversations. I haven't had any of those. And I checked the parts of the Bible that mention speaking in tongues. The Reverend was kind enough to give me the references. Not a single one covers my situation. Whatever it is that people hear coming out of my mouth, *I don't hear.* Like the time I went to see Imrahain, the guy who shot me, it happened again."

"What?"

"I didn't want to say anything about it to you. I haven't told anyone." John took a deep breath and exhaled slowly. "You're right; I'm in denial. I want to pretend it didn't happen, that none of it happened. But when I spoke with Imrahain, I could see it in his eyes. He was terrified. Janice, I have no idea what he heard. You can't have any idea what that's like, to open your mouth to say something, and to have the people you're speaking to hear something entirely different than what you thought you were saying. I don't understand how it happens, or why it happens, and it scares me. There have been times when I thought if I disappeared from view, bagged the campaign, bagged the Senate, it would all stop. "

"You can't do that."

"I know."

"Isn't it odd how we wound up here, in the U.S. Senate? First, the governor resigns, unexpectedly; then Smith surrenders his Senate seat to take the governor's job and appoints you, someone that no one expected, to replace him. Then, during your very first speech, you speak in tongues. It's an amazing chain of events. Too amazing to be coincidence."

Janice pulled out a piece of paper and started writing. "Here's Archbishop O'Connell's number. You should call him. He can help you understand all this. He has helped me."

"I'm not Catholic."

"That doesn't matter."

John smiled, "Don't you think the Reverend would be jealous?"

“Matthew Harrison Brady.”

“Excuse me?” John said.

“The character from *Inherit the Wind* I told you about, a pretentious blowhard who was willing to sacrifice a decent young man to advance his own agenda. The Reverend has his own agenda, too, and your best interest isn’t on it.”

“That man risked his life to save mine.”

“Maybe.”

“It’s amazing how you can be so spiritual in one breath and so cynical in the next. But let me tell you something, the Reverend helped me see what this ‘tongues’ thing wasn’t. After all those letters and phone calls from people who think I’m some kind of prophet, it was reassuring – I know that probably sounds strange – to have someone point out to me that I’m not the reincarnation of some Biblical character.”

“I never thought you were a reincarnation of anyone. But you have more in common with Biblical prophets than you think.”

John arched his eyebrow and gave Janice a look that clearly showed his incredulity. “Meaning?”

“Not all of them wanted the job, and they weren’t all holier-than-thou types. You mentioned Moses a few minutes ago. Did you know that according to the Bible, Moses asked God not to send him to Egypt because he was a lousy speaker? He even told God to His face that meeting Him hadn’t done much to improve his speaking abilities.”

“I didn’t realize you knew the Bible so well.”

“I don’t. But I have been reading up on prophets lately.”

“You’re sounding awfully religious, Janice. I’m not. I admit I haven’t a clue about what’s going on, but I think I’d know if God were talking to me.”

“It’s a question of faith, John.”

"How do I know this isn't a horrible nightmare that I can't wake up from? How do I know that I haven't gone completely insane and that I'm actually sitting inside a padded room wearing a straightjacket, having this entire conversation only in my head, with a bunch of doctors watching me through a two-way mirror?"

Janice shook her head and laughed. "I don't mean to make fun of you, but trust me, you don't have a good enough imagination to have thought up this storyline on your own."

Her remark and the tone with which she said it startled John. As he mulled it over, a smile appeared on his face. "No, I guess you're right. At least I can cross off the 'Am I insane?' item on my long checklist of things to worry about."

Janice pressed the slip of paper into John's hand. "Call the Archbishop, John. Maybe he can help with some of the other things on that list."

Chapter 33

When the Archbishop suggested they take a drive in the country, John had expected to be picked up in an official looking, probably black and boxy town car, not the flashy yellow roadster that pulled up in his driveway in the pre-dawn of a Saturday morning. The Archbishop's large frame was stuffed in behind the wheel, straining, like an oversized down coat jammed into an undersized travel bag, to expand back to full size. The smile on his face clearly showed, however, that the joy of driving far outweighed any discomfort he might have felt.

"Hop in," he called out.

John eased his lanky legs into the car and shifted about until he found an almost tolerable position, one in which his knees stuck up no higher than mid-abdomen.

"The seat goes back, you know," the Archbishop said.

John felt around the base of his seat and found a button, but when he pressed it, the seat started to rise, pushing his head into the roof.

"Not that one," observed the Archbishop dryly.

John finally found the right button and slid the seat back as far as it would go. It wasn't perfect, but he could at least move his legs a bit.

"Forgive me for asking, but what's a guy like you doing in a car like this?"

"Do you mean, a guy my size, a guy my age, or a guy who wears a priest's collar?"

"All of the above, I guess."

"It's my nephew's car. He lets me borrow it when I need to get away and don't want to bother my driver."

The Archbishop eased the car onto the road and headed for Route 7, an east-west road in Northern Virginia that stretched for miles from the bustling historic town of Alexandria just across the Potomac River from Washington, DC to the rolling fields of Middleburg's horse country, to the gorgeous vistas of the Appalachian Mountains lining the Shenandoah Valley.

"I thought we'd take a ride out to Harper's Ferry to visit Jefferson's Rock. Have you ever been there?"

"No," replied John.

"It's a beautiful place. It's where the Potomac and Shenandoah Rivers merge, and there's a spot nearby where Maryland, Virginia and West Virginia intersect, so you can stand in all three states at once. Most people have heard of it because of John Brown and the abolitionists' effort to seize the federal armory not long before the Civil War. A lot of people don't know that the U.S. Army officer who captured John Brown was Robert E. Lee. Obviously, that was before Virginia seceded from the Union."

"Sounds interesting." John wasn't sure what mid-19th Century American history had to do with the topic he wanted to discuss with the Archbishop, but he decided not to press the matter and to let the Archbishop work around to it in his own time and in his own way.

"There's a lot about Harper's Ferry that's interesting. But what I most enjoy isn't the Civil War related stuff. Behind the town, there is a trail that goes part way up one of the mountains and leads to a large rock that juts out over the Shenandoah Valley. The view from the rock is quite spectacular, especially at the height of leaf peeping season when the colors change. We're past peak right now, unfortunately, but it's still gorgeous. You can see the Shenandoah River far below, rushing to meet the Potomac, and across the river, the Appalachians stretch off into the distance in both directions.

"It's called Jefferson's Rock because it was one of Thomas Jefferson's favorite spots. I love the spot because the view has to be earned. It's not one of those scenic overlooks that you can drive right up to. You first have to make the climb, and for someone with my build and at my age, that can be hard work. Then you have to have enough courage to step out onto the rock, and at that height, stepping out is something a lot of people decide not to do."

A couple of hours later, the two of them sat on the top of Jefferson's Rock and gazed at the early morning sunlight sparkling off the swirling currents of the Shenandoah River below. For the briefest instant when John first looked down at the river, the sunlight's flashing silver reflection conjured the memory of Imrahain's knife, but his momentary panic passed and he was able to relax and enjoy the view. Archbishop O'Connell's face was slightly red from the exertion of the climb.

"I'm impressed," John said.

"It is lovely, isn't it?"

"Yes, it is, but that's not what I was talking about. I meant you. I'm impressed you made this climb."

The Archbishop laughed. "Don't let these old bones fool you. I still get around."

John tossed a small stone that he had picked up during the climb and watched it arc out over the river and plummet out of sight. "I guess we're a little too high up to skip stones."

"Just a bit. We're in God's country now."

"I think I've heard that phrase used everywhere I've traveled in this country, from Maine to California. Seems everybody thinks that where they live is God's country."

"Maybe they're right. Personally, I think every beautiful spot is God's country. To me, places like this, the fact that there is beauty in the world, proves that God exists."

"I've never heard that one before. I thought you couldn't prove God's existence, you either believe or you don't."

"For some people, that's certainly true. I've been blessed. To me, God is more real than any person I've ever met. But I don't think that's true for everybody. Some people need some kind of logical demonstration that God exists. That's why you hear arguments about the First Mover – the notion that someone had to get this universe started. But frankly, that argument doesn't do much for me. I mean, if God could exist without a beginning, then why couldn't the universe? Once you agree that something can have existed forever, it seems rather arbitrary to insist that it must be one entity rather than another. No, to me, if you need "proof" that God is real, the existence of beauty provides a far better argument.

"Did you ever ask yourself why people stop to watch the sunset? What is it that makes us drop everything, even if only for a few moments, to turn our eyes toward the horizon? Why do we gaze at the stars? Why do rainbows, waterfalls, and snow-capped mountains stir our souls? Ants and mosquitoes and bacteria have evolved and survived for millions of years without beauty in their lives. Why is it so important to us?"

"I've never given it much thought," John replied.

"I believe that beauty is God's gift to us, that it reflects the presence of the Divine in our lives. I believe that beauty is the bridge between this world and heaven, and that our yearning for beauty reflects our desire for God. To me, the existence of beauty proves not only that God exists, but also that we cannot approach Him through logic alone. There is a mystery to God that logic cannot embrace."

"So you're using a sort of logical argument to prove not only that God exists, but that logic cannot get you there."

"Ironic, isn't it? I'm sorry," the Archbishop said. "I have a bad habit of lecturing even when I'm not at the pulpit. And sitting on this ledge, looking out over the world below, makes me feel as if I'm am on one."

"That's okay," John replied. "It was interesting. And I have a feeling that you're going to tie this into my ... issue."

"Janice said you still have a hard time saying it out loud."

"That I speak in tongues? Yeah, it's not something I'm exactly comfortable with."

"I can understand that. I'm sure you're confused and scared. I struggled with it for a long time as well. I couldn't explain what I had heard. My rational side rejected it as impossible, and I couldn't bring myself to call it a miracle. But I've spent a lot of time thinking about it."

"So what do you think is going on?"

"I think you are here to reawaken the world to the mystery of God."

John tossed another rock into the river below and brushed his hands clean of the dirt traces it left in his palms. "As I told Janice, I'm no prophet."

"John, hear me out on this. There have been prophets for nearly every age and for nearly every people, and the differences among them are greatly outweighed by their similarities. But a prophet who spoke to one people during one age didn't necessarily resonate with a different people in a different age. Why do you think Christianity spread across the Roman Empire? How do you think Islam supplanted Christianity and Zoroastrianism so quickly and so universally across North Africa? Because their prophets were able to relate to people and bring God into their lives in a way that those before them had not."

"I'm not sure I even believe in God, so why would you think I'm a prophet?"

"You perfectly reflect our times and you relate well to the people of our times. There are a lot of people with doubts. And many others who say they believe in God, and even think they do, but only because they've been conditioned that way. They don't really believe."

"What do you mean?"

"Catholics, for example, are supposed to believe that at Holy Communion, the bread is actually transubstantiated into the Body of Christ. Think about what that means to a true believer: every Mass, we take the Body of the Son of God into ourselves. That should fill us with awe, incredible joy, and maybe even a touch of anxiety because we're not worthy to receive such a wonderful gift. It should be more soul stirring than a beautiful sunset. But what do I see at Mass? – long lines of people for communion, some in devout prayer, but others simply shuffling up the aisles, many of them wearing sloppy jeans, halter-tops, or sweat suits. Would they go to their boss' house for dinner dressed like that? No. So why are they so casual about God's house? Why are they so casual about the miracle of Communion? Because to them it's simply a ritual they go through. The wine they drink is made of grapes, not blood.

"I'm not saying rituals aren't important; they are – they tie communities together in a shared experience. But they're not miracles. They don't inspire. They don't connect us with God or our inner souls. The Church isn't getting through to these people. They need someone to inspire them, a prophet."

"I have to admit, I'm more than a bit startled at your reaction." John said. "I didn't think Catholics, or any Christians for that matter, were allowed to believe in any prophets after Christ."

"I'm not saying you're the Second Coming. And I'm not saying you shouldn't believe in Christ, but I don't believe that only Christians get to heaven. My grandmother was Jewish and no one can convince me she isn't in heaven. And how can any God-fearing person, whether Muslim or not, truly doubt that Mohammed was divinely inspired?"

"How does any of this relate to me?"

"We live in a time when people are disconnected from the spiritual side of their lives. I believe you are here to help them reconnect."

"I'm sorry, but there is just no way that is true."

"Think about it, John. We live in an Internet age, a globalized economy, and with the rise of the information age, there has been a spread of secular values – most of Europe is now atheistic. But without a sense of the Divine, people inevitably become cynical, disaffected, and unhappy. If there is no Deity, no afterlife, then this life becomes less meaningful. People need God in their lives, but science tells them He doesn't exist. Our intellectuals scoff at anyone who invokes God's name. Heaven forbid anyone even mention to a grade school student the possibility that God created the universe – no, not Heaven forbid, the ACLU forbid, and on top of that, they'll sue you. Then you come along, unknown and unheralded, and with a few short words, stir up our religious imagination.

"Look at the impact you've had. Attendance at religious services of every type is up all around the world. Religious books are on the best-sellers list. That's all due to you.

"Do you think it's an accident that you hold office in the loftiest legislative body of the most powerful government in the world? Do you think it's an accident that your message has reached people around the world? I don't think so."

John rose to his feet, shaking his head. "It's not *my* message. I don't know what it is, and believe me, I've been struggling with that fact every day since it happened. But I'm not interested in stirring up anyone's religious imagination. The only thing I want to stir up is America's political imagination and the votes that go with it. I'm sorry, but that's just the way it is.

"You're coming from a very different place than I am," John continued. "No surprise there. After all, you're an Archbishop. I met with you as a favor to Janice, but with all due respect, your Excellency, I don't think there's much point in continuing this conversation." John stood up and started to move off Jefferson's Rock and back onto the hill.

"John, before you go, answer me this. Do you know who you are? I don't mean your name, or where you come from or anything like that. I mean the voice inside your head, your consciousness. Where does that voice come from?"

John turned with a curious look. "What do you mean?"

"When you try to think about where 'you' are inside your body, you probably conjure up a notion of someone inside your head, looking out, someone who is inside your body but not wholly connected to it. People have near death experiences and tell of looking down on themselves on the operating table, their consciousness floating somewhere above their bodies. At those moments, their bodies were simply empty vessels. Do you believe that the person you are is something more than the body you inhabit?"

"I don't know."

"It's an important question. It may be the most important question. And the belief that we're something more than a physical being is under constant attack. More and more, scientists with a secular agenda claim that our minds are nothing more than biochemical reactions. These scientists argue that there is no true 'self'; that what we think of as 'identity' is just a highly structured bundle of neurons and chemical signals. According to these scientists, there is no 'you' apart from your body, and when your body dies, all of you dies with it, including whatever consciousness you have of being a 'self' apart from the body you inhabit."

The Archbishop paused and looked at John for several moments. John stood quietly. "Do you believe that's true?" the Archbishop asked.

"I just told you, I don't know."

"If it is true, if 'you' are nothing more than biochemical reactions that can be mapped and traced and measured, then how do you explain the fact that there is a part of you that has done something you cannot begin to fathom, something you say you aren't even aware of? What neurological, biophysical event can cause you to speak in languages you've never even heard of?"

John slid back down next to the Archbishop and dropped his chin to his chest. He spoke in a suddenly weary voice. "I don't know. I just don't know." He lifted his chin and turned to the Archbishop. "I'm not an idiot. I know that something is going on that defies any rational explanation. And it scares me. I admit it. If I were a man of faith, this would be easy. I'd just say, 'Lord, thy will be done,' and be done with it. But I'm not. I've got doubts. Always have. I've never been able to reconcile the notion of an all powerful, all loving God with the fact that really bad things happen to really good people. Janice didn't deserve what happened to her. Where was God when she was raped? How can that be part of His plan?"

"Those are fair questions. And I wish I had definitive answers for you. I don't. But I'll tell you what I think. I think that the fact that God is all-powerful doesn't mean he uses His power all the time. And He has enemies."

"You're trying to tell me that the devil makes bad things happen? That the devil made Darnell attack Janice?"

"I think he influences as best he can the choices we make. I think that left to our own devices, without God's help, we have a hard time recognizing the devil's role in the world and in each of our lives."

John shrugged his shoulders. “I don’t mean to offend you, Your Excellency, nor do I mean to belittle your faith. But as for me, I’ve always thought that there are enough genetic and societal influences to explain why people turn out the way they do that we don’t need the devil to explain the bad.”

“A far wiser man than me once said that the devil’s best weapon is our refusal to believe that he exists.”

“I respect the fact that you hold your beliefs deeply, but I have a hard enough time believing in God. The devil is a bit too much for me, and from where I sit, I think we should spend less time worrying about the struggle between heaven and hell, and more time over things like jobs, food and housing.“

“You may not believe in the devil, but I fear that he believes in you. I see his dark hand in some of the things that have happened. I believe God has chosen you for a special purpose, and I believe the devil will do his best to stop you.”

John shook his head. “There are a lot of things I’m not sure about. That’s pretty clear. But if there is a devil, I don’t think I’m at the top of his hit list.”

“Don’t sell yourself short.”

“I’m not a religious figure. I’m a candidate for the Presidency.”

“The two don’t have to be mutually exclusive.”

“Our Constitution and my personal beliefs say they do.”

“John, please listen ...”

“I’m no Moses. I’m no Christ. I’m no Mohammed. For you to try to link me with them ... well ... if I were the religious sort, it would strike me as blasphemous. Look, I understand you’re upset with the apathy you see at Sunday service. It’s how I feel about low voter turnout. I’m doing what I can about the latter, but I’m not the answer to the former.”

The Archbishop bowed his head and whispered softly, "I'm afraid for you, John."

John shivered as he would if he had been listening to a well-told ghost story.

"Your Excellency, do me a favor: please don't repeat this conversation or share your thoughts on this with anyone else. I don't need this sort of talk from someone as important as you floating around."

"John, above everything else, I'm a priest. I know how to keep confidences. And though you may think I'm a superstitious old fool – I can see it in your eyes – the truth is I'm pretty well grounded. I'm also hopeful, despite my fears. I have faith that in time you will understand that God has chosen you, and you will understand why. I think you're confused because you're trying too hard to figure things out on your own. If you relaxed and simply accepted it, I think things would change.

"Have you ever tried to remember someone's name, had it on the tip of your tongue, even the person's face in your mind, but couldn't come up with it no matter how hard you tried? Then, later, after you'd stopped thinking and worrying about it, suddenly the name popped into your head? At some point, when you're tired of worrying about what this all means, tired of fighting it, when you stop resisting, it will all become clear. It will come to you unbidden and unexpected, but it will come.

"But don't worry. I promise I won't say a word, not to any mortal person, anyway. I trust your request doesn't mean I can't pray for you. And I also trust you'll keep my views confidential as well."

"You can count on it."

Chapter 34

The ride back from Harper's Ferry had been a quiet one, neither man willing or able to lighten the mood with small talk. By the time the Archbishop dropped him off, John was tired, testy and given that he hadn't had any breakfast, hungry as well. He called out to Sara as he came through the door, and was surprised when only silence answered him. He walked through the house, calling out her name and Connor's a few more times before he saw the note she had left for him on the kitchen counter explaining that the Reverend had called and invited them to a service he had been asked to lead at a nearby Bible church. He had promised it would be entertaining as well as educational, as the Church had an outstanding gospel rock band and amazing audio-visual technology, with plasma TVs and stereo speakers circling the room. She thought it would be an interesting experience for both her and Connor, so she accepted the offer and expected to be back by early afternoon.

John rummaged through the refrigerator and pulled out a slice of cold pepperoni pizza and the leftovers of the roast chicken they had for dinner the night before. He also opened a couple bottles of beer to avoid making a return trip to the fridge, turned on the TV and searched for something to watch, preferably a North Carolina championship basketball game on a classics sports channel - that would improve his mood.

He had just started to cut into the chicken when he heard the garage door open. Moments later, as he was washing his hands so they would be clean for the rapidly approaching hug, Connor charged into the kitchen and wrapped himself around his legs.

"Daddy," he yelled. "We had the best time!"

"Did you? I'm glad. What made it fun?"

"There was music and singing and then I got to go to a room with other kids and some grownups told us stories and we got to play and we got to color and make things. See, I made this pretty wreath and decorated it all by myself."

Connor took a deep breath, as he had spoken in a rush and without pause, and held up a cardboard wreath that he had been clutching in his hand. The wreath was covered in strips of yarn arranged in the colors of the rainbow. Connor loved rainbows. Every drawing in every coloring book he owned, whether they were of plants, animals, buildings or superheroes, was colored in stripes of purple, blue, green, yellow, orange and red.

"That's very pretty, Connor. And you made it all by yourself?"

Connor nodded his head vigorously. "Yes. Well, I had a little help cutting out the wreath. And I had a little help with gluing the yarn. But I picked the colors."

"The colors are the best part. I'm very proud of you."

Sara had been standing a few feet away during the conversation wearing a large smile.

"And did you have fun, too?" John asked her.

"It was interesting. Different than what we're used to. I'll say one thing for the Reverend. He is a rousing speaker. He had those people up out of their seats, shouting 'Hallelujah' and screaming 'Amen' at the top of their lungs. It was quite something to see."

"I'm surprised you went."

"He can be very persuasive. He was asked at the last minute to fill in, as the minister who normally holds that service woke up with a fever this morning, and he told me how much it would mean to him if we all came. Apparently, this is a big deal church and being asked to lead services is quite an honor. I told him you were out for the morning, but he still wanted Connor and me to come. He introduced us to the entire congregation. I wasn't thrilled with that – a lot of people came up to me afterward asking questions about you. But all in all, I'm still glad I went."

Connor had wandered into the family room where he grabbed the remote and changed the program from basketball to the latest incarnation of a superhero action show imported from Japan. Normally, John would have said something like, 'Hey, ask me first. I was watching basketball,' but this time he let it pass. He wanted to talk to Sara about his morning.

"I'm not surprised the Reverend is good at what he does," John said. "It's kind of ironic, when you think about it, because I'm not at all sure he believes in God, but apparently he is very good at getting other people to believe in Him. Archbishop O'Connell seems to be the mirror opposite of that."

"What do you mean?"

"The Archbishop believes very deeply in God, but he seems almost in a state of despair that he can't get his parishioners to believe, at least in the way he thinks they should. I think he wants to use me as a way to stir up the kind of passion the Reverend generates. Maybe I should introduce the two of them to each other."

"Doesn't sound like your meeting went well this morning."

"No, it didn't. We're coming from two different places. But he is entitled to his beliefs. That doesn't worry me. What worries me is how much influence he has with Janice. I can't have someone that instrumental in my campaign operating with a different agenda than I have. I want our focus to be on the political message. I think the Archbishop has got her head turned around. She's going all religious on me."

"Do you think her being raped has anything to do with it?"

"I don't know. Maybe. It wouldn't be the first time someone turned to God for help through a difficult time. I don't have any problem with that. I just don't want her bringing it into the campaign."

"You need to talk to her about it, then."

"I already tried. It ended with her insisting that I see the Archbishop. I think she had convinced herself that the Archbishop would talk me into seeing things the same way he does. But you're right. I need to try again. If I can't get comfortable with where she is coming from or where she wants to go with my campaign, I'm going to have to find someone else to run things."

"You're not upset that Connor and I went to the Reverend's service this morning, are you?"

"No, why would you think that?"

"It sounds like you don't want anything dealing with religion to touch your campaign."

"That's not it. I have no problem having the media see you, Connor or me go to service. I think it's expected, actually. America wants its leaders to believe in God. But there is a line that can't be crossed. I can't have religion overwhelm my political message."

Sara shook her head and walked over to the kitchen table where she started cleaning up the remains of John's lunch. "Are you done eating?"

"Yes. Thanks. Why did you shake your head?"

"It's nothing."

"No, something is bothering you. What is it?"

"You'll just get mad at me."

"I promise I won't."

"It's just that all this concern about mixing religion and politics seems a bit hypocritical to me."

"What do you mean?"

"Every politician professes a belief in God. They go to church on Sundays, they ask God to bless America, they thank Him when good things happen, and they invoke His name in times of tragedy. They claim that their religious beliefs have helped form their character, yet they say that the church and the state must be kept separate. I don't see how that's possible. People are the product of their education and their experience. If those things include religion, how can they divorce it from their decision making process?"

"The Constitution doesn't forbid politicians from believing in God, but I want to be taken seriously as a politician, and religion has already had enough of an impact on my career."

Sara scraped food from John's plate into the disposal and ran the faucet. Without turning her head to look at John, she said, "It sounds to me like you want religion as background music. Let people know it's there, but don't have them pay too much attention to it."

"When you put it that way, it sounds harsher than it really is. Here, let me clean this up. It's my mess."

Sara stepped back from the sink and let John load the dishwasher with his plate and a few others items that had been left in the sink from Connor's breakfast.

"Where does all this leave you with the Reverend?" Sara asked.

"What do you mean?"

"He clearly wants to be associated with you. He thinks you're going places, and he wants to go along for the ride. You've already taken him pretty far. If he hadn't been at the press conference with you, he wouldn't have been on Melanie Kraft's show and he wouldn't have guest hosted this morning's services."

"He wouldn't have been almost killed, either."

"He probably thinks of that as a small price to pay for what he hopes to get out of it."

"It's not like you to be so cynical. That's more Janice's forte."

"Don't get me wrong. I like Reverend Jones on a certain level. He's funny and he's charming. But I don't trust him."

"You and Janice both."

"So, back to my question. What are you going to do about him?"

"I don't think I need to do anything. He's not officially part of the campaign. He did offer to give me some tips on public speaking. Based on what you saw, I think I'll take him up on it. After that, he'll go his way and I'll go mine."

"I don't think it will be that easy."

"You worry too much."

Sara was about to respond when Connor suddenly yelled, "Mommy! Daddy! Look! Look!" He was pointing at the sliding glass door leading from the family room to the deck outside. John and Sara followed the line of sight indicated by his outstretched finger and saw a large bat hanging from the perch of their bird feeder. Its wings were wrapped around its body, and its unblinking black eyes seemed to stare directly at them.

"Is that the same bat that got into our house a few weeks ago?" Sara asked.

"Could be. Looks big enough."

"What's it doing out in the daytime?"

"It must be rabid. I'll call the county's animal protection office."

Connor ran over to John and wrapped his arms around him. "I'm scared, Daddy," he said.

John picked him up and kissed him on the cheek. "There's nothing to be afraid of, Connor. It can't get in the house. I think it's probably very sick, so we're going to call someone who can come and take care of it."

"John, if that bat has rabies, and you handled it, is there any chance you've been exposed?" Sara asked.

"No. I never touched it. I wrapped it in a towel and set it free."

"Are you sure?"

"You worry too much."

Chapter 35

Dear Sara,

This has become a sort of addiction for me. When I need to share my deepest concerns with you, but am afraid to do so because of the worry and stress it will cause (is that the only reason, I wonder, or am I afraid that you'll make me face something that I don't want to look at full square), I resort to writing these letters. I will show them to you, all of them, when I'm ready.

I have never been reluctant to tell you everything on my mind before. The fact that I now am worries me. It makes me wonder if I'm heading down the wrong path. It's all so confused.

I know I'm rambling but it helps me just to get my thoughts out in whatever order they come.

You and Connor were both a bit shaken by the bat we saw this afternoon. I was too. Not for the reasons you were. Even if the bat is rabid, I'll be okay. No part of it touched me at all. What worries me is something else entirely.

That bat gave me the same creepy, eerie feeling that I got sitting next to Clark. I know it's ridiculous, that I'm just projecting something onto the bat that isn't there, but I can't shake myself of it. I keep thinking about the bat and it makes me think of Clark, and I don't get a good feeling from either of them.

I remember reading Moby Dick in high school and thinking at first that the white whale was an evil creature bent on destroying Captain Ahab. Then my teacher explained that the whale was just doing what whales do, but that Ahab, in his tormented state, had ascribed all sorts of evil motives to an animal that was simply a force of nature. I keep telling myself that's what I'm doing. That bat is just a bat.

And Clark is just Clark. I know in my last letter I was pretty harsh on him. I had just met with him and I wasn't happy with how the meeting went. And in all fairness, he really was a bit of a jerk. I'm still not sure what he's all about, other than he appears to be a man who enjoys having power. I've met people like that before – Ned's dad, for example. Ask most folks what men like that do every day, and they couldn't tell you. But they could tell you they're powerful. What does that mean? What is power? Here I am, running for President, the single most powerful office in the world, and I'm asking myself what power is. How do you exercise power intelligently if you haven't thought through what it is or what it means to have it? Perhaps men of power are forces of nature in their own way. Power impacts how they think, what they do, how they deal with others. The question is, if you have power, can you control it or must it inevitably control you? I have to believe power can be controlled. Otherwise, I wouldn't be running for office. I'm rambling again. And no matter how I hard I try not to, my mind keeps circling back to Clark and that stupid bat. I've got to rein in my imagination. I definitely watched too many horror movies as a kid.

Maybe it's Clark's eyes, the way he hides them behind those sunglasses. He looks out on the world, but doesn't want anyone looking in on him. That's bound to give anyone the creeps. It makes him seem eerie, like a character from an Edgar Allan Poe story. When I did see his eyes for a brief moment during our meeting in the coffee shop, they were black as night. I've never seen eyes like that before. He must have some sort of medical condition, but it certainly serves his purposes well. He can look very intimidating behind those smoky lenses. He's not going to intimidate me.

Tomorrow is going to be a long day. I'm not looking forward to the conversation I have to have with Janice. I've got Clark and bats on one hand, talk of prophets on the other. It's a medieval melodrama. It's time for the melodrama to end.

Love,

John

Chapter 36

The receptionist walked Hartson to the conference room door and opened it for him. He stepped inside and looked about at the spacious, dimly lit interior. The Reverend had told him not to be nervous, but he couldn't help it. He didn't know this man Clark that he was meeting, and he didn't know why he was meeting him. Soft drinks, bottled water and thermoses of regular and decaffeinated coffee were arrayed in neat rows on a narrow table against the opposite wall. He could see that the sodas and water had been recently removed from a refrigerator, as beads of condensation had started to form on them. The receptionist had told him to help himself, but he decided to wait for Clark to arrive.

Several minutes ticked by while Hartson waited. He walked over to the window and started to raise the blind to see the view when he heard a voice behind him.

"You wouldn't mind keeping the blind down, would you. The light bothers my eyes."

Hartson turned and saw a hulking figure in the doorway silhouetted against the light from the hallway beyond. As he entered the room, Hartson saw a second man, shorter, thinner and much younger, standing behind him. The two men presented quite a pair of opposites. The older man wore sunglasses and a rumpled brown suit; the young man, crisply dressed in a black suit, had eyes so blue they didn't look real. The first man introduced himself as Clark but did not introduce the younger man. Instead, he poured himself a cup of black coffee and motioned for Hartson to have a seat.

"I've looked forward to this meeting, Mr. Hartson," Clark said, "Quite a bit, actually."

"Why is that?"

"You're a rare man, Mr. Hartson. A man of action. A man who jumps into the fray without hesitation. A man to be reckoned with."

"You're talking about the shooting?"

"Of course. What else is there, Mr. Hartson?"

Hartson studied the two men across the table from him and did not like what he saw. They seemed too self-assured, and that made him nervous.

"I still don't understand why you wanted to meet with me."

Clark smiled. "I wanted to get an answer to a question that's been nagging me for some time."

"What question?"

Clark picked up a remote control device that Hartson hadn't noticed sitting on the corner of the table and pushed a button. A small whirring noise emanated from the ceiling as a large movie screen lowered in front of them. Behind them, a wooden panel slid open, revealing a projector.

Clark continued, "As I understand it, you were at Senator Peters' press conference – I won't ask how you got in; I imagine you bribed one of the hotel clerks to get you into the conference room – standing in the back, when you saw someone try to stab Senator Peters?"

"That's right."

"And you pulled out your gun and shot him?"

"Yes. I didn't want to shoot. I just didn't think I had a choice if I wanted to save Senator Peters."

"Mr. Hartson, I have a video of the incident from one of the security cameras mounted on the back wall of the conference room. As far as we know, it's the only film taken from behind the dais where the Senator had been standing when he was attacked. We managed to get our hands on it before the police did, so very few people have ever seen it. It's quite remarkable, really. It shows the crowd in front of the dais, including you and Abdul Imrahain, that's the name of the man you shot. Shall we take a look at it together?"

Hartson felt his knees shake. A clip of the incident started playing on the screen. Two yellow circles had been superimposed onto the video image, highlighting Imrahain and Hartson in the crowd.

Clark wagged his finger at the screen. "What's interesting about the video, Mr. Hartson, is that as you can clearly see, you have your gun out well before Mr. Imrahain makes it to the front of the crowd of reporters. And here ..." Clark paused the film, "You're raising your gun into a firing position while Mr. Imrahain is still at the bottom of the stairs, still out of reach of the Senator and the Reverend. It doesn't seem possible that from where you stood in the back of the room, you could have even have known he was there, let alone seen him pull a knife. So my question, Mr. Hartson, is this: just who were you planning to shoot?"

Hartson started shaking his head. "You don't understand. You don't understand."

"I believe I do, Mr. Hartson. What I want to know is, why?"

"I have nothing to say to you."

Clark sipped his coffee and sat quietly for a few moments as the young man next to him rewound the video clip and replayed it. Hartson's heart raced and he fought to stay in control of his voice.

"I don't know who you are, or what game you're trying to play," Hartson said, "but I think it's time for me to leave."

Clark raised an open palm and grinned. "I don't intend to share this video with anyone else, unless I have to. I just thought it important for you to know that I have it."

As Hartson headed for the door, the young man stood up and spoke for the first time. He had a French accent. "I'll see Mr. Hartson out. He is our guest, and one should always be courteous to one's guests."

Hartson left the conference room without saying another word. As soon as the elevator door closed, his escort turned to him and said,

"My name is Emile. I wanted to apologize for the circumstances of our meeting ... Clark can be a bit ... abrupt ... but I expect our next conversation will be to our mutual advantage."

Chapter 37

John arrived at the office early Monday morning, wet from the heavy rain that his umbrella did little to fend off, tired from a night in which sleep came only in fitful, nightmare-filled stretches, and edgy in anticipation of the blunt conversation he planned to have with Janice about the Archbishop. The coffee that he had spilled on his sleeve and hand did little to improve his mood.

Janice, to his surprise, was already at her desk despite the early hour, with a disgusted look on her face and a piece of paper in her hand that she crumpled and tossed to John.

"You're not going to believe this," she said. "I got a call from a reporter looking for a comment on this press release that he just faxed to me. John Lynch, the head of the American Confederation of Workers, just issued a press release attacking your suitability to be President."

John didn't seem at all fazed by the news. Nor did he bother to read the press release now in his hands. "So, what exactly did he say?"

"That you were dangerous. That a country with you as President would be a country he wouldn't feel comfortable living in."

"I don't know the man," John replied, "but from what I've heard of him, the feeling is mutual."

Janice was far more upset than John by this development, partly because she didn't like attacks on John, regardless of the source, and partly because securing the nomination despite Clark's opposition presented enough of a challenge. She didn't relish having to fight other powerbrokers within their own party.

"It just seems wrong for him to do this. What if you win the nomination? Is he going to endorse the other party's candidate? I highly doubt it."

John tossed the press release back to Janice. "Don't sweat it. Out of curiosity, what do you think prompted him to issue the press release?"

"It doesn't say directly, but reading between the lines, it's either Clark's influence, or he is spooked by the tongues thing. I can't think of any other reason for him to come out so early with a position like this. Normally, they don't attack their own. They simply endorse the guy they like. They save the attacks for the other side's candidate."

"Maybe it's a good thing."

"How's that?"

"I wasn't likely to secure labor's nomination over their favorite sons anyway. This way, I'm not beholden to them. I can take the stands I want to take on some pretty serious issues, from free trade to minimum wage. Most people in our party are reasonable, moderate, and decent, and I trust that they'll listen to me with an open mind, no matter what Lynch says."

"Thanks for trying to make me feel better."

"My pleasure. But before you start thinking I'm a nice guy, I do need to talk to you about my meeting with the Archbishop."

"Sure." Janice looked at her watch. "Damn, I'm late. John, can this wait until I get back? I have a doctor's appointment that I'm already late for." Without waiting for his reply, she grabbed her purse, her coat, and her umbrella and hurried out the door.

Janice stared at her doctor in disbelief. She had not been feeling well for several weeks, but had put off seeing her doctor because of the crush of work associated with organizing the campaign. Finally, though, after she doubled over one morning with abdominal pain, she realized she had to seek medical attention. Her doctor had sent her to the hospital for tests, and she had steeled herself for the worst. She operated under the theory that if one prepares for the worst, anything less comes as good news. The news she got wasn't the inoperable, malignant tumor she had feared, but it was so far removed from anything she had imagined that at first she thought she simply misheard him. He repeated the diagnosis.

"That's impossible, Doctor," she protested.

"Nevertheless, it's true. You are pregnant."

Janice's mind reeled. She couldn't be pregnant, and not just because she didn't want to be. Not just because it had to be from the rape. She couldn't be pregnant because physically, she was incapable of it. Janice called the office and left a message that she would be out the rest of the day. Later that afternoon, she visited Archbishop O'Connell. When she arrived, he was on the phone in his private office, so she curled up in the same chair she used to sit in as a girl, settling into the warm, comforting memories it gave her, memories of a time when she and her father were still close.

When the Archbishop came through the door, the first thing he noticed was how small and frail Janice looked curled up in the chair. Then he saw the tears trickling down her cheeks. He thought at first that she was upset about his meeting with John a couple of days before, but quickly banished the notion as foolish, realizing that, disastrous as that meeting was, his inability to win John over would not have caused the anguish he could see in her face. He gently lifted her from the chair and enfolded her into his chest.

Not until she had emptied herself of tears and reached that dried out, hollow feeling that follows a long cry could she bring herself to repeat what she had learned from the doctor and why it had come as such a shock. She had no way of knowing the dread with which her news would fill him. For the first time in his memory, he did not know what advice to give. He needed time to think, to sort through the conflict between his beliefs and his instincts. He treasured all life as sacred, but he feared that which grew inside Janice. He would pray for guidance, and in the meantime, he would offer Janice the support of a steady shoulder.

Chapter 38

Dear Diary,

I feel like a little girl writing that line, but I don't know how else to start. Had a shock today. That's putting it mildly.

I'm pregnant. It doesn't seem possible. I was told I could never get pregnant again, not just by one doctor but by three. Yet here I am, with child.

When I got the news, I felt scared. I felt shame. More than that, and this is hard to admit even to myself, I felt revulsion at this 'thing' inside me. I did not participate in its conception. I was forced into it. I don't think I can endure the pain of this pregnancy, of this daily reminder of what happened to me.

But I know I cannot endure the trauma of another abortion.

I don't know what I am going to do. I don't know what I should do.

I went to see Archbishop O'Connell right after I got the news. He looked even more shocked than I was. He gave me a shoulder to cry on, but he didn't try to tell me what to do next. I suppose there's no mystery in what he would say – he is an Archbishop. It's not like he'd offer me the full range of options that I'd get at Planned Parenthood.

Can I bring this child to life? Can I forgive this child for what his or her father did to me? Can I love this child?

Chapter 39

"This is for you," said Sara, handing John a previously opened envelope. It was one of the many letters that arrived at the campaign office in Rosslyn, Virginia each day. Sara had found the office space, which was only a short walk across the Key Bridge from Georgetown, and signed the lease without bothering to double-check with John or Janice, as she knew it was far cheaper than any comparable space in DC. She spent many mornings there, helping to sort the mail and answer the phones, and it reminded her of the time not so long before when she volunteered in John's district office in North Carolina. Before long, however, the flood of phone calls and mail grew beyond her ability to manage, even with Janice's help, and Janice had been forced to recruit additional staff, mostly young and idealistic college students who worked on a volunteer basis. They had been instructed to send brief thank you notes bearing John's facsimile signature in reply to most letters. The correspondents who enclosed $25 or more received an autographed 5" x 7" glossy of John, and anyone who donated at least $1,000 received a note of gratitude personally signed by John. He took a few minutes each evening to sign any such notes that the staff put on his desk.

On occasion, the staff would route a particularly charming letter to Sara or Janice for review, depending on which of them was in the office. They were always on the lookout for letters that could be used in future advertising. Letters from blue collar workers who had lost their jobs, worried parents with sons or daughters in the military, or children with serious illnesses for which cures remained just out of reach all provided fertile material. Janice envisioned stirring commercials featuring Senator Peters' profile in the foreground, flags in the background, and a voiceover that quoted the best sentences from the best letters, and finished with testimonials as to why John would make a great President.

This letter wasn't any of those. The return address on the envelope was that of the Federal Penitentiary. It came from Abdul Imrahain. John opened the letter and started to read:

Dear Senator Peters,
I do not write to apologize.
I do not write to deny that which I attempted.
I admit that I intended to end your life.
I did so for a great and just cause.
I believed you to be engaged in a great hoax.
I believed you to be the tool of an evil government.
I believed you to be a threat to my people.
I did not believe in the so-called miracle of tongues.
I agreed to meet you so that I could see for myself the type of man who would participate in such an evil deception.
But then I heard you speak in Arabic and English before my very ears.
My ears were not deceived.
You did speak in tongues.
You asked me why I did not understand.
I do not understand your question.
What I understand is this:
I understand that you are a non-believer, and as such, fall under the sway of Iblis, the Transgressor, known as Al-Shaitan, the Satan.
I understand that Al-Shaitan cannot force a man to do evil, but only incite him to do so.
I understand that you have the freedom to choose that which is good and to reject that which is evil.
But I do not believe that Allah would choose a non-believer to be the instrument of His message.
So I ask you: What did you mean when you asked me why I did not understand?
All praise belongs to Allah

Abdul Imrahain

"What are you going to do with this?" Sara asked.

"I'm going to turn it over to the authorities," John replied.

"Are you sure you want to do that?" she asked. "He talks about your having spoken in tongues. Do you want to bring that up just before your first debate?"

John stared at the letter in his hands. The first in a series of three debates among the leading candidates for his party's nomination had been scheduled for the following week. John had worked hard, thinking through his positions on various domestic and international issues and shaping them into pithy sound bites of the type that news programs loved to air. To improve his delivery, he had even studied videotapes of standup comics. Many of the more successful ones were masters at 'circling back': the art of regularly referring back to a central theme to tie seemingly unrelated jokes together and transform what would otherwise be a disjointed, rambling monologue into a seamless, integrated routine. John had also worked closely with the Reverend. For all of Janice and Sara's reservations, there could be no denying that the Reverend's tutelage had helped John polish his speaking style into one that flowed smoothly and projected confidence.

He did not want to have all that effort blown aside by the whirlwind that would surely follow the publication of Imrahain's letter. He walked over to the shredder and fed in both the letter and its envelope. The shredder's high-pitched whine always made him cringe, but he no longer depended on the trashcan to dispose of the things he wanted permanently gone.

Chapter 40

Sara felt guilty that she had misled John as to her whereabouts. She had told him that she had some shopping to do at the mall because she knew that he would have opposed her seeing Archbishop O'Connell. In truth, she had been hesitant to meet with him given the encounter at Harper's Ferry, but the possibility he extended of a scientifically based explanation for John's problem overcame her reluctance. The Archbishop had offered to secure the use of state-of-the-art medical equipment at a Church owned hospital in an attempt to detect any anomalies in John's brain. Equally important, he guaranteed that the testing and any discoveries yielded by it would remain absolutely confidential.

She flipped through the pages of the glossy brochure that he had handed her. Its pages were filled with pictures of medical equipment and diagrams of the human brain.

"Why would you do this?" Sara asked.

"Because the Vatican is as curious as you and your husband to know what happened. We want to know if we've truly witnessed a miracle, or whether there is some physiological explanation."

"Describe to me again how this works?"

"The test we have in mind is called a functional magnetic resonance imaging test, or fMRI. The MRI uses magnetic fields to take pictures of the internal organs so that doctors can see them without having to cut the patient open. The functional MRI is used to map the parts of the brain used in different activities. So what we would do first is take a high-resolution image of John's brain. That image would serve as the background that would allow us to detect any changes in brain function as the test progresses. Then we would take a series of low-resolution scans, as many as 150 images every 5 seconds. During these low-resolution scans, we would have John speak. During that time, we hope, the 'tongues' phenomenon will manifest itself, allowing us to detect the affected parts of the brain to see if and how they differ from what we would expect to see during normal speech."

"What if nothing happens?"

"We might still learn something. Perhaps there is something anatomically different about John's brain that allowed for the phenomenon in the first place. We won't know unless we look."

The overcast sky cleared for a moment, allowing the early afternoon sun to shine through the half opened Venetian blinds in the Archbishop's office and fall directly on onto Sara's face. She squinted and instinctively raised a hand to her forehead to block the glare. The Archbishop got out of his chair, apologizing, closed the blinds and turned on a lamp by the window to bring some light to the darkened room. The base of the lamp was a bronze figure of a man holding a lyre standing with his back to a woman, his head turned in her direction and his free hand reaching toward her. The woman seemed to be falling away from the outstretched hand.

"Thank you," Sara said. "Looks like we might get the sunny afternoon the forecasters had predicted. By the way, that's quite a beautiful lamp. I hadn't noticed it until you turned it on."

"I brought it back from Greece several years ago. It's a sculpture of Orpheus and Eurydice. According to the myth, he was the greatest musician in ancient Greece. His bride, Eurydice, died from a snake bite, and he went to Hades itself to get her back. He was told he could bring her back as long as he didn't look at her until they were both out of the Underworld. Just before she stepped into the world of the living, she stumbled, called out, and when Orpheus turned at the sound of her voice, she fell back to Hades."

Sara wondered quietly why the Archbishop had gone into such detail and thought that perhaps he labored under the disadvantage of never having had a close and equal relationship with another adult, a relationship in which each partner gently and affectionately reins in the other's excesses. At other times she might have found his tendency to wind on charming. This afternoon, however, wasn't one of those times – she hadn't lied to John so that she could take a class in Greek mythology. Still, she thought it better to remain patient and indulge him.

"What a sad story," she said.

"Yes, but a beautiful one, too. Not many love deeply enough to brave hell itself."

"Is that why you called me?"

"I'm not sure I follow."

"You and I have never really spoken before, so I was a bit surprised you called me, especially after your meeting with John at Harper's Ferry. I would have thought you'd have tried to get Janice to talk to him."

"Janice has enough on her hands right now, and I didn't want to bother her with this. Besides, I don't think anyone but you could talk John into having the MRI, especially as it'll be done under my authority. Will you talk to him?"

"Yes."

John lay on a rather narrow and cold table in one of the MRI rooms of the Neurosurgery Center at Catholic College Hospital. A technician fastened his head in place and pushed a button, sliding the table into the open mouth of a large magnetic cylinder. Although he had never been claustrophobic, the thought of having to lie still for nearly an hour in the humming darkness left him a bit unnerved. Fortunately, he would only feel alone for the first fifteen minutes during the high-resolution scan. For the remainder of the test, the technician would ask him a series of questions to keep him talking.

John climbed off the table slightly more than an hour later and was met with a thumbs up sign from the technician. He met Sara in the waiting room and they walked to the office of the neurosurgeon that Archbishop O'Connell had handpicked to run the procedure. Archbishop O'Connell stood in the hallway by the office door.

"Shall we?" he asked as he opened the door.

Doctor James Shaw was a diminutive man with a ferocious intellect. Archbishop O'Connell selected him because he trusted Shaw to be a tough devil's advocate against any supernatural explanation for the tongues phenomenon and to look hard for any possible natural cause. He also knew Shaw's father from the days the two of them played stickball on the streets of Boston. He trusted Shaw to be absolutely discreet.

"Good afternoon," Dr. Shaw said. "Please sit down, all of you. Senator Peters, it's an honor to meet you, and I'm honored that you've trusted me for this project."

John didn't know how to react, so he nodded and held out his hand. "Nice to meet you," he said as the two shook hands.

"Well, Jimmy," said Archbishop O'Connell, "what have you got? Anything?"

"Something quite interesting. According to the images we picked up, something unusual started to happen about twenty minutes into the low-res scan, and then faded away."

"What was it?" John asked.

"A spike of activity in an area called the limbic system. It's the part of the brain that helps control emotions. The spike was centered in a particular section called the amygdala, a small, almond-shaped structure we're just starting to learn about. There's a lot we don't know, but some researchers think the amygdala might be connected with mind and consciousness, that it might be have something to do with our perception that there is something inside us that's separate from our physical bodies."

The Archbishop and John exchanged glances. This sounded eerily similar to part of their conversation on Jefferson's Rock.

"Did anything in particular trigger the spike?" the Archbishop asked.

"We plotted it against the tape recording of the Senator. It occurred just before and during the word, 'stop.'"

"Can we listen to that recording?" asked Sara.

Doctor Shaw hit a few strokes on his keyboard and called up the fMRI image of John's brain. At the bottom of the screen appeared icons for Play, Pause and Stop. The doctor typed in the exact time he wanted to playback and hit enter. John's voice played from the computer's speakers. When he said, 'stop,' both the Archbishop and Sara gasped. The doctor and John looked at them expectantly.

"It happened, John," Sara said. "The word, 'stop.' It happened again. I could hear it resonate in a voice that wasn't yours."

"Perhaps we had better take its advice," John said, "and stop trying to figure out what's going on."

"No," the Archbishop and Doctor Shaw said simultaneously. Doctor Shaw looked to the Archbishop for permission to continue. The Archbishop nodded.

"I've never seen or heard of anything like this before, and I'm very familiar with all the literature in the field."

"You're not going to write a case study about this," John said.

"No. But I would like to do more tests."

"I think I've had enough tests. But I'll think about it and get back to you."

With that, John stood up to leave. He had no intention of coming back. As he and Sara walked down the hall away from Dr.

Shaw's office, Sara put her hand inside the crook of his arm and gave him a gentle squeeze.

"Are you afraid?" she asked.

"Wouldn't you be?"

"Yes."

"Let me ask you something, Sara. Do you think what's happening is a miracle? Do you think God told us to "stop" the MRI?"

"Do you think it was?"

John wagged his head. "No, no. I asked you first."

"I don't know what to think. And I don't think that what I think makes a difference."

"It makes all the difference in the world."

"Why?"

"Sara, you're my compass. You always have been. You make sure my head is pointed in the right direction. What you think means a great deal to me."

Sara responded without looking at John. "I'm glad to hear you say so."

"You shouldn't need to hear me say so. You know it's true."

"I know you, John. I know when something is bothering you, and I in the past, I could always count on your bringing it up with me. Lately, you've been keeping things to yourself."

John turned Sara so that she faced him, and taking both of her hands in his, he said, "Sara, I promise, I'll share everything with you from now on. I didn't want to worry you – anymore than you were already worried."

"I'm going to worry whether you confide in me or not. At least let me in on what's troubling you and I won't be worried about what you're keeping from me."

"Fair enough."

"What do you think happened back there?" Sara nodded down the hall toward Dr. Shaw's office.

"I don't know. I think somehow there is a part of me that's making all this happen, something deep down in my subconscious."

"Is that even possible?"

"How is any of this possible? It's the best explanation I can come up with."

"Then why not continue with the testing. If it's something in your own head making this happen, Dr. Shaw might be your best chance of discovering what it is."

"At what cost? Did you see the excitement in his eyes? He'd become famous if he ever figured this out. That's fine, I suppose, but I'd be finished. One story about me in a hospital gown getting poked at by psychiatrists would finish off any chance I have of winning the election. People would wonder if I was nuts."

"So you'd rather live with the uncertainty of what's happening to you?"

"For now, yes."

Chapter 41

Janice skipped her boot through the thin layer of snow that covered the grass on the Mall near the Washington Monument and watched her breath frost in the cold morning air as the Archbishop talked.

"Surely you can see how important this is," the Archbishop said. ""We have an opportunity to prove once and for all that consciousness exists apart from the mechanical structures of the brain. If we prove the materialists wrong, those who say there is nothing but the physical brain and that the perception of self-identity is simply an illusion, then their opposition to the existence of a soul also loses its strength. We could bring belief in God back to those who have lost their way."

"You're a hypocrite," Janice said, smiling, "but I love you anyway." She scooped some snow into her gloved hands and tossed it at the Archbishop, but it dispersed into a cloud of fine white crystals before it reached him. "All along you've been telling me to open my heart to belief, to accept the mystery of God, and here you are, desperate for physical proof."

"For some people, seeing is believing."

"So you want to win over all the doubting Thomases in the world?"

"Yes. I suppose that I want to do what Jesus did, bring physical proof of the Divine to those in doubt."

"That assumes you'll find such proof. There's no guarantee that even if John agreed to further tests, you would find anything. Even if you did, you couldn't get the word out unless you published what you found. John would never let you do that."

"Once he understood the significance of the work, he'd have to."

"If you really believe that God spoke through John, then why don't you accept His instruction? Seems to me that 'stop' is as clear an order as you can get."

"My heart tells me that stopping the test wasn't what the message meant."

"You sure your hopes haven't biased your thinking?"

Archbishop O'Connell paused. "Perhaps. I hope not. I think the command, 'stop,' was a call to us to stop and listen, to recognize God's hand in this. I would like to think that God has answered my prayers; that He has decided to reintroduce Himself to the world."

"Talk about a strained interpretation. You'll never get John to go there with you."

"And you call me a hypocrite." The Archbishop's voice acquired an edge that Janice had not heard before. "John is trying to pretend that none of this happened, but the only reason he is even a candidate for President is because he spoke in tongues. If it wasn't for that, he'd be nothing more than an interim Senator, headed for the door come the next election. He can't have it both ways."

Janice twirled to face the Archbishop; her eyes opened wide and she spoke in a rapid, clipped voice. "I joined up with John before any of this happened. I saw some very special qualities in him. I always knew he would go far."

She stopped, shook her head, and slowed her speech to a calmer pace. "I'm sorry. Maybe you have a point. Maybe all this propelled him to prominence a bit faster than he would have made it on his own. But talent always wins out. I am absolutely convinced the country would have discovered him sooner or later."

Janice paused as a thought occurred to her, then she looked directly into the Archbishop's eyes. "Are you jealous of John?" she asked.

The Archbishop looked startled. "Jealous? Why would I be jealous?"

"I mean, why did God pick John, someone who isn't even sure God exists, when he could have picked someone like you, someone who has dedicated his entire life to His service? Haven't you asked yourself that?"

The Archbishop turned away from her. "No," he mumbled. "I haven't."

"Come on. You must have."

"No," he said more emphatically. "Of course I've wondered why John, but I've never asked myself why not me. I know I'm not worthy."

"If you're not, how on earth could John be?"

"I don't believe the decision was made on earth, Janice. I can't see into God's mind or John's heart, so I don't know why it's John. But I do know why it's not me. Like everyone else, I have my crosses to bear, and like everyone else, some of them are of my own making."

"I'm sorry," she said. "I was out of line."

"So was I."

Janice scooped more snow into her hands and formed it into a snowball. This time, when she threw it at the Archbishop, it thudded into his chest and left a faint white ring on his blue overcoat. She laughed, "So no more arguing about it. Whether or not you're right, John will not go along with you on this, so there is no point in you and me wasting any more time on it."

"Then I'll have to keep praying for him. Just like I have been praying for you." Archbishop O'Connell looked at Janice's swelling abdomen.

"Thank you for that," she said.

"Have you decided what you're going to do about the baby?"

"I'm going to keep it."

"Are you sure that's wise?"

"What would you suggest I do?"

"Janice ... the father ..." He stumbled over his words.

"This isn't how I would have wanted to get pregnant, either, "Janice said, "but it happened. I can't go through another abortion ..."

"I would never suggest ..."

"I know you wouldn't, but the thought did cross *my* mind. For all of a second. I also considered giving the baby up for adoption, but the more I thought about it, the less I could bring myself to do it. By all rights, I shouldn't have been able to get pregnant. This baby is my own personal miracle. The baby isn't to blame for how he or she was conceived and I'm not going to make the baby pay for the sins of the father."

The Archbishop did not reply. Instead, he quietly took Janice's hand in his and started walking back to the café where they had met a half-hour before. His car was parked there and he would give Janice a ride home. He wondered again whether to tell her everything he knew, but again told himself that it would do her more harm than good. He did not ask himself whether he feared losing her friendship were she to learn of his involvement with the baby's father. Some questions probed too deeply to be asked, even of oneself.

Chapter 42

John squirmed in his chair as one of the network's makeup artists daubed powder on his cheeks to eliminate the reflected glare of the studio lights. He had hated wearing makeup ever since his mother had dressed him as a tramp for Halloween when he was four years old. She had spent what seemed like hours painting his face, then forced him to march in a circle with other children in the town's annual costume contest. He won first prize easily, largely because the judges thought the tears on his cheeks were an intended part of his look. His reward was to stand on stage by himself, in full costume, to the applause of the room. The more he cried, the louder his applause.

The memory of that incident made him uneasy, so he closed his eyes and focused on his opening statement. He was determined to deliver it from memory. As the Reverend had pointed out to him, speeches given without reference to notes appeared to come directly from the heart. He also replayed in his mind the responses he had worked out on the two issues with which he was certain to be confronted: his relative inexperience and the quasi-religious backdrop to his newfound fame. He had formulated his responses after studying the 1960 campaign conducted by John F. Kennedy. Kennedy also had to grapple with charges that he was too inexperienced to be President, and the religious issues raised by his Catholic faith loomed large throughout his candidacy.

John knew that Ned Smith sat in one of the other dressing rooms down the hall, and that he was probably still wondering how his handpicked replacement in the Senate had become one of his competitors for the party's Presidential nomination. John had tried to telephone him a couple of days before, but Ned had not returned the call. Sara sat across the room from him, thumbing through a magazine to occupy the last few anxious minutes before John had to step onto the stage. Janice had already gone to the Spin Room – the gathering place for campaign spokespeople and political reporters, a crowded room filled with noise and energy and a lot of talk that hung emptily in the air.

The makeup artist finished applying the final touches to John's face and wiped his collar clean of the few flecks of cosmetic powder that had fallen from the brush the first time John jolted his head. John stood up, removed his smock and put on his suit jacket. He leaned over for a quick good luck kiss from Sara just as one of his staffers knocked on the door and announced that it was time to go on stage.

The pundits had predicted unusually high ratings for the debate. Typically, few people tuned in for these early skirmishes; however, the promise of Senator Peters' participation added an entirely new dimension to Presidential politics. Although no one was quite sure whether it would be appropriate to market the debate as a potential miracle in the making, everyone knew that the viewing audience would be anxiously watching for one. As one radio commentator had observed, it was the inverse of televised automobile races. No one openly advocated the lure of seeing car wrecks at 200 mph, but many people watched racing at least in part in the hope that they would see one.

No one outside of John's campaign entertained the possibility that John could win the debate. He was facing formidable competition from three politicians highly experienced on the national stage, two of whom were currently governors, while the third had been the party's unsuccessful vice-presidential nominee in the previous election. The consensus in the Spin Room was that for this first debate, John would be able to call the evening a success if he could get through it without saying or doing something foolish.

Before John took his place on stage, he shook hands with the other candidates. All but Governor Smith wished him luck. Smith simply nodded his head slightly and spun away, like a prizefighter who touched gloves with his opponent only because he was required to by the referee.

By luck of the draw, John was to give his opening remarks first. He took a drink of water to soothe the tickle that had started to creep up his throat, then worried that beads of water had clung to his lip and that he didn't have enough time to wipe them off before the show went live. He rested his hands on the lectern and deliberately slowed his breathing to calm his jitters. He looked at the moderator, a well-respected television news reporter, and smiled.

The studio light flashed from red to green and the moderator welcomed the American public to the first of the debates. After thanking each of the candidates for their participation, he invited John to begin.

John looked directly at the camera and said:

"Good evening, America. The first thing I'd like to say is how much I respect the other three candidates who are here tonight. They are gentlemen dedicated to making this country greater than it already is, as demonstrated by their many years of public service. In that regard, we share more than a stage tonight. We share a deep and abiding love of country. I think it's important to keep that in mind as we move forward over the next two weeks debating our differences. We will be debating differences in ideas, not in goals. We all want what is best for this country. For that reason, I will focus on my ideas, and refrain from making negative attacks on my colleagues. So let me start with what I would do as President ... "

The butterflies he had felt before the light on the television camera turned green faded completely before he had completed that first paragraph, and his confidence grew with every word he spoke. As the evening unfolded, he started to enjoy the give and take among the candidates and the moderator. He found himself speaking with more clarity and conviction than he ever had before. Catchy turns of phrase flowed effortlessly from his tongue; on any other day they would have occurred to him only after the ideal moment to say them had passed.

Before the debate had reached the halfway point, he could sense the other candidates viewing him with newfound respect and more than a little apprehension. They increasingly tailored their comments to reply to him. His ideas shaped the contours of the debate, and by the end of the evening, he knew that he had done far more than simply survive. He had appeared more polished, more thoughtful and more creative than the other three men on stage with him.

Janice and Sara, watching from their separate posts, each sensed something unfolding far more important than John's success in articulating intelligent answers to tough questions. His easy going nature, his ability to make people feel good about themselves, and his knack for making people want to like him, seemed somehow to radiate from the television screen. The post-debate polls unanimously confirmed their instincts. Not only did John survive the debate, he won it in a landslide.

Within a few days, contribution checks started flowing in faster and in larger amounts. John also picked up a few endorsements, primarily from small town newspapers and police and fire departments, but the fact that he received them made national news and further solidified his standing as a legitimate candidate.

John prepared somewhat differently for the second debate, as there would be no opening remarks, and he knew that he would now be the other candidates' primary target. He also knew that his first night opening remarks in which he called for a debate of ideas as opposed to an exchange of insults would no longer forestall personal attacks.

It did not take long for the first shot to be fired, and it came not from Governor Smith but from the candidate that most experts, prior to the first debate, had considered Smith's chief rival. The salvo came during his answer to a question about the appropriate response to terrorism. He gave what at first seem to be a normal, clichéd response: he stressed the importance of understanding terrorism's causes, described the Middle East as a breeding ground for future terrorists, and emphasized the need to restart peace talks between Israel and Palestine. That process, he insisted, could only succeed if the United States was perceived as an honest broker, a party that did not unfairly take sides in the debate. Then he launched his missile. He bluntly challenged John's ability to be an honest broker, stating that a 'miracle-working,' apparently evangelical President would never be accepted by either side to the conflict. He pointed to Imrahain's assassination attempt as proof that Senator Peters would inspire hatred and anger toward the United States, rather than respect.

John remained calm, looked first at his attacker without any malice evident in his face, and then gradually shifted his gaze to the camera. Looking directly at the viewing audience, he said, "I believe in an America where a person's religious beliefs are his own business, where he doesn't tell others what they should believe, and others don't tell him what he should believe, either. I believe that the President should reflect that America. As John F. Kennedy once said, the Presidency, and I quote, is 'a great office that must be neither humbled by making it the instrument of any religious group, nor tarnished by arbitrarily withholding it ... from the members of any religious group.'

"Don't judge my ability to be President on preconceived, ill-informed notions of my religion. Judge me on the strength of my abilities. Judge me on the strength of my character. It's my judgment, not my religion that matters."

Governor Smith was next to speak. "I agree that Senator Peters' religion should not enter into this debate. But his experience should. That is relevant, and it's telling that Senator Peters never brings it up."

"There are many paths to the White House," John replied. "Now I don't claim to be an Abraham Lincoln, but I do think it worth noting that he served only briefly in the House of Representatives and lost his bid for the Senate before he became President. Yet no one would claim that his lack of experience proved to be a problem. What history teaches us is that the important question is not by what route I arrived on this stage tonight. The question that you need to answer, based on what you see and hear as these debates unfold, is who among us on this stage can best lead this country."

John's staff was euphoric. He had taken the worst anyone could throw at him and turned it to his advantage. Two-thirds of the way through the debate series, John had vaulted from a long shot to a serious candidate. Janice and Sara high-fived each other as the candidates shook hands at the end of the debate, and Janice started toward the Spin Room to once again work the reporters. She did not expect having to make a hard sell.

On the way, her cell phone rang. It was Clark.

"Congratulations," he said.

"Thank you."

"Your guy continues to surprise me. It seems a lot of us underestimated him."

"Well, that happens. What can I do for you?"

"Actually, I'm calling to do you a favor."

"Really?" she said with a slightly sarcastic edge to her voice.

"No need to sound so surprised."

"What favor?"

"I thought you'd want to know that Lawrence McKnight, the moderator for the next debate, has a copy of Imrahain's letter to Senator Peters."

"I don't know what letter you're talking about."

"Come on. No need to play dumb, especially now that the press has a copy of it."

"I'm not playing at anything."

Clark remained silent for a moment. Then he said, with surprise in his voice, "It seems your Senator hasn't been filling you in on everything. Ask him about the letter."

"Why are you telling me about it?"

"I just found out about the letter myself, and you're the first person I called."

"Oh, I believe that!"

"You've got me figured all wrong. I'm not that bad a guy. You have a good day, now."

The line went dead. Janice put her phone away and headed back to the stage to confront John. She saw him in a corner surrounded by reporters, occasionally looking beyond them to wave in response to shouts from the audience. Janice approached Sara, who was standing a few feet away.

"Janice," Sara said, "I thought you were going to the Spin Room."

"I was almost there when I got a phone call from Clark."

"Clark? What did he want?"

"To tell me that McKnight has a copy of a letter that Imrahain wrote to John. Do you know anything about it?"

A frown troubled Sara's face. "It came in a couple of weeks ago."

"What did it say? And why didn't you tell me about it?"

"John threw it out, and I guess we forgot to mention it to you. You weren't at the office when it came in. When I gave it to John, he shredded it. He wasn't about to write the guy back. How in the world could McKnight have gotten his hands on it?"

"I'm pretty sure that a prisoner's mail is screened and censored, so someone could easily have made a copy before the letter even left the penitentiary. What did it say?"

"Imrahain said that he heard John speak in Arabic."

"Well, what do we do when McKnight waves it in front of John during the next debate?"

Chapter 43

Clark let Reverend Jones wait in the lobby for thirty minutes past their scheduled meeting time before he told his secretary to show him in. The Reverend stepped smartly into Clark's office, flashing a white-toothed smile, his hand extended for a shake. Clark didn't rise from his seat to take the offered hand, and instead simply pointed to a chair by his desk as a signal to the Reverend to sit down.

The Reverend sat down, still smiling, determined not to show any reaction to Clark's brusque treatment.

"You've done quite a remarkable job with the Senator," Clark observed.

"How's that?"

"I can see the impact you've had on his delivery. He comes across with a lot more confidence and power than he used to."

"Thanks."

"It wasn't a compliment."

The smile disappeared from the Reverend's face. He felt his diaphragm drop and nausea filled the void it left.

"You weren't supposed to help *him*," Clark said. "You were supposed to help *us*."

"I had to gain his trust if I was ever going to learn anything of use to you," the Reverend replied, his voice rising in a defensive plea as he spoke. "I had to be able to hang out in his campaign office, chat up the staff, without rousing any suspicion. It led to my getting a copy of Imrahain's letter, didn't it?"

The Reverend knew he had done far more to help John than was necessary, and in fact had continued to help him even after he had surreptiously borrowed and photocopied Imrahain's letter off the desk of the staffer who had opened it. He was starting to like the Senator and his family, and the coaching he provided helped assuage the guilt he felt being one of Clark's operatives. He wasn't happy spying for Clark, but he didn't see any way to avoid it, not if he wanted to keep his past in the past.

"Yes," Clark said in exasperation, "but I'm not sure the price we paid was worth it. I never expected Peters to be so good on his feet, to handle himself so well under pressure, and without you, I'm not sure he would have come across nearly as smoothly as he did."

"Don't give me too much credit, or blame, as the case may be. Like it or not, Senator Peters is a fairly remarkable man."

"Are you starting to buy into all his religious mumbo jumbo?"

"That's hardly an appropriate question to ask a man of the cloth."

"Hah! The only thing *holy* about your clothes are the slits you put your buttons through. You're no more a man of God than I am."

The Reverend flinched and gritted his teeth. He paused before replying, "It has to at least make you think. Something is going on that I can't explain. It may not be God, but then again, it might be. Better to play it safe."

"You can't be on his side and mine at the same time, and you don't want to have me turn against you. It could prove very unpleasant."

Chapter 44

"Thanks for agreeing to meet with me," the Reverend said. "I hope you didn't have any trouble finding the spot." They were seated in a Spanish tapas bar in Columbia, Maryland, a town between Baltimore and DC, where the Reverend thought they were less likely to be seen or heard by someone affiliated with Clark or the press.

"No," Hartson replied. "No trouble at all." He looked over the menu and tried hard to look intrigued by the items presented. He had never had tapas and wasn't sure which if any of the various appetizer-like dishes he would like.

"How have you been?" the Reverend asked. "I still see you on commercials now and then."

"Yeah. Not as much as before, though."

"Have you found a steady job?"

"I'm in between right now. But things will work out."

"Good. Good. Listen, if you ever need help finding work, let me know. Okay?"

"Yeah. Thanks. But I'll be okay." Hartson put the menu down and decided simply to parrot the Reverend's order. "So why did you want to meet with me?"

"To talk about Clark."

"What about him?"

"I overheard Clark's friend, the French guy, mention your name to him the other day. Have you been talking to them?" He studied Hartson's face for a response, but could read nothing in his unflinching manner.

"Look," the Reverend continued, "I'm not here to pry. I only wanted to help you, if you needed help."

"I'm fine."

The Reverend fiddled with the menu for a moment. "I don't know any way to say this but straight out. I know Clark well enough to know that when he has something on someone, he uses it. He'll get you to do something you might not want to do."

"He hasn't asked me to do anything."

"He will. That's how he operates."

Hartson sat stone faced and said nothing in reply.

The Reverend's voice took on an urgent tone. "I *know* how Clark is."

Hartson leaned back in his chair and appraised the Reverend. For the first time, his voice reflected interest in their conversation. "You're a man of the cloth," he said.

"We all make mistakes."

"What has he asked *you* to do?" Hartson asked.

"That's not important. What's important is this: Clark has it in for Senator Peters. I know he does. And I know something else. Senator Peters is a decent guy. Look, you saved the Senator's life. Don't undo that good deed by letting Clark make you do something you'll regret forever."

Hartson wondered whether the Reverend had been sent by Clark to test his reliability, whether this conversation was an elaborate trap. After all, the Reverend was the one who had arranged for him to meet Clark.

"Why are you telling me this?" Hartson asked. "How do you know I won't tell Clark?"

"I don't. But I decided to take a chance on doing the right thing."

"Well ... like I said, Clark hasn't asked me to do anything."

The waitress stopped by their table and the Reverend instantly shifted into the cheerful, outgoing manner he could, with the ease of a consummate actor, summon at will. He flirted with her, asked her for recommendations and finally settled on a selection that included grilled shrimp, smoked ham, roasted pimientos and fried fish.

Hartson said simply, “I’ll have what he’s having.”

“Excellent choices,” the waitress replied, smiling at the Reverend.

After she left to put in their order, the Reverend said, “Sooner or later, Clark is going to ask you to do something for him, something you won’t want to do. Please call me when that happens. I’ll help you out. You have my word as a man of God.”

Chapter 45

Governor Smith ground his cigarette into the ashtray he had made by breaking off the bottom of a Styrofoam coffee cup, and swore. Then he waved the last wisps of smoke out the open kitchen window, grabbed a can of deodorizer and sprayed. He wasn't supposed to be smoking. Indeed, he had publicized his decision to quit as part of a public health initiative he championed, something he viewed as a rather courageous political move to make in the heart of tobacco country. But when the stress was on, there was nothing like a good smoke to calm his nerves. And he was under some serious stress.

If he was lucky, his wife wouldn't notice any lingering odors. She wouldn't be down for a couple of hours yet. She had been sleeping in every morning and going to bed early every night – sleeping had become her favorite pastime. She managed stress in her way; he managed it in his.

The morning paper featured Richard Braun's latest column, and it hadn't helped his nerves. In fact, the article had turned this into a two-cigarette morning. He should have stayed in bed along with his wife, he thought. He couldn't believe Braun had flipped. Overnight, he had switched from bashing Peters to praising him. Smith skimmed the article once more, revisiting it out of the same compulsion that makes one repeatedly probe a toothache.

> Dewey Defeats Truman. Gore Carries Florida. Red Sox Win World Series.
>
> These three headlines number among the most famous blunders in journalistic history. Okay, the last one actually happened. But the first two events (both of which, at least to this long-suffering Red Sox fan, were far more probable than the third) clearly belong on the list of blown calls.
>
> Senator Peter's amazing performance in all three debates, and

> his startling rise in the polls, have a number of my colleagues competing for a place in the pantheon of boneheaded predictions.
>
> None of them have a chance. Not in light of the columns I've written. No, I'm afraid I've secured that spot all to myself.
>
> Some say it takes a big man to admit when he is wrong. Okay. I was wrong about Senator Peters, and I'll take whatever solace I can find in the knowledge that at least I can admit it.
>
> Senator Peters has surpassed every expectation. Even the surprise attack that McKnight launched on him in Tuesday' third and final debate – confronting him with a copy of the would-be assassin Abdul Imrahain's letter -- served only to showcase Peters' ability to remain calm and collected under pressure. Without missing a beat, he asked McKnight why he would dignify comments from a disturbed man, a man who had seriously wounded one man and tried to murder another, by 'airing them on national television in the context of a debate for the Presidential nomination'. . .

Smith put the paper down, unable to finish the article. He couldn't understand what had happened. Braun wouldn't have written such a column without Clark's blessing; at least Smith didn't think he would. Unless, Smith thought, Braun truly believed Peters would win the nomination despite Clark's opposition and wanted to salvage whatever credibility and goodwill he could with Peters. No, Smith decided, that was unlikely. Braun wouldn't risk angering Clark. He didn't have that much courage.

Smith dialed Clark's direct line and let it ring several times before hanging up. He knew Clark was in his office. He was always in his office at this time of day. Something was amiss, and Smith decided to confront Clark directly before the day was out.

Clark waved Smith in with a thin, tight-lipped smile that seemed more like a grimace, as if it pained him to look pleasant.

"I assume you've read Braun's piece in today's paper?" Smith asked, holding up a copy of the morning's paper.

"No, actually I read it yesterday afternoon before he turned it in. I apologize. I should have told you about it, but I had so many things on my mind, I completely forgot. Have a cigarette?" Clark pushed a beautiful wooden cigarette box inlaid with silver across his desk toward Smith.

"No thanks, I quit."

"That's right, you did. Sorry, I seem to be forgetting a lot of things these days."

"Let's cut the BS. Why are you doing this?"

Clark extended his arms, palms up, toward Smith. "What would you have me do? Can't you see that the momentum of this race has changed?"

"So you ditch me, just like that?"

"I'm not ditching you. Try to understand the bigger picture. You need to have a long term view."

"I don't care about the long term. I care about the here and now, which is the time and place I'm getting screwed."

Clark clucked his disapproval. "What was it Disraeli said? 'Patience is the necessary ingredient of genius,' or something along those lines. Be patient. Trust me."

Smith didn't know who Disraeli was, and wasn't in the mood to ask. "Trust you? After reading Braun's column?"

"Have you ever ridden a bike, Governor?" Clark found Smith's startled reaction to the question quite amusing. The tight smile that had not left Clark's face since Smith walked into the office stretched into a grin that sliced from ear to ear. When Smith made no reply, Clark insistently asked, "Well, have you?"

"Yes. But what's that ..."

"Good. Are you familiar with the concept of drafting?"

"Clark ...," groaned Smith in exasperation.

"Are you familiar with it?" Clark insisted.

Smith sighed. He didn't like playing these games, but it didn't seem to him that he had a choice. "Isn't that where one person rides behind the other to avoid biking into the wind?"

"Exactly. The first person does the work; the one behind him reaps the reward."

Smith, who had been standing throughout the conversation, found a chair and sat down. "I'm not following you," he said.

Clark shook his head and laughed. "Governor, have patience. I'd rather help Peters rocket to an early lead than watch him build up support steadily throughout the campaign. You know the old saying, 'the quicker they rise, the harder they fall.' In the meantime, he's getting people excited about the election. He's getting people involved who never voted before. Well, good for him. The more the better. His fortunes will change, and when they do, there will be a lot of energized people looking for someone else to support." Clark pointed a long finger at Smith. "Do you or do you not want to take advantage of that? When you decide, you let me know."

Clark returned his attention to some papers on his desk without waiting for a response; his brusque manner left no doubt that the meeting had ended. Smith walked out without saying anything in reply, confused by what he had heard, troubled by what he had inferred, and desperate for a smoke.

Chapter 46

"It doesn't make any sense," Janice said more to herself than to the Archbishop. One of her friends who worked on Smith's campaign had whispered to her the other night that Smith was growing increasingly irritable when not in the public eye and that he wasn't spending nearly as much time with Clark as he had been. The rift had become so apparent to Smith's staff that some were even joking that Smith might start spending more time back in the state he was supposed to be governing.

The apparent falling out had occurred at about the time Braun's laudatory piece on John came out, and supported Janice's growing sense that Clark might be shifting his support toward Peters' candidacy.

Normally, she wouldn't confide in the Archbishop on political matters, but she needed a sounding board. Obviously, she had to discuss Clark's seeming turnabout with the Senator, but he would look to her for advice, and before she could give any, she needed to sort through her own conflicting thoughts. Her sense of danger warned her that making a deal with Clark would be risky business, but the tremendous temptation of having the party machine behind their campaign would be difficult to refuse.

Clark could arrange everything from neighborhood 'get out the vote' programs to a coordinated, multimedia national advertising campaign. Of course, she was working on all those things and more, but this was the first time she had been in charge of such a nationwide effort, and the contacts, manpower and experience that Clark could bring would be incredibly helpful, especially as the months wore on. Her pregnancy was not proving to be an easy one, and she worried that she would be unable to maintain her current pace and workload. On the other hand, Clark wouldn't offer help without a price, and that price was bound to be some measure of control over the campaign. How much control, if John and she decided to accept Clark's assistance, would depend on how well Janice negotiated the terms of the deal and how much of his not inconsiderable ego Clark would be willing to suppress. All this, of course, assumed Clark wanted to help. As she said at the outset, that notion just didn't make sense.

Clark had sunk considerable time, energy and political capital into Smith's campaign, and although John had scored some points and had risen steadily in the polls, it was far too early for Clark to throw in the towel. Janice had expected Clark to launch a dirty tricks campaign, filled with negative, misleading ads – that's the way hardball politics was played. The olive branch Clark offered instead was not only unexpected, it was a bit suspicious.

She didn't expect the Archbishop to offer any insights, but he would keep what she said confidential and give her the room she needed to think aloud. "Could it be that Clark doesn't think he can stop John from winning the nomination and is simply doing what he can to preserve his influence in the Party?" she wondered.

"I'm not a politician," Archbishop O'Connell said, "and I don't know Clark. But from what you've told me about him, he anticipates and plans for nearly everything."

"He is very smart."

Archbishop O'Connell rubbed his chin but said nothing else. After a few moments in which Janice continued to try, unsuccessfully, to put some semblance of logical order to recent events, she put her hands to her head and groaned.

"I don't know," Janice said. "Maybe I'm getting worked up over nothing. Just because Clark and Smith seem to be going through a rough spot doesn't mean Clark is throwing his support over to us."

"If he's not, then he has engaged in some pretty interesting tactics. Calling you about the Imrahain letter. The Braun column. Something does seem to be going on."

"Sometimes I feel like I'm in over my head. I should just stop worrying about everything and focus on getting our message out."

"You know I love to play chess," said the Archbishop. "The best players I've ever faced are the ones who can develop deep, long-term, not necessarily obvious strategies and implement them with well-executed and often clever tactics. Lesser players may be good at one or the other but not both. How would you rate Clark?"

Janice thought about that question for a few moments. "I'd have to say he can do both."

"And what is Clark's goal?"

"To win the election, I suppose."

"With anyone?"

Janice thought some more. "No. He'd want a President over whom he could exert a great deal of influence."

"Do you think that's John?"

"No, it's not."

"And does Clark realize that?"

"Yes, I would think he does."

"So helping John win the nomination wouldn't seem to advance his goal?"

"No."

"Then you need to ask yourself whether you have misgauged Clark's goal, and if you're convinced you haven't, and it doesn't sound like you did, you need to figure out what strategic purpose Clark would have for pushing John's candidacy. A few minutes ago, you said that it didn't make sense for him to do so. But apparently to Clark, it does. You need to figure out why."

“What if I sidestep the whole problem and simply refuse to affiliate with him?”

“Clark doesn’t sound like the type of man who takes ‘no’ easily.”

“Working with him could be dangerous. You know the saying – where is it from? -- ‘You reap what you sow.’”

“It’s in ...”

The Archbishop stopped short. A sudden realization froze him in mid-sentence and gave his face a hard, intense cast.

“What is it?” Janice asked.

Her voice brought him back. He relaxed the set of his jaw, shook his head gently and said, “Nothing. It’s nothing.”

“Are you sure? You looked awfully worried about something.”

“No. I’m fine. I’m just an old man who gets easily distracted.”

Later, alone in his study, the Archbishop pulled out his Bible and reread the parable of the man whose enemies sowed weeds among his newly planted wheat. His servants wanted to rip out the weeds, but he forbade them because his enemies had planted a special type of weed, a pernicious, diabolical plant that looked just like wheat until it was fully grown. Only then did its true nature show itself. Only then could it be safely destroyed.

That weed had a name: darnel.

Then a second realization struck him. Lenny had changed his last name from Clough to Edom – the name given the ancient Biblical land of the dispossessed son of Isaac.

This could not be a coincidence. Lenny had chosen a new name for himself that reflected who he was – a person who, because of the Archbishop’s failure, had been stripped of the innocence that is the birthright of every child. Lenny grew into a man desperate to clear his soul of the evil that had been planted there, an evil that hid its face from the world for so many years. The Archbishop sagged back into his chair, feeling more than ever the weight of his guilt. He had failed Lenny. He would not fail Janice.

Chapter 47

Hartson turned the television off and puffed on his cigar. Cigars were a new treat, not something he'd ever thought he'd try, but now that he had, he liked them. Cigars made him feel important. Not everyone smoked cigars, and those who did carried themselves with a certain demeanor, an attitude that said the world was theirs.

He thought about the kids from his hometown. They surely had heard all about him by now; if they hadn't seen his interview with Melanie Kraft, they would have read about his heroics in the front page of the local newspaper. He had expected to hear from some of them, but so far, no one had called – maybe they hadn't been able to find his number. Perhaps they hadn't thought to call his mother. He had spoken with her after his appearance with Melanie Kraft. It had been a good conversation; she seemed very happy that he had phoned.

His attention wandered back to the show he had just watched, a daily post-news, pre-prime time program filled with gossip about Hollywood and its celebrities. One of the pieces had left him a bit unsettled, and he pulled hard on his cigar as he turned it over in his mind. The article reported that the Reverend had signed a television contract for a weekly show on one of the cable networks. Hartson, meanwhile, could not even land a commercial for a local used car dealer. The energy and excitement, the buzz that had surrounded him following his shooting of Imrahain had dissipated and he could not understand why. He thought it unlikely that such an important, life-saving act would have yielded only the minimum '15 minutes of fame' normally allotted to the likes of world champion hot dog eaters. Then a curious thought occurred to him: the drop-off in commercials had started not too long after his first meeting with Clark.

Hartson wondered if Clark had somehow blackballed him from any further acting jobs. There could be no doubting Clark's ability to do so. He clearly had tremendous influence and power – even the Reverend was afraid of him – but Hartson couldn't convince himself Clark had any reason for doing it.

Perhaps his life was simply returning to its typical course. The shooting of Imrahain had given him a chance to start fresh, but as his mother used to say, 'The more things change, the more they stay the same.' Some things had certainly changed: he didn't wear the same clothes that he used to wear; he didn't eat at the same restaurants; and he didn't dream the same dreams. At the end of the day, though, he still got screwed. He had saved the Senator's life; hell, he had saved the Reverend's life. Now the Senator might be the next President, and the Reverend had landed a television show. He, on the other hand, seemed destined to watch helplessly as the promise of his new life melted away. He felt like a man who always had the ability to make music, but never the instruments. Finally, for a brief period, someone handed him a trumpet and he had blown some cool notes. Now that trumpet seemed headed for the pawnshop where so many other lost dreams sat unredeemed on dusty shelves.

Hartson had to do something. There were only two men he could approach. One was the Reverend, the other, Clark. The Reverend might be a friend, might be willing to help without extracting anything in return, but Hartson simply didn't know if he could be trusted. Clark, on the other hand, was a known quantity. Hartson faced a difficult decision: whether to open up to the possibility of friendship and risk betrayal, or deal with an enemy at arm's length, with terms clearly spelled out, and with one's guard always up. In the end, Hartson couldn't overcome a lifetime habit of suspecting the worst in others, so he picked up the phone and dialed Clark's office.

Hartson was disappointed to see Emile greet him at Clark's

office door. He looked past his shoulder, searching for Clark, but no one else was in the office.

"Your timing is quite excellent, Mr. Hartson. I was going to call you this morning even before I saw that you left a message for Clark last night."

"I was hoping to see him."

"I'm sorry for the confusion. Clark is out of the office today, but whatever you wanted to discuss with him you can tell me."

"You said you were going to call me anyway?"

Emile propped an elbow on his chair's armrest and rested his chin on his hand. He studied Hartson's face for a moment then asked in a soft voice, "I have a favor to ask of you. I need you to do something for me."

"What?"

"Something you've already tried once before."

Hartson's heart raced and his hands involuntarily clenched his chair's armrests. Emile's words frightened him. His first instinct was to refuse the request without even knowing what it was, yet he sensed that to do so would be extremely dangerous. Memories of the Reverend floated unbidden through his mind; first came his offer of help, quickly subsumed by his face on TV announcing his new cable show. Hartson steeled himself. "What, exactly, do you want me to do?"

"I think you know, Mr. Hartson." Emile walked over to Clark's desk and opened a desk drawer. "Odd. It's not here," he muttered to himself. Looking up at Hartson, he asked, "Are you a religious man?"

"Not really, no."

"I assume you never heard of Manichaeism?"

"I can't say that I have."

“It was once a very popular religion throughout Europe, as popular as Christianity. It was named after its founder, Mani, a 3rd Century Babylonian prophet.”

Hartson fidgeted uncomfortably in his chair, unable to grasp the odd direction the conversation had taken.

“Mani’s enemies had him crucified for heresy,” Emile continued, “and over the next few centuries, his followers were hunted down until nearly all were exterminated. But a few, those with enough power and influence to buy off their pursuers, continued to practice their faith in hiding. They formed a secret society, the Order of Mani. The Order still exists. “

“Why are you telling me this?”

“The Order of Mani is a very powerful group. How do you think Clark got to where he is? It can make good things happen for its friends, for you, if you do as we ask.”

Hartson wiped his mouth with the back of his hand and noticed his fingers were trembling. He hoped Emile didn’t spot that.

Emile smiled. “You think about it, Mr. Hartson. I’ll be in touch.”

Chapter 48

Archbishop O'Connell shook Clark's hand and motioned him to a chair. Moving with the quiet dignity of a man in command of his situation, the Archbishop smoothed the wrinkles in his slacks and tugged them slightly above the knees before sitting down across from Clark.

"Excuse my manners," he said. "May I offer you a drink?"

"Water would be nice, thank you."

As the Archbishop walked over to the small refrigerator he kept in his office, Clark surveyed the room. "You are a book lover, I see."

"Not a serious one. I don't run very deep in any one author or subject. When I see something I like, I buy it, finances allowing. How about you? Anything in particular you have in your library?"

"An old book or two, not much more."

Archbishop O'Connell handed Clark a bottle of cold water. "Would you like a glass?"

"No thanks. This is fine."

A ray of sunlight filtering through a gap in the blinds reflected off the top of Clark's head, bathing him in a backlight that contrasted sharply with his sunglass and shadow darkened visage.

"Thank you for agreeing to see me," Clark said.

"I was a bit surprised you called, to tell you the truth."

Clark nodded. "I wanted to talk to you about Senator Peters."

"I thought as much. I can recommend some books that discuss speaking in tongues ..."

"I didn't come to get book suggestions or advice," Clark interrupted. "I came to get your help."

"What can I do for you?"

"Senator Peters doesn't appreciate the situation he is in."

"If you're here to talk about his campaign, you're talking to the wrong person. I think it's Ms. Baxter you ought to be having this conversation with."

"You may be the only person I can talk to. Put the politics aside for a moment. What do you make of Senator Peters?"

Resting his chin on clasped hands, the Archbishop leaned forward and said, "I think he was sent by God."

"The problem, Archbishop, is that you're not the only one who thinks so."

The Archbishop furrowed his eyebrows. "What do you mean?"

Clark lifted his briefcase from the floor and set it on his lap. Slowly, he unclasped the lock, and without bothering to look up, asked in a matter-of-fact tone that suggested he already knew the answer, "Will you treat what I say to you, what I'm about to show you, as confidential?"

"Of course."

"Even though I'm not Catholic?"

"That makes no difference."

Clark pulled out a small cloth package, which he carefully unwrapped, revealing a leather bound book. "This is from my collection," he said, handing it to the Archbishop.

"What is this?"

"It will prove that the story I'm about to tell you is real."

The Archbishop eyed the title and shot a quizzical look at Clark before thumbing through the vellum pages. "How old is this book?"

"17th century."

"I thought paper had replaced animal skin by the 1600s."

Clark shrugged. "I would concern yourself less with what the pages are made of than with what's written on them."

The Archbishop reread the title. "What was the Order of Mani?"

"Perhaps the better question is, 'What *is* the Order of Mani?"

The Archbishop snorted. "Is this your idea of a joke?"

"I'm not joking."

"I'm not even sure this book is authentic – vellum instead of paper – possible but unlikely. There's quite a trade in forged antiquities. You might have been duped. Where did you get it?"

"It's authentic, trust me."

"Assuming it is, what do you want me to do with it?"

"Read it. It will explain why Senator Peters is in danger."

The Archbishop stood up. "Please don't tell me you came here to frighten me with tales best told late at night around a campfire."

Clark shook his head grimly. "This is not fiction."

"I'm supposed to believe this from a man who won't even let me look him in the eye."

Clark removed his sunglasses. "My eyes are part of the price I paid to join the Order."

The Archbishop had started to rise from his chair as a prelude to asking Clark to leave. The sight of Clark's eyes arrested his movement. "I'm listening," he said as he sat back down.

"Have you ever heard of Manichaeism?"

The Archbishop gave Clark a curious look. "Yes, I learned about it in seminary. St. Augustine was a Manichaen before he converted to Christianity. Are you telling me the Order of Mani is a Manichaen sect?" he asked incredulously. "Manichaeism is extinct; has been for centuries."

"No, Archbishop O'Connell, it is not. It has simply been in hiding for a very long time."

"That's preposterous. People don't get burned at the stake for heresy anymore."

"The Order of Mani was formed by powerful men. When organizations have power, power becomes their reason for being; it's what sustains them, and over time, it changes them. They become something different than what their founders intended. Through the centuries, the Order recruited only those who held positions of influence, men who were thrilled by being invited to secretly associate with others like them. Have you ever wondered what it would have been like to have been a Freemason back when Benjamin Franklin and George Washington were members? The Order of Mani is older, more secretive, and far more powerful than the Freemasons ever were, but most of its current members know little and care even less about the Order's origins or doctrinal underpinnings. Until recently, I never paid much attention to them myself."

"But Senator Peters changed that for you?"

"Yes."

"Why? Of what significance is he to the Order of Mani?"

"If the Order concludes he is merely a man, he is of no significance. But if the Order believes that he is a Messenger, the title of the book in your hand makes clear what it will do."

The Archbishop looked at the title again. "Why?"

"Because the Order will consider him a false prophet, sent by an evil god. If you learned about Manichaeism in seminary, then you may recall that Mani believed that the universe was created by an evil god, better known to you as the Old Testament god that destroyed cities, flooded the world, turned people into salt, and murdered the innocent first born sons of an entire nation. A rival god, your New Testament god, intervened in the act of creation, breathing some of his own essence into the universe, creating a dual natured cosmos, a universe of light and dark, good and evil."

"This is what you believe?" the Archbishop asked.

"This is what Mani taught, what the Order still holds as doctrine. Mani claimed to be a Messenger, sent to teach men how to rise above the base material from which they were fashioned by using their gift of free will to choose good over evil."

"How does Senator Peters fit into all of this?"

"Mani made it clear that he was the last of the good god's Messengers. He also said, however, that the evil god who created the universe would send his own Messengers, false prophets who would lead mankind astray."

The Archbishop shook his head in disbelief. "You actually expect me to swallow this? This is the stuff of cheap movies, not real life. Don't insult my intelligence."

"Do you believe in Satan?"

"Of course I do."

"How about angels? Do you believe in them?"

"Yes."

"Has it ever occurred to you that to some people, stories of angels and demons are as fabulous, as implausible, as you find Mani's teachings? To the Order's leaders, Mani's teachings are as real as your angels and demons. Whether those teachings are well-founded is irrelevant. What matters is whether the Order believes them. They do. And that puts Senator Peters' life in peril."

"How can the Order reconcile Mani's teaching to choose good over evil with a plan to commit murder?"

"Fanaticism makes the monstrous seem rational."

"Peters denies that he is any sort of prophet at all. Won't the Order take his word for it? "

"Have you?"

Clark's question took the Archbishop aback. "Why have you told me all of this?" he asked. "What do you want from me?"

"I want you to help me convince the Order that Senator Peters is not a Messenger. I'm not sure how, but I believe you're one of the very few men who could. If you took a public stand, for instance, stating that Peters is not a prophet ... I don't know ... a comment like that from a well-respected Archbishop, it might buy some time, change some minds."

"And have the convenient effect of undercutting Senator Peters' support among a substantial part of the voting public?"

"I care more about his life than his electability."

The Archbishop stared at Clark, wondering whether any of his tale were true, and if so, whether to believe that Clark's motives were honest. "You are asking me to denounce him, to deny that he is a prophet. I cannot do that. I believe with all my heart that he was sent by God ... the one and only God, the God of the Old and the New Testaments."

"I'm only asking you to do exactly what the Senator would want you to do."

"Who am I to doubt God's handiwork? If Senator Peters is a Messenger, then God has a reason for sending him. It's not my place to go against God's will."

"What *you* believe to be God's will. What if you're wrong? You could be condemning Senator Peters to death."

"Somebody already tried to kill the Senator once, and failed. Now he has 24 hour Secret Service protection."

"No protection is perfect."

"Then why don't you go to the authorities. Tell them instead of a priest you've sworn to secrecy."

"I can't do that. Besides, it wouldn't do any good. The best protection is to convince the Order that Senator Peters is only a politician, not a prophet."

Archbishop O'Connell gently rocked back and forth in his chair, quietly considering Clark's comments. "Every day I recite the Lord's Prayer. It says, 'Thy will be done, on earth as it is in heaven. I will not set myself against God."

"I'm sorry to hear you say that," Clark replied. "I will do what I can to help the Senator on my own. To do that, I need to gain his trust and his confidence. Can I at least ask you not to interfere in that?"

"I told you that everything you said would be kept in confidence."

"Thank you for that, at least. I guess I'll be taking my book back."

As he left the Archbishop's office, Clark sighed and gave himself a silent pat on the back. He had sprinkled enough truth in his story to make it believable, and the Archbishop fell for it. Now he could move forward without worrying that the Archbishop would steer Janice, and thus the Senator, off the course he had plotted. Clark's original plan to convince the Master that Peters was not a Messenger had failed; Peters had refused to lay low, self-destruct or wilt under the barrage of hostile press coverage, and the Archbishop's refusal to denounce Peters was its final death blow. Clark had expected as much from the Archbishop, and had planned for it. Realizing that he would probably, although reluctantly, be forced into adopting Emile's solution, Clark had the genius – for so he thought of it – of orchestrating the situation so that he could fully exploit Senator Peter's considerable gifts before turning Emile loose. Even the Master would have to be impressed ... The Master ... There was something he did not mention to the Archbishop. Clark curled his shoulders as if huddling before a cold wind. Not even Emile knew that the full truth about the Master, Clark thought, for if he did, he would not speak about him in such cavalier tones.

Chapter 49

While Clark and the Archbishop spoke, John and Sara had their own conversation about the course of the campaign. Sara had grown increasingly uneasy and unhappy as the demands on John's time increased. John was out of town almost every night, including weekends, giving speeches, attending fund-raising breakfasts, lunches and dinners, and doing interviews with local and national reporters. Sara and Connor couldn't travel with him as long as school was in session, and Sara wasn't at all sure it would make sense to drag Connor across the country, bouncing from hotel room to hotel room, even when summer vacation arrived. This was one of the rare days when John was home, and Sara took full advantage of his presence to unburden her feelings.

John sat as patiently as he could while Sara detailed her complaints, but keeping a civil tongue proved difficult. Aside from time with his family, the single biggest sacrifice he had to make in this campaign was time spent sleeping. He was weary and he had been looking forward to a restful day off. This conversation was anything but restful.

"What do you want me to do, Sara? Quit?"

"I've thought about that."

"You can't be serious. After all this, in the middle of a campaign where I've gone from the darkest of dark horses to having a serious shot at the nomination?"

Sara stirred her coffee in an absent-minded fashion, unable to meet John's gaze. She too had not been sleeping well. Each night, the bed seemed to grow larger and colder and emptier. Even the night before, John's first night back in two weeks, hadn't helped. Sara had slept on one edge of the bed while John slept on the other. He may as well not have been there.

"Sara, things have gone better than we ever dreamed possible. How can I turn my back on it now?"

"Better than *we* ever dreamed? I think not. Better than *you* ever dreamed – apparently."

"We're in this together," John replied. "I need to know that I have your support. I know it's been hard, but we knew going into this that it would be hard."

"We didn't know, in here," Sara placed her palm across her chest and patted it twice, "how hard it would be. We couldn't have known how hard it would be on Connor. Face it, John, we had hardly moved here from North Carolina when we got caught in a whirlwind, and it blew us farther and faster than we could ever have imagined."

She stirred her coffee again, buying a moment before saying what she had wanted to say all morning. "If I had understood, really understood, what it took to run for the Presidency, I would not have gone along. I would have tried my best to talk you out of it."

John's shoulders sagged. He had been under unrelenting pressure the entire time he was on the road. He didn't think he could handle added pressure at home. He loved his wife, but he couldn't talk to her about this, not now. He needed to unwind first, or he might say something he'd truly regret, so he stood up to leave the table. "Can we talk about this later, Sara? I promise we will. I just can't do it right now."

"John, when you came home last night, I told Connor that you wanted to talk to him. He walked right past you and picked up the phone. He saw you standing there, but in his mind, the only time he gets to speak with you is when you call."

"I know. I saw him do that. If you think I'm happy about it, I'm not. It will be over soon."

"It won't be over soon. And what if you win? Have you ever seen a President who didn't age incredibly during his four-year term?"

"I'm too far in it, Sara. Too many people have worked too hard for too long. I have to keep going. I don't have a choice."

"You do have a choice, John. You can go back to being that guy who just wanted to help people."

"I'm still that guy."

"Are you? I don't hear you and Janice talk about that. All I hear you talk about are voter demographics, fundraising, and battleground states. It's all about winning, John. It's about power. That's all it's about. I can see it in your eyes."

John leaned across the table and stroked Sara's cheek. She started to cry, and John pulled her gently up from the chair and hugged her.

"It's not all about winning," John said. "It's about having an opportunity to make a difference in the world. If it's about power, it's only about having the power to do good."

"At what cost?" Sara asked. "You once said I was your compass. But I don't think you're headed in the direction I would have you go."

John didn't reply. Instead, he continued to hold her as he fought back his own worries. The questions she had asked he had asked himself many times over the past few weeks. He had almost convinced himself that his motives were pure, but squirreled away in a remote corner of his conscience lingered the worry that his judgment had been clouded by his ambition. He didn't think he could easily walk away from the thrill of seeing his face on TV, his name in the newspapers, and his opinion on nearly every subject imaginable, from the national debt to his favorite musical group, quoted in nearly every magazine he picked up.

He was also experiencing, for the first time in his life, a sense that he held real power, and he knew that feeling would be magnified dramatically if he actually won the White House. Senior members of his party had already started treating him with respect and deference, and he hadn't even secured the Party's nomination. Power was intoxicating; it was an adrenaline rush. That, too, worried him.

He hated being so conflicted; too much introspection was paralyzing. Sometimes, it was better simply to press ahead and let matters fall out as they may. He would manage his newfound enjoyment of power by reminding himself from time to time that he had to be in this for the right reasons and that he had to get out if he started to lose his moral footing. He didn't think he had, but he wondered if he had rationalized his decisions to accord with his desires. It was so easy a thing to do, and so hard a thing to admit, even to oneself.

Chapter 50

John's performance in the debates translated into a surge of voter support that continued unabated into the primaries. By mid-February, he had won primaries and caucuses in Iowa, New Hampshire, Michigan, Maine, Arizona, Missouri, South Carolina, Tennessee, Virginia, Nevada, and Wisconsin. Smith barely eked out victories in DC and Delaware, while favorite son candidates took Oklahoma and New Mexico.

Most significantly, in open primary states such as New Hampshire, Missouri, South Carolina, Tennessee and Wisconsin – states that allowed registered voters from any party to vote in the primary of their choice – never before seen numbers of crossover voters showed up to cast their ballots for John's nomination. It became clear that John was a candidate who transcended party lines. It also became clear that Smith would not be their party's nominee.

So, on a cold, blustery Wisconsin morning, the day after he had lost that state's primary despite having personally visited what seemed to him to be every brewery, coffee shop and truck stop in the state, Governor Smith announced his withdrawal from the race and asked his supporters to rally behind John. He had telephoned John a few minutes before to congratulate him and wish him well, but said no more than was required of a gentleman.

Janice quickly arranged for a press conference that would mark John's first appearance as his party's presumptive nominee and wondered how long it would be before Clark tried to wrap his tentacles around her candidate.

Later that afternoon, John waited offstage for his cue to step up to the bank of microphones and deliver what he hoped would be a successful precursor to the acceptance speech he intended to give at the party's nominating convention. He planned to outline his goals and the policies he would put in place to achieve them, and voice his confidence that America would choose to walk with him toward a brighter tomorrow rather than rely on the outdated and failed policies of the current administration.

As he waited, he reflected over the improbable chain of events that had led to this moment and passed lightly over the conflicting emotions that had just a few short weeks before threatened to overwhelm him. He couldn't repress the smile that kept bubbling up to the surface, and concentrated on not appearing too celebratory. He thought about Smith's rapid decline in the polls and resolved not to be the type of leader who analyzes everything and acts on nothing.

Unable to wait any longer, he strode onto the stage before his cue was given. Janice, who had been chatting with the press while waiting for the network cameras to go live, stepped back in surprise from the microphones.

John nodded to the crowd with a broad smile on his face. "I just couldn't wait to get out here and talk with you," he said. "I guess I have to wait for the network feed before I can give my prepared remarks, but does anyone have any questions in the meantime?"

A number of hands shot up immediately. John called on a reporter he had privately nicknamed 'Breathless' because of his tendency to rush through his questions without pausing for air.

"Senator Peters," he asked, "will you make an effort to reach out to those evangelicals in the battleground states who overwhelmingly supported the other party in the last election and who are credited with putting the current administration in the White House and will you rely on the controversial so-called miracle of the tongues to convince them that you're the candidate they should vote for?"

John shook his head slowly, the way a father knowingly shakes his head at a young son's misdeed moments before admonishing him. He answered in the most patient voice he could muster as a gentle smile crossed his lips. “I guess that’s how this game is played,” he said. “You have an angle you want to pursue, so you keep asking the same questions over and over until you get an answer you like. But no matter how many times you ask, I’m going to give you the same answer. I’m not running for Pope. I’m running for President. I don’t need miracles to get elected. I need votes. And the way I’ll get votes is by convincing the American people that I am the best person for the job.”

The reporter raised his hand, “Follow up question, Senator?”

“We haven’t officially started the press conference. You’re going to use up all your questions off camera.”

“That’s okay. It’s not off-the-record, so your answers still count.”

“Go ahead, then.”

“With all due respect, Senator, you haven’t answered my question. Will you try to convince a certain segment of the American public that the reason you are the best person for the job is because you are connected with God as evidenced by the occasions you apparently spoke several languages simultaneously that you profess not to know?”

“Did you ever have the courtroom beat?” John asked.

“I beg your pardon?” Breathless looked surprised by the question.

“You used the word ‘evidenced.’ Usually, it’s only lawyers who use that word as a verb.”

“”Yes sir, I did. But could I get an answer to my question.”

“You know, it’s taken me a while, but I am coming around to the point where I actually don’t mind this back and forth so much. So I’ll try to answer your question one more time the best way I can. I’m not going to play to ...”

John stopped in mid-sentence because of a sudden and considerable stir among the crowd of reporters. A low murmur breaking from their ranks grew steadily and rapidly into a cacophony of excited chatter. Fear squeezed his stomach with an icy hand and the muscles across his chest and down his back spasmed as they tightened in panic. He turned to Janice for help, but she stood staring at him with eyes that had been startled wide open. He heard someone from the floor say, "Did you hear that? He said, 'I am coming' in Spanish." A number of voices echoed "Yes." Someone else chimed, "I heard it in French."

The camera lights turned green as reporters started shouting questions to John: "Senator, can you tell us what it means?" and "Senator, *who* is coming?"

Chapter 51

John, Sara and Janice huddled in the privacy of the Peters' living room while reporters surrounded their house, held at bay by a line of policemen and closely watched by a couple of Secret Service agents on their roof.

The room was made warm and inviting by the fire John had built in the oversized fireplace. He used only apple wood logs, seasoned thoroughly in his garage to dry out the sap and ensure a clean, fragrant blaze. Sara had once convinced him to try a four-hour-burning artificial log to decrease the number of times he had to open the grate and either poke the logs or feed more wood to the fire, but the heavy smoke and acrid smell it gave off when first lit convinced him that there were some things best done the traditional way.

John poured himself another bourbon and then opened the glass front fireplace doors to check on the fire. He grabbed the poker, got down on one knee and jabbed hard at the logs, accidentally knocking one of the logs off the andirons. It toppled to the floor of the hearth and broke into several large pieces of glowing charcoal. Embers flew up and one hit John in the cheek.

"Damn!" he yelled, jumping back from the hearth.

"Are you okay?" Sara asked.

"Yeah, I'll be fine. Surprised me, that's all." He turned to Janice. "Not much of a miracle worker if I can't even handle a little spark."

Janice laughed. "I guess you're not the kind that can walk through fire."

John rubbed his cheek. "No, clearly not." He crossed the room to the sofa by the window and peered out through the drawn curtains. "A lot of people trying to get a glimpse of me," he said. "I can't avoid them forever."

"You shouldn't," Janice replied. "You need to get out in front of this. You need to talk to the American people."

"And exactly what do I tell them?" he asked.

"The truth," Sara said. She had been sitting quietly most of the previous hour, listening to the back and forth between John and Janice over the meaning of the latest 'tongues' manifestation. Janice was as confused as John as to why some people had heard it every time it occurred, while others, Janice for example, had heard it only intermittently, and still others had never heard anything extraordinary. Perhaps most perplexing of all was why John himself still had never noticed anything unusual.

"What is the truth?" John asked. "Please, I want to know."

"That you haven't any idea what's going on," Sara replied.

Janice shook her head violently. "That's not good enough. That will hand the election to the other side."

"What am I supposed to say, then?" John asked.

"That sometimes we have to live with uncertainty. That the universe is filled with unanswered questions." Janice picked out a thick book from the built-in shelves next to the fireplace and held it up to John and Sara. It was a one-volume history of Western philosophy that she had given John as a Christmas present a couple of years before. '"How was the universe created?" she asked. "Why are we here? Those questions come up a lot in this book, but nowhere do you find any definitive answers. But the fact that we don't know how we got here or why we're here doesn't stop us from getting on with our lives, from taking care of business. What you need to tell the American people, John, is that you have a job to do, and the fact that there are some uncertainties in your life won't stop you from getting it done."

John sat down next to Sara and put his arm around her. "I thought you wanted me to acknowledge a religious significance to this whole thing," John said to Janice.

"I think it's about time you admitted it to yourself," Janice answered. "But I guess I don't think it's something you need to promote as part of your campaign. We already have the votes of those who believe it's a miracle, and I'd rather not drive away the votes of those who don't. Otherwise, it turns into a wash, and that won't win the election."

"So this is just a political calculation to you."

"To me, it's a whole lot more. But I have a job to do, too, and part of that job involves knowing when to push an issue and when to back off."

John took another sip of bourbon and remained silent for a few moments. The only sounds in the room came from the logs crackling in the fire and the ice cubes clinking in John's glass as he swirled his drink.

"John," Sara asked, "Would you get me another glass of wine, please?"

"I'll need to go downstairs to get another bottle. The glass you just had was the last of the wine left over from dinner last night."

"Do you mind?"

"No, of course not."

After John had left the room, Sara turned to Janice. "I'm glad you're not pushing John too hard on the religious front, especially given your personal beliefs. He has enough to deal with without having to worry about what God has in store for him. He may not show it, but this thing has him scared."

"I guess I would be scared, too."

"Let me ask you something. If this is truly God's doing, then why hasn't He clued John in on it? Why would He simply use John the way you would use a microphone? Why would God do that?"

"I don't know, Sara. I wish I did. As I said, some things are mysteries."

This time it was Sara who shook her head. "That's not good enough. Not when we're talking about my husband's life."

"I don't know what else to say."

"Can't you see what this is doing to him, to our family?"

"Sara, don't you think that whoever or whatever is doing this is going to keep on doing whatever it wants, no matter what you or John or I try to do about it? What if John quit the campaign packed up and went home? Then what? Reporters would still chase him down for a story, a quote, yet another miracle. He'd have to become a hermit, a recluse. Do you think that would make John happy? Would it make you happy?"

Sara silently shook her head no.

"We're all trapped by events," Janice continued, "so the only thing to do is make the most of the opportunities they present."

"John and I are trapped. You're not. You can walk away any time you want."

A look of hurt transfigured Janice's face. "I'm fully committed to this. John isn't just my boss, and this isn't just my job."

Sara crossed over to her and gave her a hug. "I know, and I'm sorry," she said. "But you have to understand the difference between us. I'm in this for the rest of my life, and I'm terrified of what all my tomorrows will bring."

Later that evening, after Janice had left, John and Sara lay on the carpet in front of the fire drinking the last of the Pinot Noir.

"Did you see the inside of Connor's closet door?" Sara asked.

"No. I didn't know there was something to see."

"He covered it with rainbows."

"Why did he do that?"

"He was afraid to go into his closet. To him, it's a big, dark and scary place. But rainbows make him happy, so now when he goes in, he doesn't think about how scary it is. He thinks about how pretty the rainbows look and how good they make him feel."

John smiled. Thinking about Connor made him feel good. Flickering shadows from the slowly dying flames played across the walls and ceiling, but what John noticed most was Sara's face glowing softly yellow in the firelight.

"You are beautiful," he whispered.

"You are drunk," she smiled.

"Maybe. But you're still beautiful."

She laughed. "Will you tell me that in the morning when you're sober?"

"I'll tell you that for the rest of my life."

On the roof, the two Secret Service men continued to monitor the grounds below when one of them noticed something moving overhead. He looked up, called to his partner and pointed to the silhouette of the biggest bat either of them had ever seen, passing like a cold, black shadow across the clear and starry night sky.

Chapter 52

The next morning, Janice planned to go John's house to help retool a speech John was scheduled to give the following day. The 'tongues' incident could not be ignored, but it could be managed. As soon as she opened her front door, however, she was greeted by a throng of reporters who had decided that if they couldn't get close to the Senator, they'd settle for the next best thing. Janice tried to make her way through the crowd, but an overly zealous television reporter thrust a microphone in front of her face and accidentally knocked into her.

Janice staggered back a couple of steps, tripped over the foot of another reporter who had been closing in behind her, twisted and fell. She lay dazed on the ground. Looking up, she saw a small circle of blue sky enclosed by a ring of reporters' heads bent down toward her while cameras clicked rapidly, capturing various angles of her sprawled on the pavement.

Janice tried to sit up, but dizziness overcame her. She would have toppled back to the ground if not for a man's firm hand across her back that arrested her fall and eased her into a seated position. As he propped her up with one hand, he took her left hand in the other and laid it palm down on her belly. She felt her hand trembling and thought that he was shaking it; when she looked, she saw that his hand lay atop hers and that both were perfectly still.

She turned her head to see who he was, but he knelt directly behind her and beyond the range of her peripheral vision. For a moment, as her equilibrium returned, everything around her seemed calm and quiet, as if time had stopped. When she tried to stand again, the man leaned forward and whispered into her ear, "Love and protect that which is precious above all else," then gently squeezed her hand before releasing it.

She slowly rose to her feet and turned to thank him, but he had blended into the crowd and out of view. She felt a fluttering in her stomach, the first movement she had ever felt, and her inner voice told her to push back the trip to John's house by a few hours so that she could see her doctor first.

The doctor's office looked like every other doctor's office Janice had ever been in: a bookshelf behind the desk, a window to her left, a wall to her right covered with various diplomas and certificates, a framed poster from a modern art museum on the back wall, an under-watered plant in the corner, and family photos on the desk.

The nurse had ushered her in and promised that the doctor would be in "momentarily." Janice picked up a back issue of *The New Yorker* magazine and started to read. Ever since she was a little girl, whenever she went to the doctor's office, she would make a bet with herself as to how many pages she could read before the "momentary" wait was over. This time, she thought, he'd be there in twelve pages. *The New Yorker* used a smaller font-size and spaced the lines closer together than most magazines. A lot of content in a little bit of space. Twelve pages would take some time.

She was mildly surprised when her doctor walked in after she had finished only four pages. He was, as always, professional, polite and somewhat distant. He was also quite handsome. That had unnerved her when she first met him, and she used to wonder what he was like behind the professional demeanor, whether he was quiet and easygoing or wild and daring. She never could penetrate his facade, and in the end, she decided that was probably for the best. Doctors dealt with such intimate matters that both they and their patients probably needed a barrier between them to avoid discomfort. Not too different from those times as a young girl she had used a confessional to confide in her priest. Of course her priest recognized her voice, but having that dark screen between them made it easier to confess. The façade of uncertainty in which both she and the priest participated made the act possible. She never could bring herself to participate in the open-air confessions that so many churches later adopted.

She and the doctor briefly exchanged routine pleasantries and comments about the weather. Then he got serious.

"Miss Baxter, we've talked about this before. I told you that if you didn't take it easy, you were going to wind up on bed rest."

"I understand Doctor, but I have a job. I can't just quit."

"You're running out of options."

"What do you mean?"

"I mean that if you don't want to lose this baby, you're going to have scale back significantly."

Janice knew that she couldn't maintain her schedule. She tired easily these days, and air travel had become increasingly taxing. But she didn't think she could quietly accede to the doctor's instruction. She needed to protest and to have her protest overruled. It was irrelevant that neither John nor anyone other than her doctor would hear her complain. For her own peace of mind, she had to convince herself that she wasn't quitting on John; that she had no choice but to step back and let others do the work.

"We're headed into the heart of the campaign right now," Janice said. "I can't let up now."

The doctor stared at her for a long moment. Then, in a matter-of-fact tone he said, "Let me put this in a way you're sure to understand. If you don't let up, you will lose her."

Chapter 53

Dear Diary,

At some point in the near future, I will have to make a choice: whether to press on with John's campaign, and in so doing, hope to realize my life's dream, or to stop and focus on having my baby, a hope I had never dared to dream of.

There is no choice, really. Once I decided to have and keep this baby, I also decided that everything else became less important. She will be my family and that must always come first. I'd like to tell my father what's been going on, that he is going to be a grandfather. I'd like him to be there, but this is hardly the news to spring on him after all this time apart. After all these years of silence.

I need to tell John. He will understand. So will Sara, but she'll probably be angry with me anyway, especially after our conversation the other night. I said I was committed and I am, but things change. This baby needs me more than John does. But I do owe him more than a mere announcement. I need to ensure that someone else steps into my role. There aren't many people I can think of who would be able to do the job well.

Clark has already suggested he'd help out. I don't entirely trust him, but in this business, if you only worked with people you thoroughly trusted, you'd spend a lot of time working alone. Besides, Clark can bring a great deal of resources to the campaign, but he won't be able to change who John is. All things considered, he may be the best person for the job. I know John is uneasy around him, but that's mostly because of the weird relationship triangle with Governor Smith. Now that Smith is out of the race, those awkward issues should go away.

I wonder if Clark would take the job. Being out on the front lines of a campaign isn't something he is used to doing. But being outside the inner circle is something he is even less used to. He might do this if only to ensure that he stays connected to the seat of power. If John wins, Clark will think he has an inside track to the President's ear. How could he turn that temptation down?

But what if he does? I can't leave John hanging. I need to lay the groundwork with Clark first before I say a word to John.

Chapter 54

John's hands trembled slightly as he thumbed through the pages in his three-ring binder. He realized that this would be the most important speech he had yet given. Although the immediate audience was that of a university lecture hall, the entire country waited beyond the auditorium walls to hear how he addressed the mystery of the tongues; the entire country waited to hear if it happened again.

It was maddening.

He hadn't felt so helpless since he was a little boy who had no say in the things that mattered most to him, but he couldn't let that show when he faced the nation. He had to appear calm, confident and in control.

He strode onto the stage to enthusiastic applause. The seats were filled with college students wondering if they would witness history.

"Good evening," John started. "Thank you for inviting me to your wonderful school and for making me feel so welcome. Your warmth has been so overwhelming that I'm almost at a loss for words ... *in any language...*" Laughter rippled around the hall. That was good. The icebreaker seemed to work.

He continued, "Tonight I'd like to talk to you about why I want to be your President. I'd like to share with you my vision for the future. And I'd like to answer some of the questions that you may have, and at least *one* that I know you have." John grinned as he said that and drew some additional laughter. He sensed that the crowd liked him and wanted him to do well.

As he looked up from his script, he saw expectation written into the faces of many of the young men and women in the audience. He suddenly realized that they weren't there to see a politician, even one running for President. He had known all along that some or even most of the audience would wonder if they might witness another 'tongues' occurrence, but now, for the first time, he fully understood how much hope they had invested in the possibility. They didn't come to see news being made; they came for something much deeper. He could almost feel their hopes and their needs reaching out to him; weighing down the otherwise empty air inside the auditorium. They came looking for a reason, a purpose, an answer. He had thought he could push the issue into the background with a few clever turns of phrase. He now realized that he had to deal with it in a far more forthright manner. He closed the binder and pushed it away.

"I came here tonight with a prepared speech," he said, looking out into the audience, "but I realize now, looking at your faces, that I need to address squarely the issue that brought many, perhaps most of you, here tonight.

"First, let me tell you that running for President has been one of the most humbling experiences of my life. When I started, I was the longest of long shots, and I got caught up in the excitement of the mere idea of it all. To be perfectly honest, I may not have given sufficient thought to the awesome responsibilities it entails. But over the past few weeks, I've thought about it more and more."

The crowd murmured. John paused, took a drink of water, and asked himself whether he was truly prepared to press on. He decided he had no choice. "I love this country" he said, "and I want only the best for it. I have dedicated my entire life to public service. When I realized that so many people were putting their faith and trust in me, I began to examine very carefully whether I deserved it.

"I can tell you that I believe I would make a good President. I *know* that I would give it everything I had. I would pour my heart's blood into being the best President I could be, and I would be as honest with you for the entire four years of my term as I am being with you tonight.

"I know that many of you are here because you think I am something more than I am. I've seen the news stories. And I get letters every day from people who think ... well, you can imagine what they think. Some of you may think the same."

John surveyed the room, over which an expectant hush had fallen, as if he were a magician approaching the denouement of a spectacular trick.

"I am a man, just a man.

"I have no insights to offer as to why, apparently, I sometimes speak in what most are now calling 'tongues.' I use the word 'apparently' because I do not hear it myself. I wish I could offer you an explanation. But as a dear friend once told me, when faced with a mystery, we can either stop to ponder it, or press ahead with the business of life. I intend to press ahead.

"I would like very much to be your President. Over the past few weeks, in campaign stops like this one, and in three nationally televised debates, you have had a chance to see me in action, to hear my views on the issues facing our nation. Over the next few months, you will have further opportunities, including a series of Presidential debates with the current Vice-President, to measure my worth as a political leader. It is on that basis and that basis alone, that I ask you to vote for me.

"I am running for the office of the President of the United States. If, come Election Day, you believe that I am the best man for that job then I would be greatly honored to have your vote.

"Thank you, and good night."

John picked up his binder, tucked it under his arm and walked off the stage.

Chapter 55

He was maddening.

After all these months, after all this effort, after all their successes, for John to throw it away with on a whim, on a sudden urge to bare his soul, was nothing short of infuriating. Candidates can't admit having doubts about their own suitability for office. If a candidate isn't sure he deserves the office he seeks, why in the hell would anyone else believe he should get it?

Janice couldn't believe that John had abandoned the carefully worded speech they had prepared. Instead, he fed raw meat to hungry lions. The media would go crazy analyzing the "candid candidate's" remarks and the opposition would run endless ads quoting from his speech: *'John Peters says he didn't think enough about the responsibilities of the Presidency before deciding to run. John Peters says that he now believes he would be a good President. What will he believe next week after he thinks about it a little more? Vice-President Rawlings has been a heartbeat away from the Presidency for the last eight years. He didn't start thinking about it yesterday. On Election Day, cast your vote for the man who has already proven he can do the job.'*

The door opened and John walked in. He had been expecting her to be upset with him – she never liked it when he strayed from the script – and judging from the look she gave him as he entered the room, his expectations had been fulfilled. His cheeks were still red from the cold winter air and in each hand he held a large takeout coffee cup from which steam escaped through a tiny slit in the lid.

"Before you say anything," John said, "Here." He handed her one of the cups. "I brought you a gingerbread latte, decaf of course."

"This is supposed to make me feel better?"

"No, just less angry."

Shaking her head, Janice accepted the drink and sipped from it. “Thanks.”

John, still standing, said “If you had seen the faces on those college kids in the audience . . . Some of them were holding Bibles. They weren’t there to see a Presidential candidate. I couldn’t go with the speech we had worked out. I just couldn’t.”

“But you didn’t have to hand the election to the other side on silver platter, either.”

John unbuttoned his coat, draped it across an empty chair, and sat down next to Janice. “How’s yours?” he asked.

“Excuse me?”

“How’s your latte? I got a mocha flavored one. Never tried it before. I don’t usually go for the foofy flavors.”

“Foofy? What’s that mean?”

“Foofy? It means fancy. Look it up.”

“I guarantee you there is no such word.”

“Well, there should be. It fits.”

“You’re avoiding the subject.”

“Yes. I am.”

Janice took another sip of her latte. “It’s good. I like it better than a plain latte, actually.” She gave John a long, hard look. “Are you happy now? Can we get back to what we’re going to do to fix this yet another fine mess you’ve gotten us in?”

John smiled. “I love Laurel and Hardy.”

“I know. You’ve mentioned it a thousand times. You like them almost as much as you like the Marx Brothers and Abbot and Costello.”

“Comic geniuses, all.”

Janice sighed in exasperation. She was tired, not feeling well, and fast losing patience. “John, you do realize that your impromptu remarks last night will be turned into campaign fodder from now until Election Day?"

"I wasn't thinking about that at the time."

"You weren't thinking, period."

"Actually, Janice, I was, but not about how my remarks would get played by the other side. I was thinking about my first interview with Melanie Kraft, the one in which I said that maybe the point behind this whole 'tongues' thing was that we needed to start telling the truth, to stop spinning. I haven't done anything but spin every day since that interview. I'm tired of it. For once, I wanted to speak from the heart. So I did. If it costs me the election, so be it."

Janice put her coffee down on the table, crossed her arms and leaned back, studying John. After a few moments pause, she said, "As long as we're going back in time, there was a time, not too long back, when you asked me if I was serious about this campaign. Now I need to ask you the same question, John. You can't make flippant decisions that undermine the months of hard work that all of us have put into this campaign. If you truly think you're the best candidate for the job, you owe it to all of us to stay disciplined, to do what it takes to win."

"*Whatever* it takes?" John studied Janice carefully as he asked that question.

She rolled her eyes in response. "Stop being so melodramatic, John. You're not being asked to sell your soul. I'm only asking that you stay on message when you give speeches. Otherwise, you're going to get crucified."

John swirled his cup to melt the last of the foam clinging to the sides of the cup into the espresso. "Was that a pun?"

"Give me a break," Janice replied. "Listen, John," she continued, "I'm upset because we're drawing close, really close, to winning this thing. You're up solidly in the polls – at least you were before last night – and I was hoping I could ... ease up a bit. You know I went to see my doctor the other day. Well, it doesn't look like I'm going to be able to pull you out of the fire every time you decide to jump in."

Chapter 56

Neither John nor Janice anticipated the dramatic impact of his latest pronouncement in tongues. Nothing they could have contrived, neither carefully scripted speeches nor impromptu remarks, would have lessened the foment that followed.

Weekly supermarket tabloids were the first to react. They showed pictures of John standing next to either angels or aliens, and in one issue, both. That tabloid also published what it claimed to be secrets of his private life, including his favorite brand of underwear, diet tips and preferred sexual positions.

In-depth scholarly articles appeared in Sunday newspapers and weekly magazines, examining prior examples of those who allegedly spoke in tongues, especially St. Vincent Ferrer, the 14th Century Dominican whom Janice had read about the day the Senator first spoke in tongues. A new biography of the saint entitled, *Angel of Judgment*, concluded that the reemergence of the miracle of tongues foreshadowed the end of the world, but offered as a salve St. Vincent's belief in the penance of Judas -- salvation was possible even for those who thought themselves hopelessly lost. The book shot to the top of the best-sellers list and was quickly reissued in an illustrated version and packaged in a boxed gift set that included an unauthorized biography of Senator Peters and the Book of Revelations. The fascination with St. Vincent extended to the church bearing his name in Manhattan's Upper East Side, where day after day lines of worshipers wrapped around the block, waiting their turn to light a votive candle by St. Vincent's statue and pray before the preserved remains of one of his finger joints.

Posters to Internet blogs debated the meaning of, "I am coming." Many expressed anxiety or fear, only to suffer the barbs of self-righteous responses that they must have done something for which they were ashamed. A handful of disturbing posts suggested that the best way to alleviate any fear was to kill the messenger. The Secret Service did its best to track down those responsible for those posts, but a couple of them had been routed through overseas internet accounts that could not be further traced.

Millions of letters and cards from dozens of countries clogged the Senate mailroom; most fell into one of two categories. They either asked Senator Peters for his prayers and blessings or they cursed him as a false prophet. John, with his face blazoned across newspapers, television screens and magazines, became one of the most recognizable and controversial figures on Earth.

Political pundits, accustomed only to debating typical campaign issues such as the economy, abortion and defense spending, scrambled to place Peters in context. What was the nation to do with a prophet for President? He couldn't be marginalized as he had already secured his party's nomination, and he couldn't be ridiculed because the 'miracle' he had performed was witnessed, not by a small group of illiterate children in a remote country village, but by jaded reporters and their worldwide television audience.

A column by Richard Braun, who for the first time in many years wrote from his heart, summed up the mood of a nervous world:

> 'These are the times that try men's souls.' Those words, penned by Thomas Paine more than two centuries ago, have never been truer than they are today.
>
> Can anyone doubt that we are witnessing an epochal event – one that will be discussed and debated for years, if not decades or centuries, to come?
>
> Unless, of course, as some fear and others hope, when "I" arrives, he brings with him the end of days.
>
> To all you cynics and skeptics, pop psychologists and pseudo scientists who have been blanketing our airwaves with your nay saying, I say to you: shut up

and listen. There is a voice you should hear.

Senator Peters himself would have us turn a deaf ear to the message he brings. We cannot.

Whatever it means, whoever is responsible, it bespeaks a power far greater than any of us possess.

What are we to do in the face of this power? Continue, as Senator Peters' would have us do, with business as usual? How can we?

I empathize with the Senator. He wants no part of this, and I don't blame him. It must be unspeakably hard to have millions of people hanging on your every word when you don't even know what it is that you're saying.

But Senator Peters, for better or worse, you are our messenger.

What will that message be? I am reminded of the philosopher, Pascal, who suggested that even an atheist should believe in God when death approaches. I don't know if "I" is coming, and I don't know who or what he, she or it is. In the meantime, though, just to be safe, I'm examining my conscience, healing wounds that I have caused, and reaffirming to those I love how much they mean to me.

Chapter 57

Archbishop O'Connell sat alone in his office with a West Highland Terrier puppy jumping about his lap. His nephew had given it to him as a birthday present in the hope that it would pick up his spirits. The Archbishop named him MacGregor, or Mac for short, and he was still small enough to fit in the palms of his hands. Mac's eyes and nose formed a small triangle of black dots that stood out against his white fur; one ear was folded over while the other pointed straight up, and a small semicircle of pink tongue poked out of his mouth as a result of a slight under-bite. Whenever Mac nipped his fingers in an effort to draw attention, the Archbishop would smile briefly, play with him for a moment, and then drift off, his thoughts circling back to Janice, her unborn baby, and his role in the sad story of Darnell Edom's life.

Although he had confessed his sins to a priest long ago and received absolution from God, he had never forgiven himself, and after the events of the last few months, he wondered if he ever would. The lamp of Orpheus and Eurydice that he had shown Sara Peters sat before him, casting its soft light, and as the Archbishop looked upon it, he pondered the fine line between heaven and hell. Orpheus had been so determined to save his wife, but in the end, his instinct to help, his unthinking turn at her cry of distress, brought about her doom. Archbishop O'Connell had always tried to do that which he believed would best help those in need. 'The road to hell is paved with good intentions,' he thought.

He worried that the protective cocoon of the Church, one that had shielded him from the scrutiny of the outside world for so long, could not protect Janice from the evil he had wrought. He agonized continually over whether he should tell her what he knew of Darnell's past and what he dreaded lay in her future. He was afraid of how she would react if he told her about Darnell's medical diagnosis and explained that schizophrenia might be hereditary, and wondered whether she would blame him as he had blamed himself. That which haunted him most, however, was something he had decided he could never tell her – his fear that Darnell had been possessed by evil itself and that his attack on Janice was directly related to John's speaking in tongues.

Janice had admitted that she was not capable of getting pregnant, so how did it happen? Was the baby the Devil's response to John's message? What would happen now in the aftermath of John's latest message? What could or should he do about it?

The Archbishop remembered his college Ethics class debating whether it would have been morally acceptable for someone who could travel back in time to kill Hitler before he rose to power. Some argued that preventing the evil to come justified such a homicide, while others argued that to murder someone who had as yet done no harm would have been morally repugnant. The arguments were trite and superficial because entirely hypothetical. The dilemma posed by Janice's baby, however, was very real.

If Janice had decided to have an abortion, the Archbishop wondered how forcefully he would have tried to talk her out of it. Such a decision would have given him the moral cover of protesting in public while privately heaving a sigh of relief. But Janice had not given him that out.

Archbishop O'Connell shook himself out of his melancholy reverie and mentally slapped himself in the face. Abortion! What was he thinking! Life was sacred, and he would not, could not judge or condemn an innocent baby.

Mac jumped up and licked his face, then plopped on his back, eager to have his belly scratched. Archbishop O'Connell smiled and complied, grateful for the dog's company. In that moment, a sudden clarity gave him respite from the confused swirl of his thoughts. The

Archbishop realized that he had been in danger of letting his fears overwhelm his faith. He would not sink like the Apostle Peter into the waters of doubt. He accepted the fact that he was just a man. The only way for him to stay afloat in the troubled waters surrounding him was to surrender to the will of God. He got down on his knees and started to pray, "Our Father, Who art in Heaven . . ."

Chapter 58

John arrived home from an exhausting campaign trip in which he had fended off innumerable questions about the Apocalypse and tried instead to focus the discussion on the weakening U.S. dollar. He had been hoping for a few quiet moments by the fire, perhaps to read a story to Connor or share a glass of wine with Sara.

Instead, he was greeted with a stack of telephone messages, the most important one from Janice saying that she needed to talk to him as soon as possible, in person. He climbed back in the car and drove to Janice's home. Two hours later, he returned, more tired than ever. Sara looked at him expectantly.

"She's been having a hard time with the pregnancy," John explained, "and I guess the doctor put it to her in no uncertain terms that she had to cut back. You know Janice; she only does one speed, all out. She's been trying to cut back for the past couple of weeks, but just doesn't know how to do it well. So she thought she better watch the race from the sidelines for a while."

In a soft, still voice, Sara said, "All along, I've wondered whether she would go through with having the baby or whether it would be too hard – you know what I mean, whether seeing the baby would remind her of the rape. I don't know that I could handle it. But I guess in the end a mother's love outweighs everything else."

"Maybe," John replied in a weary voice. "I'm trying to be sympathetic, but her timing couldn't be worse."

"Did she have any ideas in mind for a replacement?"

"Yes, interestingly enough, she suggested we try talking to Clark."

"Really?"

The next morning, following a brief phone call, Clark arrived at Peters' home, set his brief case on the foyer floor and took a long look around before removing his coat. He noticed the meticulous effort put into cleaning even the nooks and crannies where dust usually collected unnoticed and the small personal touches that adorned the walls of the rooms off to either side, touches designed not to impress the casual visitor but to make the house's occupants feel at home. Pictures of the Peters' family, especially of Connor, decorated the mantle over the fireplace and the staircase wall, but Clark didn't spot a single photograph of the type that he typically saw when visiting politicians' homes – posed autographed shots of the homeowner with other dignitaries or celebrities.

"You have a nice home," Clark said. "Thank you for inviting me over."

"You're welcome. Thanks for agreeing to meet me here. Connor's at school and Sara is off somewhere on a fund-raising drive for children with cancer, so we have the house to ourselves."

Clark laughed. "Inside maybe. Outside is a different matter, with all those reporters camped on the street. The fact that I'm meeting with you is not likely to be a private matter much longer."

John shook his head. "It's unbelievable. Even the paparazzi follow me around now."

"The price of fame," Clark observed dryly.

John shrugged his shoulders in reply. "Would you like some coffee? It's not as good as what we had at the coffee house, but it's plenty strong."

"I'd love a cup."

The two men settled into the study.

"You may have heard," John started, 'that Janice has decided to cut back on her day-to-day role in the campaign."

"I assumed that's why you wanted to meet with me."

"Janice thought I should talk to you to see if you were interested in helping out."

Clark leaned back in his chair and sipped his coffee. “You sold yourself short on your coffee making skills. This is an excellent cup.”

“Thanks. So how about it?”

Clark held up two fingers and said, “Two questions: would you have called me if Janice hadn’t suggested it and what is it you want me to do?”

“I don’t know and I’m not sure. The second question is precisely what I wanted to talk to you about.”

“Well, I guess whether you would have called me absent Janice’s suggestion is irrelevant. You did call me, and here I am. The second question, however, is critical. I don’t do things halfway. I’m either in charge or I’m not in at all. And, frankly, you need me more than I need you.”

“How’s that?”

“Whatever happens to you and your campaign, I’ll still be around when it’s over.”

John set his coffee cup down on the table beside him and folded his arms across his chest. With a wry smile on his face he said, “You have an interesting way of negotiating for a job.”

Clark peered at John over the top of his sunglasses. “I’m not negotiating. You either want what I can bring to the table, or you don’t.”

“Okay. Enlighten me.”

“You’ve come pretty far on the back of what to date has been an amateurish campaign – no offense to Janice, she’s never done one of these before and she was in over her head – but now you’re headed for the home stretch, and amateur hour just won’t cut it any longer. You don’t have a coordinated advertising campaign; you haven’t identified who will negotiate the terms of the Presidential debates let alone, from what I hear, figured out what shape you want the debates to take – town hall, single moderator, time limits, that sort of thing;

and have you even started thinking about who your running mate will be?"

John uncrossed his arms and reached for his coffee. "Let's take that last one first. How would you go about picking him?"

"You need to set up a screening committee, people who will draft a questionnaire for any prospective candidates, vet their backgrounds and credentials, and narrow the list down to a final few for you to meet with. That's the formal process. The real process is far simpler. There are some people you have to meet with because it's expected. It gives them credibility back home as national figures, and if you don't meet with them, they'll screw you when it comes to getting out the vote on Election Day. So Burke from Idaho; Tanner from Ohio; Coombs from Connecticut; Masserti from New Jersey, and a few others will be on the list. At the end of the day, after you've gone through this extensive process and tell the press how impressed you were by all of the men and women with whom you met, you go with the guy you planned to run with all along."

"You're back to my initial question. How do you pick that guy?"

"I already know who your running mate ought to be: Governor Smith."

John rested his chin in the palm of his hand and studied Clark, who continued to drink his coffee, unperturbed by the prolonged silence. The only sound that could be heard was the rumbling of a passing garbage truck and the occasional banging of empty trash cans as the workers tossed them back onto the street.

"You hear that," John said.

"What?"

"The garbage truck that just went by."

"I didn't notice."

"It just picked up my trash from last night. In that trash was some shredded paper, which, before I shredded it, contained a list of potential running mates that Janice and I had discussed. Burke and Coombs were on it. Tanner wasn't. Masserti wasn't. And neither was Smith."

"Who were you leaning toward?"

"That I hadn't decided. But let me ask you, why Governor Smith? I mean, he's from North Carolina, too. How does he bring anything to the ticket?"

Clark stood up and tipped his cup toward John, showing him that it was empty. "Do you mind if I pour myself some more coffee?"

"Here, let me have your cup. I'll get it for you."

"That's okay. I can help myself." He nodded in the direction of the kitchen. "That way to the kitchen?"

"Yes," John replied. "I'll come with you. I could use another cup, too."

As they walked toward the kitchen, Clark said, "You know what they say about generals, that they're always fighting the last war. Well, you're running the last election. This election won't be decided by the ticket with the best geographic coverage. This election is all about you, John. It's kind of funny, you know. The Vice-President doesn't quite know what to do about it. He was all set to run on the current administration's record over the last eight years. Now, nobody cares about that. It's all about you."

"It's all about my speaking in tongues, you mean."

"Absolutely."

"But I've made it clear that I don't want that to be the focus of my campaign."

"Forgive me for saying this, but you've been an idiot."

"What?"

"You're like one of those aging rock bands that go on a reunion tour but only wants to play songs from their new record, not what their fans came to hear. You've got to give the fans what they want, John, and what they want from you has nothing to do with tax reform, minimum wage or foreign trade policy."

"What, exactly, am I supposed to say?"

"Something that plays to their hopes and fears. Something that makes them think they can't afford not to vote for you."

"They think I'm some sort of prophet. I don't. How can I sell something I don't believe in?

"Do you think you'd be the first politician to sell something he didn't actually believe? Does 'read my lips' ring a bell? How about 'I did not inhale'? Mondale told the truth in 1980 when he said that if he were elected, he'd raise taxes. His reward was to get slaughtered at the polls on Election Day. Truth, my friend, is a highly overrated virtue."

John shrugged off Clark's last comment as symptomatic of someone who'd been a Washington insider for a long time, fixed himself another cup of coffee and leaned against the kitchen counter. "Religion and politics don't mix. How can I run for the Presidency as a religious figure?"

"Jesse Jackson and Al Sharpton both ran for President, and they're Reverends."

"They both lost."

Clark chuckled, "I wasn't running their campaigns." Then his face assumed a serious aspect. "During the 1984 Democratic convention, Jackson gave an absolutely marvelous speech during which he compared himself to Jesus, saying that they were both born in slums. Did it hurt him? Far from it. The next election cycle, he ran for President and entered the Convention with 1200 delegates, second only to Michael Dukakis. When he stood up to speak, he delivered his message in the up-and-down, rolling cadence of a Sunday preacher; he quoted from the Bible and even from the Lord's Prayer – 'Thy will be done.' Did he get crucified for it? No. He got 18 standing ovations in a speech that lasted less than an hour. That speech was later hailed as the greatest Convention speech since William Jennings Bryan's Cross of Gold speech in 1896."

John smiled at the mention of Bryan, recalling that Janice had compared Reverend Jones to him.

"Did I say something funny?"

"No, I'm sorry. Janice used to refer to Bryan sometimes, that's all. But let's put the message issue aside for now. Why Smith for a running mate?"

"You need someone who speaks your language." Clark paused in the awkward silence that followed, and then said, "I didn't mean that as a joke. I meant that he comes from your neck of the woods. He understands how you think; he'd be a good partner, someone you could rely on. And it would show some gratitude. He was the one who appointed you to the Senate in the first place, and but for you he'd be the nominee. So why not repay the favor he did you? It'd be the nice thing to do."

"I'm surprised to hear you say that. Nice and politics don't seem to go together in your book."

Clark started walking back toward the study. With his back to John, he said, "Oh, I can be as sentimental as the next guy." Then he turned to face John directly. "Seriously, though, Smith would be my recommendation. My *strong* recommendation."

"You told me once before that Ned does whatever you tell him to do. I'm not at all sure I like the idea of having my campaign manager being closer to my running mate than to me."

"What's more important to you, running for President or being President?"

Chapter 59

The Reverend opened the envelope containing his latest monthly bank statement. He already knew what it would say, as he checked his brokerage and bank statements on-line on a daily basis, but there was something special about holding a piece of paper in his hand that detailed his growing net worth. He was a tactile sort of man. He needed to touch something before he'd believe it was real.

His association with Senator Peters had rewarded him handsomely. Contributions for his ministry flowed in ever increasing amounts. He had been generously paid for appearing as a guest preacher at churches across the country and on numerous television broadcasts, and he had even received a lucrative advance on a book he was preparing to write about his life and mission. If John got elected, things would get even better.

Even his relationship with Clark had paid off. The Reverend recalled that disastrous first meeting and smiled. Now that Clark was running John's campaign, all the adversarial gamesmanship was over and he could devote himself to honing John's presentation with a clear conscience. He filed the bank statement in his desk drawer, took out his red editing pen and turned once again to the speech he had written for the Senator to give on his next campaign stop:

I stand before you tonight not as a prophet, not as a politician, but as a man. I stand before you tonight not with a prophesy, not with a promise, but with a message.

We are all here by the grace of God. Some of you believe that I have been specially chosen by Him for some special purpose as yet unknown. I say to you that we have each been chosen by God for a special purpose, and it is our responsibility, our destiny, to fulfill that purpose.

There was a time, many years ago, when America believed it had a special purpose in the world. There was a time, many years ago, when Americans believed it was their Manifest Destiny to rise to greatness.

Our forefathers fulfilled that destiny. They made America the envy of the world, the shining light on the hill, the beacon of hope for the tired, the poor, the huddled masses, and for anyone yearning to be free.

How did our forefathers accomplish this great feat? They did it by honoring their heritage. They did it by striving for better tomorrows. They did it by trusting in God.

Some say that America has lost its luster. Some say that America has lost its way. Some say that America is no longer home to the tired and the poor, but to the wealthy and the arrogant.

They are wrong.

This is my message to you.

We are Americans. We have it in us to be great because it is our heritage. We have it in us to be great because we will never stop reaching for better tomorrows. We have it in us to be great because we trust in God.

'Trust in God' is not just a hollow phrase on the back of the dollar bill. It's a belief embedded in our hearts and souls.

We are a diverse people of diverse faiths, but we are all stewards of the great hope of mankind that is America.

I believe in America. I believe in you. I believe that together, we will rekindle the beacon on the hill so that all the world will see America shine.

The Reverend put his pen away. The speech was perfect, capturing the religious flavor that Clark wanted without violating John's admonition not to go over the top. Most important, it would give the voters what they wanted to hear. Everyone would be happy, and that was a good thing.

He had a hard time believing how well life had been treating him of late. He was still a little afraid of Clark and probably always would be, but everyone had to answer to someone in life, and with the way events had unfolded, with Clark in charge of John's campaign and Smith named as the running mate, Clark probably wasn't too concerned about keeping the Reverend tightly under his thumb.

The Reverend emailed the speech to Clark and John, confident that neither one would change a word. The next step was to help John master the delivery, and for that, he would download tapes of Jesse Jackson and Martin Luther King, Jr. and have John listen to them, over and over again. Their cadence, combined with John's soft North Carolina accent, would make him quite the orator.

Chapter 60

The first day of spring brought a surprising and rare thunder snowstorm to Washington. Within twenty-four hours, nearly a foot had fallen, and in DC, an inch was all that was needed to bring the city to a screeching halt. The driving wind whipped around Janice's building, its more ferocious gusts rattled her windows and howled through the narrow passage between her street and the homes across the alley. Lightning flashes reflected off the snow as it fell, illuminating the sky with an eerie glow.

Janice snuggled into her armchair and tried to read a book. She had been feeling a bit queasy for most of the day, more so than usual, and she had hoped that a good mystery novel would keep her mind off her discomfort and the disquieting sounds outside.

She occasionally looked up at the television to monitor the snowstorm, amazed at the ferocity of the blizzard. According to some reports, it was the heaviest March snowfall in Washington since 1891. This storm was becoming one for the ages.

Suddenly, a pain seized Janice's belly, doubling her over before it subsided. It couldn't be contractions, she thought, as she was only in her twenty-third week. She tried to calm herself and mentally reviewed the various books and articles she had read about this stage of pregnancy to figure out what was happening. Then the pain struck again, and this time, Janice feared the worst.

She called her doctor's office and left an urgent message at the beep, worried that no one had made it into the office given the treacherous conditions outside. When the third contraction came, she dialed 911.

Janice packed quickly and kept an anxious watch by her front door window. The hospital was only a five-minute drive away, but it took nearly half an hour for the ambulance to arrive. The city's road crews had not been prepared to handle a storm of such magnitude, and as a result, many of the streets had neither been plowed nor sprayed with sand, and driving even the shortest distances proved to be dangerous and difficult.

While she waited, her doctor called. Fortunately, he was already at the hospital visiting other patients and was able to meet her when she arrived. Unfortunately, his efforts to delay the delivery failed, and a short while later, he stood by Janice's bed and introduced her to a neonatologist, who explained the risks that lay ahead.

"Ms. Baxter, your baby was born during one of the most critical periods in a pregnancy. If she had been born even a week earlier, her chances of survival would not have been very high, but as it is, she has a good chance of making it. We have her in an incubator to keep her warm because she hasn't yet developed any body fat – that's why you could see her veins through her skin. She is too small to take breast milk directly from you, but since that's the best nutrition we can give her, we'll want you to pump regularly, and we'll give it to her through a tube that will go from her mouth to her stomach. We'll have to feed her slowly to avoid an intestinal infection that premature babies are prone to get."

"When can I see her?"

"When your doctor says it's okay for you to be up and about, you can come up to the NICU, the neonatal intensive care unit. That's where she is going to be for a while. Oh, by the way, do you have a name for her? The nurses in the NICU are absolutely wonderful, angels really, and they'll want to call her by her name."

"Lilith, her name is Lilith."

"Lilith. What a pretty name. Ms. Baxter, after you've rested, we'll need to talk a bit more. Lilith will have some special needs, and I want you to understand them so you'll understand why we'll be doing certain things in the NICU."

"Tell me now. I won't be able to sleep for worrying anyway, and I'd rather know what I'm dealing with."

The neonatologist looked at Janice's obstetrician, who nodded his assent, so he pulled up a chair and sat down next to Janice. As he explained the challenges that lay ahead for her baby, Janice felt suddenly emptied, as if the doctor's words had hollowed her out. She bit down on her quivering lower lip and focused on quelling the nausea in her belly.

"What are her chances?" she asked.

"Technically, they're fifty-fifty at this stage. But from what your doctor tells me, you're quite a strong young woman, a real fighter, so Lilith has those genes working in her favor."

"How long will she be in the hospital?"

"She'll need time to catch up to where she would have been if carried to term. I can't predict exactly how long that will take, but you should plan on having her in the hospital until her original due date in June." The doctor stood up. "We'll talk more later, but for now, you need to get some rest. The nurse will be in later to take you up to the NICU."

As the doctors left, they dimmed the lights in her room. Janice had never felt so alone. She ran through the list of her friends, of those she could call for help and comfort, and came up empty. There was the Archbishop, but for some reason she couldn't explain, she did not want him to be the rock upon which she leaned.

Then she thought of her father. They had been so close, once upon a time. So many times during her pregnancy she had wanted to call him, to hear the reassuring voice that she remembered from her childhood. So many times she had reached for the phone, only to draw her hand away as she thought about how harsh and unforgiving he had been after her abortion. She always thought that he should have taken the first step toward reconciliation, that if he had shown he could forgive her, then she would have been able to forgive him.

The more she thought about him, however, the more she realized how badly she needed him. She also began to understand that her refusal to reconcile on any terms other than hers reflected the triumph of pride over love. In this, her hour of greatest need, she could no longer let pride determine her conduct. She needed her father's help to remain strong for her daughter. Janice picked up the telephone and dialed his number. When the answering machine came on and beeped for a message, she felt her breath catch. "Daddy," she said, "It's Janice. I'm in the hospital. I need you. Please come."

After she hung up the phone, a great weariness came over her. The snowstorm continued to rage outside, and as she drifted to sleep, she dreamt that the doleful cry of the wind echoed the pained cry of her heart.

Chapter 61

The storm beat against the walls of the house, shaking the walls and whistling through minute gaps in the window frames. To Connor, the wind's plaintive moans sounded like the cries of a ghost, and he had been unable to fall asleep until John lay down beside him to ease his fears.

John, too, had difficulty sleeping. The sounds of the storm made for a fitful night, and just as he drifted off, Sara shook him awake.

"John, there's something in the house."

John propped himself up on his elbows, yawned, and lay down again. "It's just the wind, honey," he said.

"No, I heard something."

"If there was something in the house, the Secret Service would have heard it. Go back to sleep."

"Please, John, check it out."

John sat up and flicked on the light by his bed. An out-of-place shadow caught the corner of his eye, and as he turned toward it, he gasped. Hanging from the ceiling, its wings wrapped around its head and body, was the bat he had caught so many months before. He pointed to it with a nervously shaking finger, and Sara screamed. Within seconds, two Secret Service agents burst into the room with guns drawn.

The bat slowly unfurled its wings. The four of them stared in morbid fascination as its face emerged, a face with two large black eyes and bloodshot corneas, a face that they all knew very well, the face that belonged to Clark.

Sara grabbed John as the Secret Service men fired at the bat.

"John, John, wake up."

John opened his eyes to see Sara shaking him by his shoulders. A branch was hitting against the windowpane, sounding very much like the pop of a gun.

"John, you were shouting in your sleep."

John sat up in bed, shook his head to wake himself up, and flicked on the lamp. "I'm sorry."

"You're sweating. That must have been a very bad dream."

"Unbelievable."

"What was it?"

John briefly described his nightmare but finished by saying, "It was just a dream. Nothing to worry about."

Sara disagreed. "Your subconscious is telling you something, John. It's warning you."

John fluffed his pillow, turned off the light and tried to find a comfortable sleeping position. "You're reading too much into it," he said. "The brain does funny things when you're asleep, puts things together in weird ways. I've been under a lot of stress lately, and I've been spending a lot of time with Clark. That's all there is to it."

Sara continued to sit up in bed, turned half way toward John. "My face would never show up like that in one of your dreams, at least I hope not, so that can't be all there is to it."

John turned his head toward Sara, "Well, if it had been you in my dream, I'd have seen other parts of your body as well as your face, and I would have been grinning, not shouting."

John craned his neck forward for a kiss, said "Let's go back to sleep," and flopped his head back onto his pillow.

"Okay," Sara replied, but she stayed awake long after John had fallen back asleep, trying to quiet the vague uneasiness his dream had stirred in her.

Chapter 62

Hartson found the box, wrapped in plain brown paper, sitting on his bed when he returned from his morning run. He knew that Clark had sent it, and he also knew that it would contain no indication that Clark had anything to do with it.

When Hartson met with Emile a second time – Clark was again unavailable – Emile had been gracious, all smiles actually, but his grin was that of a crocodile's, structurally imbedded in his face and devoid of any genuine goodwill. When Hartson asked for help landing commercials, perhaps for Senator Peters' campaign, Emile smiled, shrugged his shoulders, and said "I'll talk to Clark. I'll see what we can do." That had ended their meeting, but on Hartson's way out, Emile gave him a brief pat on the back, an unspoken assurance that a deal had been made. Hartson knew that he would be asked to do something soon, and that intuition was validated by the package in front of him. He didn't stop to wonder how someone had made his way into his apartment without any sign of forced entry. He simply assumed Clark could get accomplished pretty much anything he wanted.

With nervous fingers, he ripped off the paper wrapping and opened the box. Inside he found a small ring box, a manila envelope, and a metal attaché case. The ring box contained a key; the envelope held a map of Camden Yards –home of the Baltimore Orioles – with one of the suites circled in red, directions to a specific room in an office building in downtown Baltimore, a piece of paper bearing a date (just two days away) and a time; and in the attaché case, Hartson found a disassembled sniper's rifle. He recognized the rifle type as one that only law enforcement officials could legally import. He had first seen it in a catalog shown to him by his group of friends back home and later had a chance to handle one at a private firing range. It had lived up to its reputation of being incredibly accurate over quite a distance with only limited recoil, so that if a second shot were necessary, it could be fired without much time being lost between rounds.

Hartson pulled out the sports page and looked up the Orioles' schedule. In two days, they would be playing their home opener and Senator John Peters was scheduled to throw out the first ball. Normally, the President would have done that, but he had opted to throw out the first ball for the Nationals, the baseball team that had moved to DC from Montreal.

So, Hartson thought, he had come full circle. His first ride to fame and glory had started with his failed attempt to assassinate Peters, and if he wanted another ticket to ride, he needed to finish the job.

John had finally acceded to Clark's request that he attend opening day at Camden Yards. It wasn't that he had anything against baseball, or the Orioles, or their opponent, the Boston Red Sox, it was simply that he didn't want to make a fool of himself in front of a national audience. He had never been much of a baseball player – football had always been his game – and he was afraid he would toss the opening pitch into the ground or over the catcher's head. But one of the Secret Service agents measured out a strip of dirt 60 feet 6 inches long – the distance between the pitcher's mound and home plate – in a protected spot in back of John's house, and worked with John on his delivery. By game day, he felt relatively confident that he could get the ball to the catcher, maybe even with a little zip on it.

On the way to the ballpark, John and Clark stopped at the hospital to visit Janice. She looked tired, but in good spirits, and her father was there, a man John had never met before. Lilith had been responding well to her medication, and each day as her prospects improved, Janice's spirits lifted higher. John said he would dedicate the opening pitch to Lilith on national television, and promised to bring back a baseball autographed by every player on both teams as a souvenir of the tribute.

Hartson took the elevator fourteen stories to the fifteenth floor (there was no thirteenth floor) of the nearly century old Bromo-Seltzer building, which had been modeled after the Palazzo Vecchio in Florence, Italy. Hartson entered the room to which he had been given the key and quickly noted that the window faced the open end of Camden Yards and looked directly onto the suite behind and to the left of home plate that had been circled on his diagram. The suite was a mere 500 meters away – an easy shot for a rifle designed to hit a target five times more distant. He assembled the rifle, set it on the tripod, and waited. He found it unnerving that Clark knew of his expertise with rifles. 'What else did Clark know about his past'? Hartson wondered. A few minutes later, Peters took his seat, and Hartson gently slipped the rifle's safety off.

As he waited for a clean shot, he grew increasingly nervous, and for the first time, began seriously to wonder why Clark wanted him to carry out this assignment. Clark could have found any number of professionals to do the job, and it finally occurred to Hartson that his life was in jeopardy regardless of what he did. If he went through with the assassination, Clark was likely to have him killed to eliminate any possibility that he would talk. He was a patsy, nothing more. He was a tool that Clark would use and then discard. The conspiracy stories he had heard about John F. Kennedy's assassination floated back into his memory – Oswald had been killed shortly after his arrest, and many believed that was done to silence him forever. Hartson even wondered whether Clark had been involved in the Kennedy shooting; he certainly looked old enough.

If he refused to do the job, Clark would probably have him killed anyway. By failing to do Clark's bidding, he would have outlived his usefulness, and the knowledge he carried would make him nothing but a liability.

Hartson pondered his options. He could move back home. He could try to run. But if Hartson had read Clark correctly, someone would be coming after him. No. Neither going home nor running away would be permanent solutions to his problem. There was only one sure solution. Hartson had to go through with the shooting, but his target wouldn't be Senator Peters. It would be Clark.

He shifted his aim until Clark's head appeared in the crosshairs. He began to slowly squeeze the trigger when someone popped up in front of Clark, forcing Hartson to wait. When that person moved out of the line of fire, Hartson started once more to pressure the trigger, but then he stopped. He emptied the rifle chamber, disassembled the gun and left the building. He couldn't put in words why he had been unable to pull the trigger, but he felt better about himself for walking away. He knew that his life span would now be measured in moments stolen from the fate Clark had decreed for him, but he also knew that he would live each of those moments a free man, a man defined by his own choices and not by a choice someone else had selected for him. It occurred to him that perhaps simply walking away was not enough. After all, he knew that Clark and Emile were not likely to give up their attempt to kill the Senator, and he wondered if he ought to do something – warn the Senator, call the press – to foil them. But the thought of Melanie Kraft telling the world that he had never been a hero, that instead he had been a foiled assassin, was more than he could bear. If there was a God, then Senator Peters' life was in His hands. If Peters was meant to die, so be it; at least he wouldn't be the tool by which it occurred.

Chapter 63

Imrahain sat in his jail cell working through the crossword puzzle from an old Sunday newspaper. The rest of the paper, including the front page, lay in a loose pile on the edge of his bed. He had read the conflicting articles about the significance of Senator Peters' latest 'miracle' and was more confused than ever.

Following the incident, Imrahain had received another round of requests from the press for interviews, and, as he had with respect to the requests received after the public airing of his letter to Senator Peters, he turned them down. He wasn't interested in speaking with reporters. They would filter his words through their own lens, edit his remarks to make them fit into their narrative.

He did, however, very much want to speak with Senator Peters one more time, and prior to the last of the primary debates had hoped that Senator Peters would answer his letter. He now realized that he was unlikely to either hear from or speak with the Senator ever again.

Imrahain focused on the next unanswered clue in the crossword puzzle, 15 down -- a four-letter word for "the land of Jacob's brother." He hadn't any idea what the answer could be, and as he started to skim for other clues to solve, his mind drifted back to what Senator Peters' had said to him in Arabic.

What didn't he understand?

Every day he asked for insight, but none came.

He surveyed his world, a largely naked eight-foot by ten-foot cell, with an overly bright light bulb overhead, a toilet in the corner and next to it a sink without a mirror and from which hot water ran only sporadically. There was nothing of him in the cell except for him. For now, it was an empty hole into which he had been placed. He suspected that over time he would somehow find it more tolerable, that he would invest his personality into the things that made his cell unique – the cracks on his ceiling that he would turn into something else, the way children transformed clouds in the sky into familiar objects. He wondered if he would ever again see his true home, whether he would ever again kiss his wives and hold his sons. He thought it unlikely. He didn't have any friends in the prison, and his name guaranteed him a certain number of enemies.

As Imrahain reflected on the incredible chain of events that had led him to prison, he worried about whether he had completely misunderstood what had been asked of him, or if he simply hadn't been worthy enough to accomplish the task. He looked at another clue in the crossword puzzle, a five-letter word ending in 's' for "His name is synonymous with betrayal." The person who put this puzzle together clearly had religious themes on his mind, Imrahain thought. The answer was obvious, even to a non-Christian.

Imrahain wondered why Christians believed that God would orchestrate the salvation of Man by pivoting it around betrayal. If Christ had been predestined for crucifixion, then Judas had been a marked man since the time the story of the universe was first written. He had no say in the matter. He was nothing more than a hapless tool, used to accomplish great things, and discarded as soon as his usefulness had expired. It hardly seemed fair.

Imrahain put the newspaper away and lay down, marveling at how little any man comprehends of his role in the unfolding of the world.

Chapter 64

The day dawned warm and sunny, the type of day made for tossing a ball around, and with the last of the snow melted off that was exactly what John intended to do. His perfect pitch on Opening Day had inspired him to teach Connor how to throw, so he pulled out his old baseball glove and checked on the new one he had picked up for Connor at the Orioles gift shop. He had kneaded it with mink oil to break it in, and it was now soft and pliable in his hands. Connor's small fingers would have no trouble closing it around a ball.

"Connor?" John called. He didn't know which part of the house Connor was in, and didn't feel like searching each of the rooms.

"Yes, Daddy?" came a voice from upstairs.

"Let's go outside and play catch."

"No thanks."

"What do you mean, 'no thanks'? It's a gorgeous day outside, and I'm actually home for a change."

"I'm watching cartoons."

"I don't think so," John laughed. "Come on down."

"In a minute."

"Now." John knew that Connor's definition of a minute had no relationship to actual time transpired. He couldn't go onto the front yard, as reporters and their camera crews kept a steady presence on the street below, and he wasn't about to subject Connor's first attempts at throwing a ball to national scrutiny. He walked out to the back yard, calling to Connor as he went, and started tossing the ball up in the air in a game of one-man catch. As he stretched his glove to catch his third toss, the world went suddenly black.

Blood spilling from below his ear pooled on the grass by his head, turning it a sickly reddish-brown. One of the Secret Services agents drew his gun and charged over to cover John's body. The other agent radioed for help and scanned the trees looking for the shooter. The reporters, sensing that something dramatic had occurred, scurried around the house to the backyard, and the sounds of their frenzied voices and clicking cameras disturbed what had been the peaceful atmosphere inside the house.

Sara rushed to the back door. When she saw the agent huddled over John, she turned and directed Connor, whose favorite cartoon show had just ended, to go back upstairs and watch another cartoon. Then she ran outside, shouting at the reporters to give way, and knelt beside John. Her world stopped in that moment. Everything except John's face faded to black, and all she could hear was the pounding of her heart. One reporter at the scene later observed that in the moment that Sara looked upon her husband, her face took on a look that he had only seen in paintings, that in tragedy, she looked sublimely beautiful.

A few days later, the news was still dominated by the shooting and its aftermath: Who did it and why? Would Senator Peters ever wake from his coma, and if so, what kind of shape would he been in? How long would the Party wait before deciding whether to choose another nominee and who would it be? What psychological effect would the shooting have on the nation?

Not since Bobby Kennedy in 1968 and George Wallace in 1972 had a candidate for the Presidency been shot. Never before had a party's presumptive nominee been shot. Talking heads vied for airtime to espouse their theories of how this tragedy would ripple through the cultural, political and religious fabric of America. Conspiracy theories abounded, coming in flavors to suit every predisposition. Some believed that religious fanatics were responsible, fingering either atheists acting out of fear that a President Peters would tear down the wall between church and state, or high priests (including the Pope) who feared that Peters' message, whatever it would prove to be, would somehow undermine their doctrines or upend their positions of power. Others thought the attempted assassination the work of political extremists, but whether of the far right or the far left depended on their own political persuasion. Yet others blamed it on radical Muslims, for no other reason than a Muslim had previously tried to kill him.

Throngs of people filled the sidewalk and grounds surrounding the hospital where John lay. They cried, they prayed, they held candles, they chanted, and they demanded answers. The Secret Service and the FBI, working with state and local police, put every resource they could spare on the hunt for the shooter. Reports leaked into the press of bickering between the agencies as the pressure for answers increased.

The shooter was never found. A few days later, another story appeared briefly in the news: the discovery of Mark Hartson's body, an apparent suicide.

Chapter 65

Sara's hands lay folded together in her lap as she looked with empty eyes out the hospital room window onto a gray, bleak morning that perfectly reflected the feeling in her soul. John lay beside her, tubes and wires running into and out of his body, monitoring brain and heart activity, keeping him breathing. It had been three months since the shooting, and John still lay in a coma. The doctors said he might never come out of it. She knew differently, but the waiting was hard, very hard.

For the first few weeks following the shooting, Sara had to battle her way through the mobs of reporters and well-wishers that gathered outside the hospital. But as time passed, both groups went elsewhere, the reporters returned to the pursuit of more timely stories, and the well-wishers returned to the routine of their everyday lives. John's name faded to the occasional explanatory note on the evening news: "Governor Smith, the likely nominee in the wake of Senator Peters' shooting..." Of the millions of people who had followed John's every word during the campaign, waiting expectantly for another miracle, only a few kept him in their prayers. The rest put him aside. There was only so much time and attention they could devote to any one person or thing, and when the likelihood of a miracle dissipated, so did their interest.

It was by John's bedside that Sara started making plans for his permanent care. She read brochures on nursing homes and hospices in North Carolina and she called Connor's old school. She wanted to move before the new school year started in the fall. 'John, how long? What am I going to do without you in the meantime?' she thought.

One afternoon, she sat next to John looking through the contents of a cardboard box that she had found in his study. It was filled with old photographs, letters she had written to John many years before, and several recent letters that John had written but never given to her. She had just finished reading the last of John's letters when a nervous hand knocked tentatively on the door. The drawn face of Ned Smith followed behind. He looked as if he had aged considerably in the few weeks since Sara had seen him, and his voice sounded thin and weak.

"Hello, Sara."

"Ned." She waited quietly for him to explain the purpose for his visit, though she already knew why he had come.

"Still the same?" he asked.

"Still the same," she answered.

"Even now, I can't believe what happened."

"I know," she replied.

"How are you holding up?"

"Okay, I guess. Janice comes by pretty often. Her baby is in the NICU a couple of floors up. She's been a great comfort."

"How is her baby doing?"

"Great. Janice says she might be going home soon."

"That is great. How is Connor?"

"Better. He keeps praying for a miracle. He says that God will answer him. That God will send him a sign that everything will be okay."

"It's good to have faith."

Sara didn't answer.

"Sara, I need to talk with you."

"I know," she said.

He came around to the side of the bed where she sat and took her hands in his.

"Not here," he said.

"Okay."

He pulled her gently out of the chair and led her out of the room. The walk to the elevator, the ride down to the ground floor, and the walk to the cafeteria were marked by silence. Smith ordered two coffees that he knew neither of them would drink and studied her face a long time as he searched for the right words to say. Sara cut the silence short.

"So, next week is the Convention."

"Yes."

"And you'll be nominated?"

"According to Clark, yes. Apparently, there are no rules for something like this. The Constitution only deals with the succession of actual Presidents, not Party nominees. How a Party selects its candidate is its own business. But Clark is confident that I'll be the one picked."

"Well, he would know."

"He's not as smart as he thinks."

"Congratulations anyway."

"Sara, I didn't want it this way."

"You've wanted it ever since I've known you."

"Please, Sara, believe me. Not like this."

"Clark must be happy. You were his guy from the start."

"Sara, no one is happy about what happened to John. Not me, not Clark, no one."

Sara brushed her hair back from her eyes. She hadn't combed it since the day before. "What is it you want from me, Ned?"

"I need to hear you say that it's okay for me to accept the nomination "

Sara's shoulders sagged. "Ned, I'm tired and I'm scared. Sometimes I fall asleep by John's bed and when I wake up, I'm afraid to open my eyes. I'm afraid of what I'll see. I never thought anything like this could happen. But I have to open my eyes. I have to be strong for Connor. That takes everything I have. So you'll understand when I tell you that right now, I don't care about the nomination, I don't care about your needs. I only care about getting John back. But if my blessing is that important to you, you can have it, for whatever it's worth."

Sara returned to John's hospital room alone, refusing Smith's offer to walk back with her. Janice was there.

"Ned Smith came by," Sara explained, feeling a need to explain why she hadn't been by John's side when Janice arrived. "We went to the cafeteria for a cup of coffee."

Janice nodded. "It should have been John making the acceptance speech."

"A lot of things should have been different," Sara said as she sat down beside Janice.

"I know. It's hard to understand why things happen the way they do, hard to accept. After I was raped, I kept asking, 'why me?' Archbishop O'Connell helped me to understand a little better. He said that we don't understand why things happen because we can only see a tiny sliver of eternity, a single grain of sand on an infinite beach. He said that things that seem arbitrary or cruel to us take on a wholly different meaning from God's point of view, from the perspective of eternity. A grain of sand is nothing more than an irritant to an oyster, but for us it becomes a gorgeous pearl."

"What good does that do the oyster?"

Janice gave Sara a quizzical look. "I'm sorry?"

Sara bit her tongue and let her anger pass. "I'm glad your faith has been of such help to you, Janice, but don't ask me to accept what happened to John as part of some grand plan. He didn't deserve to be shot."

"I'm not saying he did. I'm only trying to tell you that we have to trust in something greater than ourselves, or none of this makes any sense."

"Maybe sometimes things just happen. Maybe sometimes they don't make sense to us because there is no sense in it."

"Janice, I know you're in a lot of pain. I also know that things people tell you to make you feel better don't work. I won't lie to you, Sara. Time doesn't heal all wounds. Some things never fully heal. You just learn to live with the pain and move on."

"You're making it sound like John is dead. He's not dead. He is going to get better. We have too many things left to do together. We're going to watch Connor graduate from college. We're going back to Venice to drink cappuccino at a café in St. Mark's Square. We are going to grow old together."

"That's what I'm praying for, Sara, with all my heart."

Janice gave Sara a hug. "I'm going to check on Lilith. I'll talk to you soon."

As Janice got up to leave, Sara put a hand on her arm. "I'm sorry, Janice. I didn't mean to yell at you."

"It's okay."

"How is Lilith?"

"She's great. She has such a sweet disposition. Never fusses. Sometimes I even think she understands me when I talk to her. She seems so ...," Janice paused for a moment, searching for the right word, "... focused. I mentioned it to the doctor once, but he laughed at me." Janice gently shrugged her shoulders. "I guess I'm not the only new parent who sees more in their child than is actually there."

After Janice left, Sara took John's hand in hers. "Ned came to see me tonight, right after I finished reading your letters. I wanted to confront him with what you had written about him and Clark, but I decided to put my anger away. I don't have the time for it, or the energy. All I can think about, all I care about, is what will happen to you, to us, to Connor."

Sara leaned over the bed and kissed John's forehead.

"Come back to me, John. Please come back."

Chapter 66

Melanie Kraft sat in a glass booth high above the Convention floor, waiting patiently as the hair stylist and make-up artist applied last minute touch ups before the camera went live. The noisy bustle of activity from the crowded floor below echoed off the rafters, making it difficult to hear her producer even through the earpiece she wore. His voice started to take on an urgent tone, so she squirmed out from under the stylist's hands and pressed the earpiece against her head.

"What did you say?" she shouted so as to be heard above the noise, forgetting that from the producer's position in the trailer outside the arena hall, he could hear her just fine as long as she spoke into the microphone.

"Change of plans," he shouted back. "Ned Smith is coming out first, to open the Convention."

"Okay. Is that a big deal?"

Melanie was a student neither of history nor of political science. She hadn't a clue that the presumptive nominee is supposed to take the stage on the last night of the Convention, his speech marking the crowning event to a weeklong parade of speeches building him up as an American hero.

"Yes, it's a very big deal. You're going to have to wing this. We don't have time to get a script up on the teleprompter."

The camera went live, and Melanie looked directly into the lens. Her face and voice were made for television and she knew it. Even when she didn't know what to say, she said it with style.

"Good evening, America," she smiled. "Tonight marks the first night of what promises to be a most unusual Convention. As you know, until three months ago, Senator John Peters was going to be the Party's candidate for the Presidential election. Then, tragically, he was shot. As we gather here tonight in this festive hall, John Peters lies in a hospital bed in a coma from which he may never wake. His replacement is almost certain to be his running mate, Governor Ned Smith. We understand that Governor Smith will open tonight's Convention. We are all waiting anxiously to hear what he has to say to America."

The arena's lights went dark, and a lone spotlight shone on the microphone stand on the stage. Ned Smith strode from behind a curtain up to the microphone, blinked as hundreds of cameras flashed in his face, and savored the hushed silence of the expectant crowd.

"Good evening. Tonight represents an occasion for both celebration and reflection. We celebrate the free and democratic process by which our leaders are chosen, and we reflect on the price sometimes paid by those who fight to keep us free.

"I am here tonight in the place of my friend, Senator John Peters. Senator Peters fought for what he believed in. He fought for his country. And he has paid a heavy price. But I know that he would want us to carry on the fight, to set America back on the path to success, and I am here to give you my word that I will do just that.

"I spoke with John's wife, Sara, last week. She is a remarkable woman, a strong woman, and a woman of deep and abiding faith. She wanted me to tell you that she knows you are praying for John and for her and for their son, Connor, and she is grateful. She also wanted me to let you know that she is praying for you, and for me, for all of us. Even in this her time of greatest need, she is thinking of us.

"I think it would be appropriate to start the evening with a prayer, and I have asked my dear friend, Reverend Creighton B. Jones, to lead us all in that prayer."

Smith stepped back a couple of paces as the Reverend took his place at the microphone stand. The lights came on and the Reverend looked out over the thousands of people crowded onto the floor and in the seats around the hall. Their earlier festive chatter had given way to a somber mood. They had been keyed up before Smith took the stage, and Smith's remarks left them wide open to an emotionally powerful prayer. He could move them to tears. He knew that millions of people were watching on television and that he could move them as well. This prayer could make him a star. This was the moment he had dreamt of for years, but somehow, he couldn't savor it. He grown to care for John and his family, and he did not want to make his fortune by taking advantage of their tragedy.

He had made a career out of delivering powerful prayers that held more meaning for his audience than they did for him. Now, for the first time, he would invest his soul into his words.

He began to pray. The booming, charismatic voice in which he normally spoke gave way to a softer, heartfelt, soothing tone. The crowd had to strain ever so slightly to hear him, but being drawn in, they listened more closely. He talked about the mystery that had surrounded John ever since that day he delivered his first speech on the floor of the Senate. He talked about the marvelous, indeed miraculous changes that had been wrought in people all over the world – people who, in struggling to understand what they had heard, came to the realization that their lives had been spent walking down an errant path. People of every faith, people of little faith, even people of no faith, had awakened to the reality that a successful life was measured not by how much one made, but by how much one served.

"Was it God's handiwork?" the Reverend asked the audience. "Does it matter?" he answered. Whether it was God or some natural phenomenon that man, with his limited knowledge, could not yet comprehend, the end result was the same. John had delivered a message that would echo throughout time. When he finished, the crowd remained silent. Not until Clark told the band to start playing did the crowd come out of its reverie.

Chapter 67

The next morning, Janice and her father stood expectantly outside the hospital nursery. The day had finally arrived when she could bring Lilith home. There had been many anxious moments over the previous three months, but Lilith was a fighter, and the doctors, nurses and modern technology had been miracle workers. Now Lilith had reached the developmental stage of a full-term newborn and she was ready to start her life anew. To Janice, even the weather seemed to be joining in the celebration. The morning had been misty and damp, but the sun had started to break through the clouds; in the distance, a beautiful rainbow arched over the horizon.

"Hello," a voice called out. Janice and her father turned to see the Archbishop striding down the hall. "I didn't want to miss the big moment. And I come bearing gifts." He pulled out a small case and opened the lid. Inside was a gold chain and crucifix. Janice smiled and gave the Archbishop a hug. He had been a regular visitor to the hospital, checking in on both Janice and Sara. At Janice's request, he had already made arrangements for Lilith's formal baptism ceremony at the Cathedral, and he would be the one to administer the sacrament. Whatever fears he had concerning Lilith's paternal legacy he hoped to wash away with the waters of the baptismal font.

A nurse carried Lilith out to Janice. She was bundled in a pink blanket and tiny bubbles played about her lips. Janice had never been so happy. The Archbishop looked down at Lilith and smiled.

"Hello there, sweetie," he said.

Lilith's eyes turned toward the sound of his voice. She seemed to fix her gaze upon him, but he knew that wasn't possible for such a young baby. Then Lilith smiled at him, and he knew that wasn't possible either. He gently brushed her cheek and felt a warmth and calmness from that touch that he didn't understand. He told himself that it was nothing more than the fanciful imaginings of a doting old man; nevertheless, he felt it, and it brought joy to his heart.

In a recessed window across the street, barely visible among the dark shadows with which it blended, a bat watched, still as death.

Two floors down, and on the opposite wing of the hospital, Sara and Connor sat in John's room watching television. Connor had been invited to a friend's house for a play date, but insisted on accompanying Sara to the hospital. He wanted to be with his father. As Connor flicked channels on the remote control looking for cartoons, they heard a stirring from John's bed.

Sara and Connor rushed to his side, and in the brief moment that it took to reach the bed, Sara prayed harder than she had ever prayed in her life. To her great joy and relief, John's eyes flickered open. He took in the room about him and a weak smile played across his lips as he recognized Sara and Connor. He turned his head toward the window and they followed his line of sight. Outside shimmered the largest, most richly colored rainbow they had ever seen as the morning sun broke through the clouds and shone through the mist that still hung in the air.

Sara clasped John's hand, tears streaming down her face. She heard him laboring to speak and leaned close. As John's eyes closed for the last time, three words passed through his lips, words that resonated with the musical, magical tone that had first brought him to the attention of the world: "I am here."

For a brief instant, as Connor gazed at the rainbow and before he realized that his mother was sobbing, before he understood that his father had passed, Connor was as happy, as filled with joy, as it is possible for a little boy to be.

Printed in the United States
117449LV00003B/170/A

9 781430 325123